NOSTRADAMUS

A SCIENCE FICTION KIND OF STORY

An Original Novel by
Bud Seligson

Lost Age Publishing

2017

NOSTRADAMUS © 2014 Bud Seligson

The following original novel has been filed and registered with the Writers' Guild of America, West, under the name of Bud Seligson.

Printed in the United States of America.

ISBN: 978-1-946480-04-0

9018 Balboa Boulevard
Suite #562
Northridge, CA 91325

DEDICATION

Apart from doing the research and touring locations, the life of a writer tends to be very solitary and often boring. Never more so for me as when I am working under a deadline. Every year, my wife, Diane, puts up with the long hours and the fact that, even when I am home, I am often mentally elsewhere. I am a lucky man to be married to such an awesome and understanding woman.

INTRODUCING NOSTRADAMUS

Nostradamus, the popular name for Michel de Nostradame, was a sixteenth-century physician, astronomer and astrologer. He is best remembered as the prophetic writer of future predictions that quite often came to pass. A world-famous French futurist, he was born in mid- or late December of the year 1503, in the little town of Saint-Rémy-de Provence, in the south of France. The eldest of seven brothers, he had only one sister who was older that he was. His father was James, a local merchant and self-made lawyer, and his mother, Reynière, was a very strict Catholic who brought up her eldest son within all the strict ways of the Church.

Michel Nostradamus was an exceptional athlete. He highly excelled in the extraordinary use of the sword, which was the preferred weapon of the day. His writings were always quite controversial, and many people believe that his words have been twisted about by others in order to fit events that had already happened. Others believe that if his ideas are carefully interpreted, future warnings are being told to us, and their unclear meanings are there for the taking.

Whatever your perspective on Nostradamus, it can be safely said that people have always been fascinated with his clear thoughts and ideas. It is our intent to present the facts as we found them through our detailed research. Hopefully you will agree that his life story is different from any other figure that history has thrown at us.

Michel de Nostredame, usually written as Michel Nostradamus, was a French apothecary (pharmacist), reputed seer (one who predicts the future), and doctor.

Nostradamus published collections of many prophecies that have since his death become famous worldwide.

He was born on December 14, 1503, in the small village of Saint-Rémy-de-Provence, in Provence.

He died on July 2, 1566.

He is mostly known for his book entitled The Prophecies, which has rarely been out of print since his death.

Nostradamus has attracted a following of millions of people as well as newspapers and the popular press. These followers credit him with predicting many major world events. His birthplace in France has been rebuilt and acts as a sacred place to his fans.

Nostradamus was one of at least nine children born to his father Jacques, a lawyer and notary. The family had originally been Jewish, but his grandfather on his mother's side gave up the Jewish faith and became Catholic.

At the age of fifteen, he entered the University of Avignon in France to study medicine. Due to the terrible Black Death that was sweeping the continent, the university and all other public meeting places closed down for several years. Nostradamus never went back to school to finish his medical degree. He went to work and was certified by several licensed doctors as a full doctor.

During the time that the plague was strongest in Paris, he moved to the countryside and spent eight years doing private research on plants and herbs. He came up with a combinationn of herbs that he called the "rose pill," which made him a rich man. The pill was supposed to cure the plague.

In 1534, his wife Henriette and their two children died of the plague, and there was nothing he could do to save them. He remarried with a rich widow in 1547, and they had six children who lived past the death of their parents. There were three boys and three girls.

Following the popular trends of the day, he wrote a short book of future predictions, which became so successful that he put out several new books each year. He continued with his writing up to his time of his death. The most famous book, of which he was proudest, was called *The Nostradamus Book of Updated Prophecies*.

Many people thought Nostradamus was evil, a fake, and insane. Others thought he was touched by God and could see into the future.

He spent much of his time traveling about and writing out predictions for wealthy patrons. The queen of France, Catherine de' Medici, was one of his greatest followers. She made him the royal court's physician to keep him close at hand.

Nostradamus was always careful to keep his relationship with the Catholic Church in perfect order.

In 1566, Nostradamus became seriously ill. He was sixty-three years old at that time. In the sixteenth century, the average life expectancy for a male child born in Europe was not more than the early forties.

It was reported that Nostradamus told one of his loyal servants his prediction for his own death. He is supposed to have said, "After tonight, my friend, you will never see me alive again." Nostradamus was found dead the next morning by the same servant. He was lying at the side of his bed in his night clothes.

He left a request in his will that he be buried in the family church and that he be buried standing upright. There are many different interpretations as to the meaning behind that request.

This, then, is the story of Nostradamus, the man, the myth, and the truth as we understand it.

—Bud Seligson

CHAPTER ONE

The lilting strains of a Strauss waltz filled the room.

The music waxed and waned beneath the sensitive fingers of Michel Nostradamus, and through his half-closed eyes, he could recall seeing the whirling figures pirouetting about the highly-waxed floor of some luxurious private home of a seventeenth-century nobleman.

This was a most interesting phenomenon, since Michel was sitting in his private home playing this waltz in the year 1533, about three hundred years before the famous Johann Strauss was even born.

Music always affected Michel in a very special way. It filled his mind with dreams of sheer beauty, and transformed his room into a paradise of sound. His hands flickered over the piano in the last delicious combination of tones and slowed reluctantly to a halt. He sighed and for a moment remained absolutely silent, as if trying to extract the last essence of beauty from the dying echoes. Then he turned and smiled faintly at the other occupant of the room.

Benjamin Franklin, of the time of the American Revolution, smiled back at Nostradamus.

Franklin had a great liking for Michel but very little understanding. They were worlds apart—literally—for Franklin, the product of the American War of Independence, from the late seventeen hundreds, and Nostradamus, who was born in the year 1503, were physically centuries apart—and yet here they were spending a quiet evening together.

Franklin was saying, "What really impressed me the most about you so far, Michel, is your complete command of so many languages. In our brief time together, I have heard you speak your native French, my American style of English, which is quite different from the language spoken in England, and finally some very fluent Spanish, with the proper accent of the royal court of Ferdinand and Isabella, in the late fourteen hundreds.

"If you hadn't met me in Philadelphia as I was coming out of my print shop, and somehow or other 'time-traveled' the two of us back here to what is your present and my past, I would have assumed that one of us was in need of immediate medical help. A bit of an explanation would be greatly appreciated, and I must tell you that you have all of my attention. But before you begin with what I hope will be a long and glorious adventure story, perhaps another glass of that wonderful vintage wine that you poured for us earlier, would be in order."

When the two new friends were finally seated in front of the warming fireplace, and each of them obviously enjoying each other's company, Michel Nostradamus slowly and clearly began to tell his unbelievable story.

CHAPTER TWO

The standing, sometimes called a small castle, had been the home of the Nostradamus clan for generations beyond counting. It had served all their various needs with calm efficiency.

When Michel had inherited the ownership of the castle, he had the castle dismantled stone by stone, and had it and all its contents shipped to the small town of Saint-Rémy-de-Provence in the south of France, where he had always made his home. It was reassembled surprisingly quick by a small army of fanatical stone masons. You can do things like that when you inherit a small family fortune.

The standing was his whenever he decided to plant his roots. All that was required of him was that he preserve it and hold it in trust for future generations.

This was assuming that he would get around to marrying and producing the next generation. His mistress was a delightful sort, but not at all the kind of person one married. As head of one of the oldest families in France, he had a duty to marry someone of his own rank and station. And he would. Eventually.

Michel remembered looking thoughtfully at the giant picture on the wall opposite his bed, showing the original Nostradamus in all his fearsome aspect and martial glory. He was a warrior prince of the French Empire, and founder of the clan that still bore his name. He looked a bit rough-and-ready in his thick furs and steel mesh tunic, bristling with weapons, his head shaved in a mercenary's scalp-lock.

According to the family history, he'd been the greatest fighting man of his day, unanimously elected warrior prince, and elevated to the peerage by popular acclaim. He was a hard man by all accounts, and a bit of a bastard, but the French public liked that sort of thing in their heroes. He bloodied his sword in a hundred battles and never backed away from an insult or a war.

Michel thought that it was a pity about what happened to him in the end, but that's a warrior's life for you. He often wondered what the old man would have made of his most recent descendant, which was himself.

Personally, Michel did not give a damn about what anyone thought. He had always known that he was a writer and not a fighter. Of course, he'd had proper training in weaponry and all the martial arts, as befitted his station and inheritance, but it never really interested him.

His interest lay in researching and piercing together the French empire's somewhat tangled history and the lessons to be drawn from it. Nothing excited him more than reaching into the past and finding one new indisputable event that he could hold up and make it as clear and as defined as finding a diamond in a coal mine.

And if he'd learned one thing from all the histories he'd read, and the tales he'd investigated, it was that most of the time there was no glory and damn little honor to be found on the battlefield. Only blood and mud and the endless bitterness of lost hopes were out there.

Whenever Michel looked in the mirror, he saw himself tall and rangy, with dark hair and darker eyes. He prided himself with always moving about with the quiet grace of his breeding and long martial arts training.

These days, in his mid-twenties, Michel had lost some of the athlete's leanness. Good living and satisfied appetites had softened the lines of his muscles and padded his stomach. Not excessively so by any means, but his old weapons master would have thrown up his hands in despair at how out of condition his pupil had become.

It was a thought that never failed to please Michel. The two of them had never got on well, and despite all that, Michel still worked out most days, when he could spare the time, if only so that he could keep up with his mistress.

Nostradamus directed his best smile at Franklin as he carefully set his wine glass down upon the small hand-carved table that stood next to his chair. "It was not by chance that you and I met outside your printing shop, Benjamin. I was standing outside your front entrance, where I was partly hidden by a nearby doorway, waiting for you to come out. I was waiting there with a purpose in mind.

"I must admit that I reviewed dozens of strong candidates before I decided that you were the one person that I had to have help me with all the things that I am planning to do. You are most intelligent, quite fearless, and have a relaxed and easy manner that I believe would fit into the time-travel experience that we will certainly be having. In my opinion, you are the right man for the job, and your skill with weapons would be hard to match for any other twenty-six-year-old that I might come across.

"At lunch that afternoon, when I went over some of the details of who and what I am all about, it pleased me to no end for you to say to me as you did, and I quote, 'Let's get on with it.' That is probably my favorite English expression because it always goes right to the heart of the matter. And so, we did 'get on with it,' and here we are right at this moment, discussing plans about who, what, when and where we shall be going with this time-travel thing.

"You need to know that with the fine control I now have

over the wand and sun mirrors that make all this work, I will be able to bring you back within minutes of where we first met outside your print shop. No time will have passed from that point for the people living there, but since you will have been alive and moving about with me, you will age as many days, months or years that you spend with me jumping around the time continuum. For example, if we spent six months doing whatever we are going to be doing, and then we return you to where we first met, nothing will have changed back home, but you will be six months older. I am very sorry to say that I can move us about in time, but I can't stop our bodies from continuing to age. Father Time, as they say, waits for no man.

"Speaking of time, it is late for me, as I have been up for about thirty hours now, and I believe a good night's sleep will do us both some good. You will find some blankets and pillows on the bed in that room behind you that will act as your bedroom for the night. Please consider all the things that I have been throwing at you, and have your questions and thoughts in good order for us to continue this conversation in the morning. There is a very fine shop down in the lower village that offers a good breakfast menu, and I think that we shall spend the rest of the day walking and talking. And now, I bid you a good night and welcome you to my world and my timeline."

As Nostradamus quietly stepped away from the bedroom where Benjamin Franklin was getting ready for some much-needed sleep, he reviewed in his mind once again as to why, with all the choices that he had to pick from, he had decided on Benjamin.

Actually, Franklin was an easy choice, and once he settled into looking into the future years of his life, he threw out consideration of anyone else. He would never tell him that he had spent several weeks moving up and down the Franklin timeline, there as an eyewitness at every major event in his life. Nostradamus was always in the background, just watching, listening and silently observing. It was fascinating to watch Benjamin become the foremost American of his day and one of the most pivotal figures in colonial and Revolutionary America.

This man was a fantastic study in what a person could do with his life if he dedicated himself to all of the right causes. He was a wit, diplomat, scientist, philosopher, businessman, inventor and general ladies' man (the French word *"un homme à femmes"* comes to mind). Nostradamus watched Benjamin evolve into America's first Renaissance man, and he was extremely proud of him. He carefully studied Franklin as he grew from a penniless runaway to a highly successful printer. He observed his change from a most loyal subject of Great Britain to the architect of an alliance with France that ensured the independence of the United States of America.

Benjamin Franklin went from complete obscurity to become one of the world's most admired figures, whose circle of European friends included the likes of Voltaire, Hume, Burke and Kant. Nostradamus was absolutely fascinated by the guest who was getting ready to go to sleep in his downstairs bedroom. He realized that sleeping under his roof that night was a future eighteenth-century genius full of greatness and general humanity. He concluded that he had taken a magnificent tour of a future legendary and historical figure and watched him grow into his legacy.

CHAPTER THREE

Morning came early to the castle of Michel Nostradamus as sunlight streamed into the room where Benjamin Franklin lay sleeping. It was not the sunshine coming through the open shutters that awoke Benjamin, but the loud clanging of pots and pans coming from the kitchen.

He had slept rather well in the featherbed that Nostradamus had provided for him. The strangeness of being two hundred years in the past from his own timeline of the seventeen hundreds did not bother him at all.

It was, rather, an exciting intellectual stimulation that had him up, dressed and walking down to the kitchen where the delicious smell of coffee called to him.

"*Bonjour*, good day, Benjamin," was the greeting waiting for him as he stepped into the large kitchen where a smiling Nostradamus greeted him with a large cup of coffee for him in his hand. "Please help yourself to milk and sugar that you will find on the side pantry by the window. I myself like my coffee black. When you are ready, please join me in the dining room for some rolls and jam to get us going for today's adventures."

Benjamin added a little sugar to his coffee as he looked around the pantry that was adjacent to the large kitchen. The first thing that he noticed was that everything was sparkling clean and all the utensils and dishes were lined up in perfect order. The unspoken message that Benjamin received from this well-organized area was that the master of the castle was clean, precise and detailed in his lifestyle. This fit in perfectly with the image of Doctor Michel Nostradamus that he was forming in his head.

With a smile on his face, Benjamin found the good Doctor, and sat down opposite him across the large dining room table that was neatly set up with knives, forks, spoons and napkins. There were fresh flowers in vases through-out the room to provide bright colors to the gray and white walls of the castle. If Nostradamus was trying to achieve a mood of uplift and openness, he was quite successful.

Interestingly enough, even though Benjamin knew that there were several servants moving about, he never heard them and never really saw them. He merely sensed them being there as secondary background to the image that was being created.

Nostradamus opened up the dialogue by offering up a toast.

Benjamin touched coffee cups with him and listened carefully to the words that Nostradamus offered.

"I propose a special toast to the beginning of a long and prosperous journey for the two of us, where we will go into and out of times present, past and future. And let us never forget the beautiful women and exciting adventures that are out there waiting for us."

Both men sipped at their cups and were silent for a few moments as the words sank into their awareness.

It was Benjamin who broke the silence. "A most wonderful toast, Michel, and I sincerely hope that all those things come true for us. But what I think that you have to do right now is to explain to me how this time-travel thing works, and how you are able to control our comings and goings. I have not yet achieved a comfort zone for all of this."

It was only a few minutes later that Benjamin had to hurry

to keep up with the rapidly moving Nostradamus as he led him down the long and brightly lit internal castle's passage way. The obvious destination was the beginning of a very wide, circular and winding staircase that would take them to the central high tower of the castle that opened up onto a large, flat roof area. There was very little if any conversation, as each of them was deeply involved within his own thoughts as they walked along.

Nostradamus was going over in his mind how to simply explain things to Benjamin in terms that he would understand. Nostradamus had personally and privately been experimenting with time-travel for well over a year. He finally was able to control the time-transfer with very little problems, and he was able to make it take him to when he wished and where he wished to go with very good accuracy. It was not yet one-hundred-percent accurate, but he was improving with each trip.

He was never really able to figure out just how his bending of solar light rays into a steady and repeating pattern caused an opening in the space-time-continuum, which allowed him to be able to step into and out of. He was finally ready to try an experiment with it, and he thought it was wise to take someone with him. This was just in case something came up where he would need some assistance.

He had taken a local village friend along with him on this first visit to the future, and it was a good thing that he did. He had learned a very important lesson about always having a companion with him, and from that time forward he always tried to have a backup. By holding the hand of his fellow traveler, Nostradamus was able to take him with him back and forth on his time jump. He gave his friend some very wonderful gifts, and later sent him on his way after they returned from what turned out to have been a most difficult and dangerous trial run. The important lesson that he had learned from that very brief jump a few years into the future of Paris was that he never knew what dangers he might be stepping into when he arrived at a new destination and timeline.

They had arrived without any problem into one of the squares of central Paris, where they seemed to be having a protest of some kind about unfair conditions in the local jail. The screaming and yelling coming from the marchers into whose midst they had landed was something about turning all the prisoners loose from the local city jail, called the Bastille. Things got pretty rough in the streets for a little while, and it started getting ugly as the crowd worked itself up into a frenzy.

If it wasn't for his young friend, he never could have worked his way out of the crowd, and he might have lost the time-travel wand that controlled his ability to get back home. If he had lost it or dropped it, they would have been forever locked into that terrible timeline for the rest of their lives. This would have been a disaster, and he learned a lesson on the value of having a dependable traveling companion with him at all times.

Upon his return home from that awkward time-jump, it took him several days to make a list of all the possible candidates that would fit his needs. He briefly, on his own, time-jumped into the future and into the past to find someone that he would be comfortable with. It had to be someone that would be reliable, loyal, smart, and good with weapons in case things got out of hand.

His first thoughts were to look for a fellow Frenchman, with whom there would be a natural bonding.

The past only gave him names of men-at-arms from the thirteenth century, and all that he could find in that timeline was an interesting group of powerful individuals called the Knights Templar.

Detailed investigation brought him to an awareness that they were probably mostly a group that was strong in the muscle department, but not mentally up to the tasks that he thought an associate had to handle. He left the Knights Templar open as an outside possibility.

He came to the conclusion that he probably needed to find someone from his own future, who would be a product of a more advanced society, and therefore someone who would have better skills at dealing with the problems of the societies that they would be coming in contact with.

CHAPTER FOUR

Time, Michel Nostradamus thought, *has been with us from the beginning, invisible, untouchable and ever-present.*

Early people were aware of it, watching the stars gradually change their position, experiencing the shifts of seasons, measuring their days, knowing when it was time to eat and time to sleep.

As civilizations evolved, so too did the concept of time. The scientists believed time resided in the heavens, as surely as destiny and astrology. The mathematicians were certain it was their arena, filled with numbers and calculations. The historians knew that they were the true owners of time. How else can we record achievements as well as conflicts? And the philosophers, not to be forgotten, maintained that wisdom and experience were the true manifestations of time. The fact that we started as helpless babies, blossomed into functional adults and then progressed into decrepitude was a cosmic message for the only animal that demanded to know the meaning of life, namely mankind.

Michel believed along with the historians. Time, as he understood it, was related to the duration of historical incidents, great and small.

Michel recalled vividly the very first experience that his new time-traveling ability gave him. He still shuddered mentally as he recalled the events of the special but terrible day that he decided to go out alone once more. He broke his own rule and paid the price.

He had just waved the crystal wand and allowed it to take him where it wished to take him within the time of the twelfth century. He wished to stay within the confines of western Europe. The twelfth century was dominated by the Knights Templar, and he was planning on taking a look at them to be sure that he was correct when he decided to exclude them from his list of possibilities. They seemed to be too unstable, and not as reliable as he needed his companion to be. As he waved his crystal wand, there suddenly was a flash of bright light and a mild disorientation that lasted only for a few moments.

As his attention returned, he saw that he was standing alone in the middle of a huge flat area of land, surrounded by some small foothills off in the distance. From the look of the familiar shape of the surrounding mountain range, he thought that he was somewhere near the border of France or possibly Spain. The timeline may change but the mountains seem to go on forever.

He turned around to get a better look at his surroundings and saw a mounted, armored figure bearing down on him quite rapidly from one of the nearby covering foothills. The knight was sitting astride a huge black war horse that was pounding toward him at a very rapid pace.

Michel quickly drew his sword as he noted that his assumed enemy had his sword already out and was waving it around his head as the great steed drew nearer to where he was standing. As part of Michel's martial-arts training was the practice of defending against an attack such as this. As such, Michel went into defensive mode, which was to stand perfectly still in direct line with the charging horse, which was trained to run down any human standing directly in front of him. The theory was that if the horse was going in a straight line toward the standing person, then the sword of the mounted knight would not come into play.

Michel stood perfectly still and watched the waving sword and the huge steed drawing nearer and nearer to him. Everything was in the timing. The horse was perhaps a dozen yards away when Michel unexpectedly jumped across the path that it was taking toward him. The knight was leaning downward on his left side to strike at what he saw was a right-handed opponent, when suddenly he wasn't there anymore, and his horse went on by where Michel had been standing only moments before.

As Michel leaped across the path of the oncoming mounted man and horse, he also swung his sword with all of his considerable strength behind it, and struck the shoulders of the horseman as he went by.

The horseman, having taken a mortal blow to the neck, began to slide off his mount on the left side that he was leaning, and that caused the horse to lose his stride and fall onto his side, pinning the knight beneath his considerable weight.

It was only a few moments until Michel had disarmed the helpless knight and led the horse to an upright position and let it run away across the field. He then turned his attention to the needs of the unconscious knight.

Michel noted that the knight was dressed in chain mail, an early form of body armor. He had a 'croix pattée' (an eight-pointed Templar cross) imprinted on a white sleeveless robe slit from the waist down for ease of movement. He wore a matching cloak knotted beneath his chin.

Michel, a doctor of medicine back in his own timeline, tried to find a pulse in the neck of the fallen knight, but could not find any. The knight had obviously broken his neck during the fall, besides having that fatal slash across his shoulders.

Being the religious man that he was, Michel said a few proper words over the body. He felt no guilt whatsoever in his having caused the death of the man lying there before him. The knight's attacking a stranger without notice was wrong, and Michel felt justified in his defending himself. He was also a little bit proud in how well he had defended himself on such short notice. His old martial arts instructor would have been smiling from ear-to-ear at him.

He rapidly reviewed what he had learned about this religious order from his detailed investigation into this timeline. He was trying to see if there was something in what he had read about them that would explain their attacking a stranger upon a moment's notice.

It seemed that the Knights Templar stimulated changes throughout Europe by them just being there in these very early years. They had accumulated great wealth before they were declared outlaws and were arrested, tortured and completely disbanded. Their controversial origins, true beliefs, and the sudden disappearance of their vast treasure has remained shrouded in great mystery.

Michel felt somewhat better than he had a few minutes ago; this knight that he had to kill in self-defense would have killed him without giving it a second thought. The Templar group that he belonged to was outlawed by the Church, and it was therefore not such a bad thing, what Michel had to do to save himself. He knew that he would be talking about this when he went to confession at his local church.

Until he was able to clear up his thinking on all of these things, he knew that he had to get back to his home base and organize himself better than just randomly time-jumping into the vast unknown. But before he left this area, knowing that he was never going to return, he needed to bring back a few items so that he could examine them at greater length and put them into the museum that he planned to start up about the places that this time-traveling thing would be taking him. It occurred to him that perhaps, if he kept good enough notes, someday he could write them up in the form of future predictions and make himself look intelligent and smart for the history books.

Michel carefully removed the long and very fancy sword from the hand of the dead Templar, and also removed the chain-mail glove that he wore on his sword hand. With these two memorable items in one hand and his own sword back in its scabbard, he used his free hand to transport himself back to the rooftop of his waiting castle where this adventure had started.

With the usual flash of light, Michel Nostradamus disappeared from the open field, and reappeared in his own timeline about thirty minutes after he had disappeared into the past.

CHAPTER FIVE

A special and most unusual note to the readers of this story from author Bud Seligson:

The Knights Templar always held a special fascination for me, and so, when the opportunity came up to be able to include them in the Nostradamus story, I, of course did so.

This chapter is a sidebar and should fill in the spaces on the story of the Knights Templar. Our Nostradamus story will continue right after the side bar.

Due to the rapid pace of the storyline of the Nostradamus novel, I could only touch upon the Knights Templar, and had to leave the impression that they were the "bad guys."

I decided to add this sidebar in order to briefly tell their special story and conclude with their sad, terrible, and quite tragic ending.

Well-known author Dan Brown, in his great, world-famous novel *The Da Vinci Code*, referred to the Knights Templar and left the impression that they are still around somewhere underground within our society.

I agree with Dan Brown; I also believe that they are well hidden and are very, very rich.

I do wish to refer you to a reading or a re-reading of that wonderful book, *The Da Vinci Code* (Dan Brown).

෨෨

Not too long ago, my wife Diane and I had dinner with our former editor, Beth Schindler, and her husband Ed.

At dinner Beth always came up with something unusual to talk about, and this night's conversation was upon the origin of the bad-luck superstition of Friday the thirteenth.

It was rather embarrassing that here I was, a Renaissance history major, and I really did not have the answer at my fingertips.

Most everyone has had the experience of riding up in an elevator listening to the so-called elevator music, and seeing that the call buttons for the stops went from the 12th floor directly to the 14th floor.

Obviously the 13th number became a bad-luck number, and Friday the 13th, which was the cause of the problem, became a universal bad thing.

I took this as a challenge, and mentally I thanked Beth and Eddie for such an interesting topic.

The first thing that I explored was the common conception that the last supper where Jesus and his apostles held their Friday night services was the source of the superstition.

This was the Friday night service where Jesus said that someone present was going to betray him.

It was very easy to see how this concept could have covered over the real story that I was after.

After all, it was a Friday night dinner, and there were thirteen people present at the dinner, and the actual date was the thirteenth.

As right as all of the above sounds, it was all wrong.

I soon discovered that the key to this riddle was buried in what Dan Brown, the author of the famous *The Da Vinci Code*, and Ron Howard, the director of the movie with the same name, called 'the knights of the temple of Solomon' or, as we know them, as the Knights Templar.

ॐ☯

Both the History Channel and A & E television stations carried the story of the Knights Templar. They have hinted that a newer and even greater mystery surrounds them in today's modern world, and it has a lot to do with the mystery surrounding Mary Magdalene.

Mary Magdalene, history tells us, was a reformed and repentant woman. However, within the story of *The Da Vinci Code*, she was portrayed as the wife of Jesus. And the story of her life, the real life of Mary Magdalene and not the twisted story that has come down to us, is a fantastic story—and perhaps if there is enough interest in her, we might go ahead and put something together on her at another time.

As follows, here is what I believe to be the true story of the Knights Templar, and the major effect that they have had on the world from the twelfth century to the present.

ॐ☯

By the year 1118, the Christians once again controlled the Holy Land, as the first crusade had been a resounding success.

Even though the Muslims were defeated, their lands confiscated, and their cities occupied, they had not been vanquished at all. They considered being forced out of the city to be a very minor setback in the grand scheme of events. And so, they remained on the edge of the newly established Christian kingdoms, wreaking havoc and mischief on all persons who were brave or foolish enough to venture to the Holy Land.

Safe pilgrimage to holy sites was one of the reasons for the crusades, and a fee or toll was now being charged for the true believers to be allowed to pass safely through the outskirts of the city. The new money-making machine was thought up by the conquerors, who called themselves the "Christian kingdom of Holy Jerusalem." Pilgrims were streaming into the Holy Land, arriving alone, in pairs, or sometimes as entire uprooted communities.

Unfortunately, the roads into and out of the city were not really safe and secure. Muslims lay in wait, and non-army Christian bandits roamed freely about. And even the Christian soldiers themselves were a threat, since robbing, stealing and rape was to them a normal way of doing business.

When a knight from Champagne, France, named Hugues de Payens started a new religious order consisting of himself and eight comrades-in-arms, it was to be a monastic order of fighting and religious brothers of the church who were dedicated to providing safe passage for pilgrims. The idea of protecting pilgrims on religious missions met with widespread approval.

The nobleman Baldwin II, who ruled Jerusalem, granted the new order a shelter under the Al-Aqsa Mosque, a place Christians believed to be the former temple site of the long-dead Jewish leader King Solomon. So, the new order of Templars took its name from its headquarters location: "the poor fellow soldiers of Christ and the temple of Solomon at Jerusalem," and thus was born the special order of the Knights Templar.

They owned nothing individually. All of their worldly goods became the property of the order. They lived in common, and took their meals in silence. They cut their hair short, but let their beards grow. Charity supplied their food and clothing. The emblem or seal for the order was particularly symbolic: two knights riding one horse—this was a clear reference to the days when knights could not afford their own mounts.

A religious order of fighting men was not comfortable to

the minds of most medieval people. However, this new order appealed, due to both religious and martial prowess. Its creation also solved another problem, namely one of manpower, since there would now exist a constant presence of trusted fighters.

In 1128, the fellowship had expanded, finding great political support in many powerful places. European princes and prelates donated land, money and materials to the order. The Pope ultimately sanctioned the holy order, and soon the Knights Templar became the one and only standing army in the Holy Land.

Extremely strict laws governed them. Hunting was forbidden. No gambling, hawking or females. Speech was rarely used and had to be without laughter. Ornamentation was banned, and they slept with the lights on, dressed in shirts, battle vests and pants, ready for battle at any time of the day or night. The head master was the absolute ruler and his generals acted as seconds-in-command. By an order of the Pope in 1148, each knight was allowed to wear a red cross with four equal arms, wide at the ends. It was impressed on top of a white shirt called a mantle.

These knights were the first disciplined, fully outfitted and regulated standing army since the early days of the powerful Roman empire. These brother knights participated in each of the subsequent crusades, always being the first group into the battle. They would always fight to the death as they would never allow themselves to be captured. They believed service to their order would clean their soul with heaven, and over the course of two hundred years of constant warfare, twenty thousand Templars gained their martyrdom by dying on the battlefield.

In 1139, the order was placed under the exclusive control of the Pope, which allowed it to operate freely throughout Christendom, unaffected by kings and royalty as they came and went upon the world's stage. This was something that had never happened before, and as the Templars gained political and economic strength, they began to put together a huge reserve of wealth.

This huge reserve of wealth is the whole point of this written piece. Great kings and other wealthy nobles left them great sums of money and valuables in their wills. Loans were made to barons and wealthy merchants on the promise that upon their death, their lands, castles, houses, vineyards, gardens and serfs would be taken over by the Knights Templar. Riches beyond riches were pouring in. Pilgrims in the Holy Land were now forced to pay for their "free" passage to holy locations.

By the beginning of the fourteenth century, the Templars rivaled the entire world with their net worth. The kings of France and England kept their treasury in the Templars' vaults. Even their enemies, the Muslims, banked with them. This had never been done before, and never again has something like this been seen.

The Templar's central city of Paris, France, became the center of the world's currency markets, as the organization slowly evolved into a financial and military complex that was self-supporting and self-regulating. Eventually, Templar properties numbered over nine thousand large estates, and all of these never had a tax bill. This led to many conflicts with local priests and landowners, who were struggling to pay taxes to the king. It was this jealousy that ultimately led to where our story is headed, and with the sudden downfall of the order. And the answer to the Friday the 13th question.

During the 12th and 13th centuries, control of the Holy Land seesawed back and forth between Christian and Arab forces. The downfall of the Knights Templar began with the rise of the great Saladin, a ruler of the Muslims. Saladin provided the Arabs with their first great military leader, and Christian Jerusalem finally fell to the Arab forces once again.

In the chaos and confusion that followed the fall of Jerusalem, the Templars moved all men, material, money and valuables to the small fortified city of Acre, which was a stronghold on the greater Mediterranean shore. For the next one hundred years, the Knights Templar were not a factor in or near the Holy Land, but with all their riches, they grew stronger and stronger in Europe, until they were the equal of the kings of England and France.

And here is the key to the riddle: finally, and after much deliberation, the king of France, Phillip IV, decided in the year 1307 that he had enough of the "upstart Templar order." He ordered that all their lands and finances should belong to him, since they were a French organization subject to his absolute rule. And so, in complete secrecy, King Phillip ordered his troops to surround each and every Templar location, and on the night of March 13th—a Friday of course, he ordered the deaths of every member of the Knights Templar to be found.

This day and date, Friday the 13th, has come down to us throughout history as bad luck. It truly was not good for the Templars. The king also ordered all of their personal holdings and properties to be brought to his treasury, and overnight he doubled his wealth. Many Templars, of course, escaped what history has correctly called "The Night of the Long Knives".

Those who survived that terrible night took themselves and their personal fortunes to Scotland, where they set themselves up once again as a very secret society. There is, or was, a definite connection with the royal order of Masons, which is still a functioning organization existing today. And since the Masons are also a secret organization, only myths, stories and speculations have leaked out.

The Knights Templar were greatly involved in the story of Mary Magdalene, as given to the world in *The Da Vinci Code* by Dan Brown, as we previously stated.

Perhaps, if we get a good response to this sidebar story of the Knights Templar, we could sit down and research a new story that would take history down the road of knowledge a little bit more.

Once again, my thanks to Beth and Eddie Schindler.

Thanks,
Bud Seligson

❧

And now back to our story of Nostradamus.

CHAPTER SIX

Benjamin finally huffed and puffed his way up the winding staircase, following the swiftly moving Nostradamus, who took to the stairs with the ease of a natural athlete. He promised himself that he would get in better physical shape if things went along as planned and as promised. He looked around at the large, flat roof area of the small castle that they were now standing on.

Benjamin estimated that they were twice as high as the nearest trees that grew in various clumps surrounding the castle. He was able to see the few large buildings in the far distance, he could see sunlight being reflected off of the rapidly flowing waterway and source of its drinking water.

Benjamin came to a halt a few feet behind Nostradamus who had stopped in what must have been the very center of the open roof area.

Nostradamus took hold of a multi-colored cord of thick rope, and with a great smile that he directed at Benjamin, pulled it firmly and quickly, causing the covering of a tent like material to fall to the roof floor.

What was revealed was a low-standing central stage with three stairs leading up to it. Surrounding the stage were eight extremely tall, full length mirrors whose upright angle caused the extremely bright sunlight from each one of them, to be focused upon a special table that was standing in the middle of the raised area.

The sunlight from these focused eight mirrors was being concentrated upon a large glass crystal wand that was standing upright in a holder. An open box held several extra crystal wands a few feet from the center.

An extremely interested Benjamin Franklin walked slowly around the mirrored area. He understood the basic principal behind the focus of all the mirrors upon one very small area as represented by the crystal wand. He walked over to Nostradamus, whom he knew was watching him move about, his eyes recording every move Benjamin made.

Benjamin, speaking in a very soft voice, said to his soon-to-be best friend, "The very concept of time-travel makes no sense at all, since time as we know it does not flow. The fact that we think that time passes is just an accident of our nervous system, or so I always thought." He continued, "In reality, it is not time that passes, we pass. Time itself always seems to be unmovable. It always seems to just be there, moving along at one specific speed and one specific pace."

Nostradamus said nothing as he listened carefully to the thought process that Benjamin was expressing to him.

Benjamin continued in the same soft voice. "Time itself has to be a non-variant. It never changes. It exists and just is. Therefore, past and future are not separate locations, the way London and Paris are separate locations. You seem to have set up a sort of doorway that goes from one location such as the one we are standing in right now, and the location you wish to step into by bending the concentrated light beams and anything else standing in the general area." A smiling Benjamin stopped speaking and stood there quietly waiting for a response from Nostradamus.

Benjamin had just said that it was impossible to time-travel, and yet both men accepted the fact that they were standing there at that moment, men from two separate timelines, interacting with each other. Benjamin could hardly wait for the response.

"Everything you have said is quite true, and has always been the rule that has guided the world we live in." Michel said. "I can't tell you why it works or the reality of how it works. I can only tell you that it works, and our both standing here is all the proof we really need. The best thing to do is for us to move into the flowing stream of time, and carefully jump into a safe timeline that will show you how this thing works. I propose that we take a few necessary items with us such as some small pieces of gold and silver so we can purchase food and other necessary things if we decide to stay for a while. Weapons carefully concealed within our clothing are also a must so that we can protect ourselves from the unknown hazards that we might be stepping into.

"I have spent a great amount of time thinking about what our first timeline adventure should be, and I have come up with something that I think will be of interest to the two of us. Let us retire from this area, and sit down and talk about my proposal over a hot cup of coffee that I am sure we can find in the downstairs kitchen."

Both men turned around and retraced their steps, heading back to the kitchen.

❧

About thirty minutes later, once again Michel and Benjamin were comfortably seated in the dining room with a steaming cup of coffee in hand, and a few tasty breakfast sweets spread out before them. Michel found that breakfast was his favorite meal, and he always put together an interesting table for friends and guests who came into his home.

He got right down to business. "I have researched in great detail our first adventure. It will take no adjustment on our part to fit into the location because I will only be taking us about twenty-five years into the future from now, and not many changes will be happening to the French countryside within that timeline.

"The adventure for us is to be at the jousting match of our present King Henri II of France in the year 1559. Our King at that time will be forty years old, and he will be wanting to show to the world that he has not slowed down at all. Jousting, of course, is a tournament-combat fought with breakaway long lances between two knights. Only royalty may joust as it is above the station of the average man in the fifteen hundreds."

"The two contestants come at each other on specially trained horses, holding long lances in front of them. Usually the contest is for show and bragging rights only, and the winner is considered to be the better man, and he always becomes a great favorite of the ladies. It usually has a carnival- or fair-like atmosphere where everyone has a wonderful day, but this time something will be going very wrong.

"In order to protect the knights from any harm other than being knocked off their horses, both contestants wear heavy body armor. There is no place on the armor that they can be struck and harmed in any way, except for one vulnerable area so small that it was always thought to be impossible that anything could happen. The only opening in the entire suit of armor is a one and one-half inch wide eye slit in the helmet. This of course is so that the knight could see where he was going.

"Well, Benjamin, the impossible happened. A splinter from the shattered lance of the King's opponent flew up and entered the opening and went into his eye and onward to his brain. The King fell to the ground and was pronounced dead within minutes."

"I am proposing that we travel twenty-five years into the future from where we are now, and watch this amazing happening for ourselves. I would like to write up this event in a journal that I wish to start up on predictions that I would make based on actual events that I would see as an eyewitness. Think of the great reputation that I would have in history, if my predictions would come true. We both know that they will be accurate because we will have seen the real thing happen and so I would only be reporting on the reality of what I predict.

"This puts forth an interesting concept that I believe you would agree with. See the event in person, go back to the past and predict the future with a knowledge that it will actually happen because it was already seen as happening. Confusing, isn't it?"

The two men continued to talk for the rest of the day and on into the early evening. Finally, they both agreed that a good night's sleep before tomorrow's big adventure began would be a good thing.

CHAPTER SEVEN

At the first whisper of sound, Benjamin was fully awake. He had left Nostradamus to his coffee and excused himself by saying he was very tired and was going to try and get some sleep. The adventure that they had planned for the next day sounded exciting, and it took him some time before he fell into a deep sleep. And then the sound that awoke him happened.

He became aware that the noise he heard was the soft *snick* of the well-oiled lock on the door leading into his room from the hallway. Someone had quietly cracked open the door and slipped into the room. Of this, Benjamin was certain. Even though the door was again closed and the room was in semi-darkness, he knew that someone was inside the room with him. His hand closed upon the hilt of the dagger he always kept under his pillow. Habits of a lifetime are hard to break.

Unable to clearly see, the room's intruder was probably waiting to orient himself within the complete dark-out of the bedroom. Ever so silently, Benjamin slid from beneath his blankets and crept toward the almost indiscernible sound of soft breathing.

As he stealthily closed upon his unseen visitor, Benjamin suddenly relaxed his tense grip upon his dagger. To his sensitive nostrils came the piquant fragrance of perfume. He swept out his arm and gathered in a startled female form.

The girl gave an involuntary yelp of surprise, then subsided in his embrace. A quick brush with his arm made it plain to him that the woman carried no weapon.

"I might have gutted you, young lady. It's a good thing that I heard your breathing and smelled your perfume. And wasn't that door locked? I do remember snapping the lock closed before I went to bed."

"Anyone can pick those locks. I have done it before. That doesn't matter, does it? The most important thing that counts is that I am here with you."

She was wearing only a thin shift. Benjamin, who was wearing rather less, was keenly aware of the warm female body that was pressed against his own bare flesh.

The girl was saying, "The master asked me to spend the night with you, and that I was to be very good to you." As she was saying this, she pressed herself tightly against him.

Benjamin was thinking to himself that Michel really knew how to make a guest in his home feel very welcome. And now he was wondering if all the things that he had heard about French girls were true or not. He realized that he was about to find out.

As he ran his hands in a brief caress, he determined that her shoulders were straight and almost mannish, her breasts were full and high, and her hips slender but generously curved. What more could one ask of so willing a female?

She rose on tiptoe to fully mold herself against his large and powerful frame. Her mouth opened to receive the heated branding of his searching tongue. A soft moan escaped her lips as she felt a simmering heat in the very depths of her being.

Benjamin's ears were filled with the soft sounds coming from deep within her throat. He held her crushed against him as his lips left her mouth and he tasted the softness of her cheek, the fragile curve of her jaw, and the slim line of her throat. As he placed moist kisses along the upper edge of her shoulders, he felt the straining fullness of her breasts. He lowered his lips and placed feathery kisses between the valley created by her breasts, while his fingers brushed against the hardened tips.

The girl inhaled sharply as she felt the soft caress of his fingers going down her spine. But she released her held breath just as quickly, as his head lowered once again down to her breasts. Sheer carnal desire flamed throughout her body as his lips settled over one rose-colored nipple. As he suckled the tender tip, her limbs weakened and she felt herself slipping to the floor.

Before she could fall very far, Benjamin gathered her up in his arms and stepped carefully into the small alcove that contained his large bed. Gently he laid her down upon the rumpled coverlet.

His mouth consumed hers with its searching demand as his tongue pushed forward, and finding no resistance from the compliant female, he sought out and touched each and every curve of her body as he once again traced a tempting path down to her ever-waiting breasts. As he drew a sweet nipple into his mouth, her body trembled with a deep, wanton desire that left her clutching at his head and pressing herself fully against him.

It seemed only seconds later that she lay upon the coverlet with nothing covering her body. Her gown had been discarded upon the floor beside the bed, and for a breathless moment Benjamin stared down at the wonderful curves of perfection that he could see in the darkened room.

The heated flames within his eyes seared every inch of her flesh, as he gazed upon the fullness of her twin globes with their dusty rose-colored buds. His eyes roamed down the length of her trim rib cage to the tiny indent of her navel, and across the womanly flare of her hips, and down the long, shapely legs.,

Benjamin, at age twenty-six, had bedded down a fair share of girls so far in his lifetime. Most of them were local girls from the

British Colonies, scattered over the eastern seaboard of America.

There were also a few native Indian girls who came into and out of his life; all sexy and exciting, as were all the others.

But, he thought quickly, as he was really quite busy with the young lady who occupied his full attention at that moment, *French girls were everything said about them and more.*

CHAPTER EIGHT

Benjamin's gaze caressed the delicate ankles and slim feet of the beautiful French maid that his new friend, Michel Nostradamus, had sent to him. He knew that he now owed Michel a big favor, and one he would definitely make up for in the future. But for the moment he was having one of the highlights of his young life.

He drew himself halfway up, eyes filling with burning desire as he looked down upon the junction of her womanhood, with the feathering of dark, curling hair lending a definite contrast to the creamy, pearl iridescence of her skin.

As his eyes returned to her face, she was parting her lips as if to speak, but seeing the desire in his eyes, she was content to know the power her woman's body had over this man. At that moment, she knew that her master's guest desired her above anything else in his life. This indeed was raw, female power and her own passion laced desires welcomed his seduction.

The irresistible pull of pleasure's promise grabbed her body as Benjamin's mouth again roamed over her. Feathered kisses, licking and nibbling, he ravished her breast once again. His straight white teeth caressing the under-flesh and driving her mad with her own desire. A soft moan escaped from her, deep within her throat, and at the same time his dark head lowered to her ribs and the tempting curves of her waist and hips.

The taste of her sweet flesh and the feel of her satin-smooth body combined to seduce Benjamin into a physical wanting that knew no bounds. His hands splayed over the firmness of her belly and then pressed on closer to her hips. His tongue sent flames shooting throughout the lower portion of her body, as he rubbed the inside of her thighs. As his mouth touched her woman's jewel, she bucked as sweet forbidden pleasure snaked through her womb and thrashing limbs.

Without mercy, Benjamin kept up his love play, his tongue plunging into her moist, sweet depths, and lingering over the extremely sensitive nub as she shuddered again and again. Her cries filled his ears and fueled his desire to pleasure her to the fullest.

As the trembling of her body slowly subsided, and the fingers within his hair lessened their tight hold, Benjamin rose from his position between her thighs. His lips seared branding kisses over her body, as he finally pressed his length of manhood against her. His eyes witnessed the sated passion on her face before he covered her mouth once more with his own.

The girl opened up to him, too swept up in the steaming rapture of the moment to do otherwise. As Benjamin's tongue filled her mouth, he felt the sculpted marble head of his love-tool pressing at the opening between her parted thighs.

His buttocks drew upward and as he entered her, just an inch or so, he felt the tightness of her passage. Another thrust and another inch as he felt the velvet trembling of her inner sanctum. A low rumbling came from within his own chest and filled the entire room with his animal-like noises. He moved back and forth, going slowly deeper and deeper, and then withdrawing back to the very lips of her moist opening.

Over and over he plied her with his skillful seduction, until she was clutching his back, with her head thrown back wildly, as the fullness in her loins drove her toward a frenzy of mindless desire. Each time the brand of his lance drove into her depths and stirred her, her body moved toward completion. Her legs slowly rose and fell as she sought to capture and hold onto the entire length of him that was deep within her.

Still holding himself back somewhat, Benjamin caught hold of her buttocks, and with a talent born of past love-making, he maintained his inner control. Even as he felt the shuddering coming from the lady beneath him, he was able to inhale deep breaths of air, willing himself not to release the final fury of his passion.

Benjamin knew the power of her climax, and for a moment or two, he fought his own heated need that was racing through his own loins. He watched her passion-filled face and heard the climatic moans escaping from her throat. Each thrust was now torture-laced for him as he fought off the aching need for his own fulfillment.

Only when he felt her climax receding did he allow himself to give full vent to his own desire. His mouth covered hers, and as he plunged just a fraction deeper into her soft velvety depths, wildfire absolutely caught within him. Scalding pleasure burst forth from the center of his being, and showered upward, racing through his most powerful lance.

It took Benjamin several minutes to regain his normal breathing and to conquer the disbelief that filled his brain as he thought about the wonderful moment that had just occurred between himself-and this woman. A slight shudder coursed through him as he realized that he had never before been driven to such powerful feelings of lust and surely, he thought, she must have felt the same thing. Turning his face so that he could gaze into her eyes, he found her eyelids closed, her breathing soft, and her arms caressing his neck.

She slept peacefully in his arms, and a small smile filtered over his lips. It seemed quite silly, but he did not even know her name.

Tomorrow would be soon enough for all the adventures that Michel had promised him. For now, he just wanted to enjoy the moment. Sleep, slow and pleasant came to him in the most wonderful manner. Everything was quiet within the darkened room.

CHAPTER NINE

Morning came too early for the utterly exhausted Benjamin Franklin as he stood next to Michel on the rooftop of the castle. Neither man made any reference as to how they had slept last night, although Benjamin was sure that he saw a twinkle and a slight smile each time Michel looked over at him.

Benjamin vowed to himself that when the time was right, and he had Michel in Benjamin's own timeline, he would do something to top Michel's gift to him from last night. He would have to do something extraordinary to beat or match Michel's gift but he had lots of "time" to think about it.

Right now, Benjamin was paying close attention to Michel, who was handing him small but deadly weapons that he was to conceal within his clothing. Michel said that the last few times he had time-traveled, violence was happening all around him, and he did not want them to be caught without a way to protect themselves.

Benjamin had given up his English style of clothing, and was now standing there looking like a stylish French lord, as was Nostradamus. Michel had filled Benjamin's money purse with a great amount of gold and silver coin, and he concentrated upon what Nostradamus was saying.

"On this, our first time-jump together, we shall only jump into the near future, and we should try to arrive just after sundown, so that our arrival won't be noticed by any of the locals who will be moving around. I'll tell you more about what we're going to be doing a little later. Right now, I would really appreciate your taking a few minutes out to read my last entry in my time-travel journal to see if I am clearly reporting what I experienced in a different timeline. I am open to any comments or suggestions that you might have for me so that what I personally experienced will sound like predictions."

Benjamin sat down in his favorite seat in the kitchen and positioned himself so that the sunlight streaming in through the high windows would brighten the papers that Michel had given him to read. He put his excitement about their time-jump out of his mind for a few minutes as he settled down to read Michel's adventure. He was curious about where and when the famous Doctor Nostradamus had taken himself to.

Michel excused himself from the room so as to give Benjamin some quiet time to concentrate on the papers.

The first thing that Benjamin noticed was that the report must have been written in French, which was Nostradamus's natural language. It was obvious that he had translated the French into English so that Benjamin could comfortably read it. Benjamin was going to suggest that he leave his report in the original French or else have a professional language translator do the conversion since some of the English words did not quite satisfy what he knew Nostradamus was trying to express. He wrote that comment down on the blank paper that had been provided to him.

He began to read Nostradamus's translation of his timeline adventure:

The subject I wanted to find out more about was none other than the famous Leonardo da Vinci.

The facts about the great Leonardo are well known throughout the world, and I decided to follow through on one of his famous paintings, perhaps the most famous painting in the world—the Mona Lisa.

༺༻

Leonardo was born on April 15, 1452, in Vinci, Italy.

He was born out of wedlock, the love-child of a respected notary and a young peasant woman.

He was greatly concerned with the laws of science and nature, which greatly influenced his work as a painter, sculptor, and draftsman.

His greatest paintings are the last supper, and the *Mona Lisa*.

Leonardo's most well-known painting and arguably the most famous painting in the world, the *Mona Lisa*, was a privately commissioned work and was completed sometime between 1505 and 1507. The picture of the Mona Lisa is a half-length portrait of a woman. In the Italian language, the *Mona Lisa* is *La Giaconda,* and in French it is *La Joconde*. It has been said that Mona Lisa had jaundice, that she was a pregnant woman and that she wasn't actually a woman at all, but a man in drag. The *Mona Lisa* is considered to be the source of countless advertisements, poetry, songs and sculptures.

For the great Leonardo, this painting was always a work in progress, as it was his attempt at perfection. The painting was never delivered to the person who commissioned it, in that Leonardo kept it with him until his death.

Toward the end of his life, an ailing Leonardo was invited to spend his years in France at the court of King François the First. Once there, Leonardo was highly honored and greatly respected. Rather than being simply a court painter, he was given the title of premier architect, engineer and painter to the French court.

King François, by all accounts, had a special place in his

heart for Leonardo, and the feeling appears to have been mutual. Leonardo presented his favorite painting, the *Mona Lisa*, as a gift to the king. Upon Leonardo's death, the king gave the painting to the louvre museum where it was looked upon as just one more nice picture by Leonardo da Vinci. It stayed in the museum as just another picture for many long years.

And here is where the story of the *Mona Lisa* gets interesting.

It was the art theft that gave it its fame and fortune. On August 21, 1911, someone stole the not-so-famous painting from out of the museum. It was the theft and the interesting story of how it was done that brought the picture into the public consciousness and worldwide fame.

The resulting story of the theft, its final recovery and the story that lies within, is what I, Michel Nostradamus decided to investigate, and as follows are the results of my investigation.

CHAPTER TEN

On August 21,1911, a small-time French portrait painter was setting up his artist's easel in the Salon Carré in one of Paris's most famous museums, called the Louvre.

There are well over twenty very small side rooms in the Louvre that directly face the location where the portrait of Mona Lisa smiled out at her admirers.

Louis Béroud, the painter, was planning to paint his copy of the *Mona Lisa* portrait as he had done many times before. But this time, something was very wrong. There was a completely empty space where the picture should have been hanging.

When he first asked the guard, who was walking around, where the *Mona Lisa* was supposed to be, he was told that it probably was in the photography room where copies of portraits were made. Louis Béroud waited for the painting's return, but finally he was getting impatient, so he asked the guard once again about where the *Mona Lisa* portrait was, and why it was taking so long. The guard checked with his supervisor and then went back to Louis Béroud. The artist was now pacing back and forth in front of the empty space where the *Mona Lisa* should have been.

The guard, with a definite shake in his voice, admitted that the portrait was … gone.

It seems that the most famous painting in today's world, Leonardo's *Mona Lisa*, was not very well known in the 1900s. The painting, up to that point, only was appreciated by art professionals and a very few others. The general public was almost completely unaware of the painting. But the news of the theft caught the public's collective imagination, and it transformed the simple painting into a cultural icon. The whole civilized world was talking about it, not only the local French.

Suddenly, the whereabouts of the *Mona Lisa* became a red-hot item. The picture's likeness began to show up on posters, postcards, coffee mugs, in nightclubs, on movie screens and anywhere else that was imaginable. Perhaps the strangest part of this whole story was the fact that record crowds of people from around the world, began to show up at the museum just to look at the empty space where the painting used to hang. The burning question of the moment was: where was the picture of *Mona Lisa*?

All kinds of theories were being talked about in France. With the First World War just getting ready to start, many people thought that the Germans, who were the number-one enemy of France at that time, had taken it in order to humiliate the French. Others thought that it was probably an elaborate practical joke that was intended to stir up interest in the museum.

It took well over two weeks before the detailed search of the entire museum was completed. They never found the portrait, but what did turn up was the painting's empty frame. They located it at the very top of a tall staircase in the rear of the museum. It was believed that this location was probably the escape route taken by the clever thief.

The months passed by quickly, and for two years there was no sign of the painting. The fascinating question at that time, was what would an art thief have done with the portrait? It was valued at five million dollars, and in later years it would be beyond belief in value.

To whom could the thief sell the painting? Even if a buyer was found and was willing to spend that much money, wasn't the painting too highly profiled to be passed easily along the art-thief network? It would have been too easy to trace. The crook would have been caught without difficulty no matter where in the world he tried to sell it.

The answer finally came on November 29, 1913. A very wealthy art dealer, Alfred Gert, had a note passed to him one evening at a dinner party that he was attending. The note was from someone whom he did not know. The note, from a person who called himself Leonardo Vincenzo, offered to return the Mona Lisa portrait to him for a fee.

Alfred Gert thought it was a hoax, another practical joke among many having to do with the painting. He was intrigued enough, however, to put together a meeting at a local Florence hotel. He invited the museum's chief of staff and the local police to attend the meeting with him.

The two men walked into the hotel room, and the police waited patiently outside and out of sight. Once inside the room, they encountered a short, mustachioed Italian man, who told them that he left Italy and moved to Paris at the time of the art theft. He then reached underneath the unmade bed and pulled out a long object that was carefully wrapped in red silk.

The museum director, who was an art expert, unrolled the covering and examined the painting in great detail. His examination was very careful and very complete. He declared that the painting in front of him was authentic. It was the real Mona Lisa portrait.

The bottom line, or the end of this story, was that Leonardo Vincenzo, the thief, did not receive his ransom money. Instead he was arrested right on the spot and taken to the local police station where he freely admitted that he was the one who stole the *Mona Lisa*.

On the morning of the theft, he explained, he entered the museum dressed in a flowing printer's smock. He went straight for the famous *Mona Lisa* painting, and he recalled that there were no other visitors or guards anywhere in sight. He then removed the painting from the four wall hooks, and hid it under his loose-fitting smock, frame and all, and then he simply walked out of the exhibit hall. When he reached the rear staircase, he removed the painting from the frame and continued his way. The entire theft took about twenty-five minutes from start to finish.

So why did he do it? Why did he take the *Mona Lisa*?

He said, "It was for love of my country, which is Italy." He said this clearly and loudly when he had his day in the French court system (and I was sitting there taking in every word). He said that the Mona Lisa belonged in Italy, not France. He said that when Italy's greatest artist, Leonardo da Vinci, painted the portrait, his intention was to leave the picture within the country of his birthright, which of course was Italy. He made an impressive and interesting defense for himself, and the French press took hold of it and ran many days' worth of headlines with it.

The French judge who was hearing the case later remarked to the press that he had thoughts of letting the little thief go, but his past criminal record of burglaries, along with other various offenses, convinced him that Leonardo Vincenzo's motivation was much less than patriotic. The judge sentenced him to seven months in jail, and when Vincenzo died in 1927, he was still bragging about being one of Italy's greatest patriots. The people of Italy were not really sure if he was a hero or just another confidence man, and mostly they left him alone.

As for the now-famous picture of Mona Lisa, it made a triumphant return to the museum in France where today the

Mona Lisa smiles out from behind her impregnable, climate-controlled, bulletproof case. The picture averages about five million admirers each year with tourists and locals who simply come to the museum just to see her famous smile.

Benjamin turned the last page face down, and sat at the kitchen table for a few minutes.

He was starting to get a feel for just who Michel Nostradamus really was. Michel seemed to be a most intelligent, well-meaning and deep individual, who had a great curiosity about many things. Benjamin thought that he personally could learn a lot about people and places just by being with Michel.

And personally, he began thinking about himself starting up an interesting little paper back home in the American colonies. Maybe it could be his view upon everyday life that was going on around him. He thought of a good name for it while staring out Michel's garden window. How did the name "*Poor Richard's Almanack*" sound? It sounded pretty good to him.

He got up, stretched, and gathered up the papers as he went in search of Michel.

It was time to start their great adventure together.

CHAPTER ELEVEN

It was perhaps an hour later that found both men finally walking up the steps that led them to the raised platform on the roof of the Nostradamus castle.

The bright sunshine focused upon the area where they now entered caused Benjamin to cover his eyes. He knew that the eight mirrors were directly pointed at the very center of the platform but that didn't help him with the glare.

Michel quickly walked over and removed one of the fully charged crystal wands. With a very little twist of his wrist, Michel, who was holding Benjamin's arm in a tight grip, made a rapid series of motions with the crystal, and with a blue flash and a low-frequency rumbling, the two men vanished from view. If anyone were watching, they would have seen their two bodies dissolve in a maelstrom of sparkling blue light and then into nothingness.

Again, Benjamin felt only a momentary touch of dizziness which quickly left him.

No longer were they standing on the roof of the Nostradamus castle, but they now found themselves on a slightly hilly area somewhere in the countryside, not too far from where the center of Paris was to be found. There was no moon, and the sky was black and filled with stars and the occasional drifting cloud.

Michel led them down the hill into a large area full of small trees.

Benjamin was surprised to find out that once his eyes adjusted, he could actually see quite well by starlight. Probably because there was no air pollution, night vision was easier. He remembered reading that in centuries earlier than his own seventeen hundreds, people could actually see the planet Venus during the day, just as everyone was clearly able to see the moon in his own time. He was also surprised by the utter silence of the night. The loudest sound they heard was their own feet moving through the grass and scrubby bushes.

"We'll follow the path," Michel whispered. "Then down to the river."

Their progress was quite slow. Frequently they paused, crouching down to listen for two or three minutes before moving on. They did not want to be seen wandering about at night.

Almost an hour passed before they came within sight of the final dirt path that ran from where they were, and then on down to the river. The path was a pale streak against the darker grass and foliage that surrounded it. Dawn was finally breaking, and the two time-travelers were able to come out of hiding and join the hundreds of local Frenchmen who were going to watch the jousting.

It was not very often that the King consented to try his hand in competition with the knights of his realm.

Since the body armor was so complete, the worst that could happen to any of the combatants was to get a bruise or two if they were knocked off of their horse.

Henry II of France was a forty-year-old male. He was considered to be in excellent physical condition.

His opponent was a much younger knight, the Count of

Montgomery. There was much excitement in Paris at the thought of actually seeing the King.

When Michel and Benjamin finally reached the top of the hillside, they were able to look down on the famous castle of the King.

Benjamin was most impressed with the dark and sinister-looking castle that stood high above the largest buildings in France. It was called the Fortress of La Rogue, and it had been assaulted by enemies many times but never conquered.

On the east and south sides, the castle was built atop a huge limestone cliff with a sheer drop of over five hundred feet. The castle could never be attacked from those approaches. The other two sides of the castle walls had huge water-filled moats and a series of drawbridges. The king and nobles of France were well-protected within the castle walls.

The rules for the joust were very simple. Two knights on horseback would charge at each other and each try to unhorse their opponent by means of a breakaway ten-foot lance. The joust between knights usually ended in a draw, since both lances frequently broke on the armor of the knights, and everyone went away happy.

Michel and Benjamin joined all the other minor nobles and townspeople as they stood and watched the goings-on from raised areas surrounding the arena. They had an excellent view of the action.

The higher nobles and many Church representatives were sitting in shaded and raised viewing stands. Most of them brought servants along to see to their personal comforts. The overflowing crowd was noisy, and quite colorful, as they were all dressed up in their finest clothing.

The time-travelers, who were dressed as nobles, were able to get seated in the front row of an excellent viewing location.

The crowd was treating the event like a huge party where

everyone was having a good time. A good time, that is, until the final event when the King and the Count met in the last face-off of the day. The crowd came to an absolute silence as the heralds blew their trumpets for attention and quiet.

The King and the Count took their proper places at the very end of the long horse run that was divided in the middle with a series of large wooden panels to keep the horses from running into each other. As the trumpet sounded, both men spurred their horses into a fast gallop as they pounded along their way. The lances were carefully held chest high so that if and when they made contact with the opponent, the contact point would stay chest high, and maybe one or possibly both of the fighters would be thrown from their mounts but should emerge basically unhurt.

As fate would have it, each lance hit the other rider chest-high, and both riders were lifted off of their saddles by the violent strikes. But after a minute or two, when the Count staggered to his feet, the crowd went silent when the King did not move. The King was rushed off the field on a stretcher, and it was later announced that a splinter had broken off from one of the wooden lances and, astonishingly, had flown into the one-and-a-half-inch eye-slit opening, and penetrated into the King's brain. He had been dead before he hit the ground.

Michel and Benjamin did not wait around to hear all the wailing and crying that would follow the turmoil that history said followed the royal death. Nostradamus grabbed a flag showing the coat of arms of the now-deceased King Henry II of France for his growing collection at home.

The two men worked their way through the crowd to a nearby stand of trees that would hide them from any onlookers. Michel waved his wand, and again with a blue flash, the two men disappeared from view and reappeared on the rooftop of the Nostradamus castle.

They were both exhausted but happy at the experience.

Michel had his trophy, and Benjamin saw the time-travel process in action. Michel was going to stay up for a-while and write up the day's adventure in the form of a prediction, and promised to read it to Benjamin when they met the next day.

Benjamin wished Michel a good evening, and quietly went off to the servant's quarters to look for the no-name serving girl. Benjamin knew that he had a good thing going here.

CHAPTER TWELVE

Twenty-four hours had passed, and both men were quite relaxed and enjoying the discussion upon the remarkable ending of King Henry II's life.

Benjamin had once again made the point that it was an almost impossible thing that had happened with the splinter finding its way into the tiny eye-slit. The odds against that happening were absolutely enormous, but they had both seen it happen right in front of their eyes.

Michel had given Benjamin the paperwork that had kept him up all night writing. He had written a publication for the local news letter that was to be well circulated in the small town. It was his prediction of the death of an important noble in the near future.

Michel was careful not to mention names and actual events, and tried to be unclear as to exactly what happened. He seemed to enjoy putting to paper, events that he had witnessed and could write up as educated predictions.

Benjamin could not see anything of great interest coming from Michel's writings, but he complimented Michel greatly as he read the writings so as to keep him happy and in a good mood.

Benjamin himself was a happy man as he sat there with Michel. While Michel was concerning himself with scholarly things, Benjamin had found his previous night's companion and worked upon things not quite as proper as Michel's.

He learned that her name was Mimi, and she worked as the upstairs maid and sometimes backup cook. She was twenty-three years old and looked better to Benjamin in clothes that she had without them.

In a short period of time, Benjamin would have Michel transport Mimi with him, back to Philadelphia in colonial times, and she would live as Benjamin's mistress for many years. Benjamin would be very kind to her as she was to him. But this is another story for another time, and it is interesting to note that comments from Mimi about Colonial days as compared to her life in the fifteen hundreds are very interesting and offer a different viewpoint on day-to-day happenings in those special days.

Putting all thoughts of Mimi out of his head for the moment, Benjamin sat and looked over the new papers that Michel had given him to review. The original copy was in Michel's handwriting and were written in French. An exact copy followed with an English translation that Michel put to paper for Benjamin to read:

LE LYON JEUNE LE VIEUX SURMONTERA.
EN CHAMP BELLIQUE PAR SINGULIER DUELLE,
DANS CAIGE D'OR LES YEUX LUY CREVERA:
DEUX CLASSES UNE, PUIS MOURIR, MORT CRUELLE.

The English translation is as follows:

THE YOUNGER LION SHALL MEET THE OLDER

ON MARTIAL BATTLEFIELD IN SINGLE DUEL.
IN A CAGE OF GOLD HIS EYES HE'LL PUT OUT
TWO FORCES JOINED, THEN A DEATH MOST CRUEL.

Several hours passed and Michel, in a most gracious mood, asked Benjamin where he would have them go upon their next adventure. He had prepared a partial list of places that he thought would be both safe and interesting for them to physically travel to.

He asked Benjamin to take one of the next few days off and wander into town on his own and see the local sights. They could talk about Benjamin's thoughts for their future travel any time in the next few days.

Later that night, Benjamin retired to his room and had his dinner sent up. He was anxious to take a look at the paperwork that Michel had given him. This time-travel adventure thing still caused his adrenaline to flow, and the excitement of famous dates, events and people were beyond description.

The only negative thing that he saw in all of this was that after a few more fantastic adventures with Nostradamus he would be completely worn out, and perhaps it would be time for him to get on with his own life. And, speaking of his own life, he knew that he would never allow their travels to go to his own lifetime in Colonial America. He realized that no man should be allowed to know his own future. It could, and would, cause terrible things to happen.

With that thought in mind, Benjamin opened up the letter that he had been given in regard to future time- travel events with Michel.

The letter, as usual, was neatly printed out in Nostradamus's precise lettering. Everything that Michel did, always seemed to be done with a great deal of thinking involved. The letter read as follows.

My dear Benjamin:

I have spent a great deal of time thinking about the many possibilities available to us by route of our time-traveling. Needless to say, I am sure that you realize how pleased I am that you have consented to be my partner in all things. We both know that your joining me will be only for a limited time, and until you have had your fill of adventure and fantastic events, I am honored with your friendship and companionship.

It is my plan to have us do five more time jumps together into the flow of time. With the predictions that I shall make based upon what you and I actually see and what we will be experiencing, I believe that my credibility will be established for all time as a great prophet of the future. I shall be extremely happy with that kind of reputation.

I also promise you future rewards of the most generous kind when I finally return you to where and when you want to stay. I know that you believe me when I say that I shall make you a wealthy man for the rest of your many years of life.

And so, my dear friend, adventurer and traveling companion, please find a partial list of my suggested five stops in the order that I believe we should make them. I'll fill you in on my reasoning for each selection in greater detail-before we would actually do our jump.

Please feel free to submit an entry of your own to our travel agenda. Nothing is locked and everything is open to our discussions.

I remain your humble and trusted friend.
Michel Nostradamus

CHAPTER THIRTEEN

Here are my suggested time visitations in the order that I believe would be best: First, Philip the Second, King of Spain. We shall be visiting him while his country is at war with England and he is getting ready to send out his Spanish armada against them.

Philip, a thoroughly religious man, wants to achieve two things out of his conquest of England.

He wanted to bring England back into the fold of the Catholic Church. Under King Henry the Eighth of England, who was the present Queen Elizabeth's father, England had changed to a Protestant country because of an issue that came up with the Pope over his many divorces. He was looking for a male child to take the throne after him, but sadly for him, his many wives only gave him female children. And so, Philip of Spain wanted to throw out Elizabeth and put himself on the throne.

The second reason why he would send his huge fleet of fighting ships was that the defenses of England were very poor and he saw a good chance to gain the wealth of England for his own.

I believe that it would be interesting for Michel Nostradamus and Benjamin Franklin to appear at Phillip's court in 1558 and see for ourselves what was really happening there. It would be a wonderful story for me to write up as one of my predictions of future happenings.

My suggested second time stop would be to visit with the times of Napoleon Bonaparte.

Napoleon is a most fascinating man who should have been able to conquer the world. I wish to see just what the few mistakes he made, that cost him his conquest in the eighteen hundreds. We could probably spend months and months observing this important timeline, but I wish to limit us to only Napoleon's final defeat at the Battle of Waterloo.

I am open to your thoughts of whether or not you also would want to see how he actually became the dictator of France. Let us talk about possibly doing both. Either one or both would be fine with me: the dates for these two Napoleon events are June 18, 1815, for the Battle of Waterloo, and he became Emperor of France in 1804.

I forgot to mention to you that we will need to put out heads together and figure out how we will get proper clothing to wear for each different time period that we decide to go to.

My third suggestion for our time jump is to visit Cesare Borgia, who lived in the late fourteen hundreds.

Cesare Borgia died violently at the young age of thirty-one. He was the son of a pope and was a great Italian military leader. He was made a cardinal of the Catholic Church by his father. What was interesting about this era was that the Borgia family was very big on poisoning their enemies. Let us be very careful about what we eat and drink if we decide to visit this timeline.

My fourth suggestion is Julius Caesar, senator of Rome, its greatest general and first dictator/emperor.

In this early timeline of the Roman empire, we shall also meet Mark Antony and the fabulous Cleopatra. We would be going the farthest back that I ever went time-traveling, about twenty-five hundred years to the years around 49 BCE.

What I really want to see is the killing of Julius Caesar by his most trusted friends (of which the famous Brutus was the leader of the plot)—Brutus was always one of my heroes from the story associated with the saying "Beware the ides of March."

I also would like to watch Cleopatra as she moved from one great Roman empire leader to another.

Cleopatra moved around from Julius Caesar, (the father of her son Octavian), to Mark Antony, who was with her toward the end of her life, when she chose to die from a deadly bite from a snake. The snake was an asp, whose bite was absolute death within minutes. She chose the snake rather than personally surrender her country to the Romans. This was such a waste because the Romans took over Egypt anyway. They wanted Egypt because of the Nile River's tremendous production of food to feed its army, which was spreading out in all directions.

I am especially excited to see Julius Caesar being stabbed to death by sixteen of his trusted Roman senator friends.

The final Roman scene that has my interest is when Cleopatra has herself smuggled into Caesar's room, and has herself unrolled from the rug that she was hiding in. Can you imagine Julius Caesar's surprise when this beautiful woman was unrolled in front of him?

The fifth choice was one that I left open for you in case you had a suggestion, Benjamin.

If you don't have anyone in mind, then I would like to visit Merlin at King Arthur's court. The Knights of the Round Table have always been one of my favorite stories, and I would like to see Sir Lancelot in person.

I am looking forward, as always, to seeing you at breakfast. Please bring with you an opinion upon the worthiness of my above list. If nothing else, our time-travels should be interesting.

> I remain your humble friend.
> Michel Nostradamus

CHAPTER FOURTEEN

The next morning arrived right on time, and with it the bright sunshine that came into the large second-story bedroom where Benjamin Franklin was just waking up. He turned over and reached across the huge bed for Mimi, but once again she had completely disappeared.

He knew that she had to be up and about before anyone else in the household was moving around. She had to have the fires lit in the kitchen and the rest of the castle, and she had to have the coffee ready for the master when he came down. She took her duties as housekeeper of the Nostradamus household very seriously.

A large and very lazy smile played across Benjamin's pleasant looking face as he thought about last night's love-making. Mimi had shown him several new positions, which he enjoyed tremendously, although he was not quite sure that he had got them all right. Practice, as Mimi had said with a little smirk on her adorable French face, will make things perfect.

Benjamin planned to get in as much of that practice as he could with this remarkable bedmate that his new and good friend Nostradamus had provided him with. It was with a positive spring to his step, that Benjamin showered, shaved, and dressed and made himself presentable.

This morning, for sure; the two of them were going to walk to the village. Michel had promised to point out some highlights of the little town. The plan was to end up in the local coffee shop that overlooked the peaceful river that could be seen quietly rushing by.

Benjamin thought that Michel was the actual owner of the little shop, and probably several of the other local establishments. The Nostradamus family had been in the area for many generations, and they surely had their fingers into a lot of the local activities. Obviously, not much that was happening in and around the town escaped Michel's notice, and everyone seemed quite happy with whatever arrangements they made in and around the prosperous little area.

Before he left his room, Benjamin opened up the windows to let some fresh air into the room, and he drew up a large sitting chair. He had some very serious thinking to do before he got into the discussion with Michel over their next few time-travel adventures. He had read over carefully the list that Nostradamus had provided him with, and one obvious problem had occurred to him.

From the notes that Michel had given him, it was quite clear that he was most interested in going back a tremendous amount of years to the time of Julius Caesar, the Roman Empire, and Cleopatra.

The problem as Benjamin saw it, was a simple but not easily fixable one. Whenever Nostradamus had time-traveled, either by himself or with a companion such as Benjamin along, the arriving time-travelers had never stood out from the crowd and could not be identified as not belonging there.

The example for this was when Nostradamus went back and had to kill the one Knight Templar who had tried to kill him. No one saw Nostradamus, and he then disappeared without a trace. This was nice and clean and would have no effect upon the delicate fabric of time.

It was also true when the two of them went back and watched the King of France die with a tiny wood splinter in his eye. They had looked just like the crowd who watched the jousting and no one in the crowd was the wiser.

All of the above was well and good as far as it went, but now that Nostradamus wanted to personally witness the killing of Julius Caesar and his earlier love-making with Cleopatra, perhaps he was going a bit too far with his personal risk taking. Benjamin thought that he could not suddenly appear on the scene without the guards surrounding this most famous Queen and this great General of Rome striking him down instantly. He would have absolutely no chance of surviving those scenes, and it was Benjamin's thought to talk him out of such foolishness.

He planned to put several objections to Nostradamus later that morning when they walked to breakfast in town at the coffee shop. Benjamin hoped that Nostradamus would be reasonable and listen carefully to what he had to say. If Benjamin was with Nostradamus when he was killed, then Benjamin would spend the rest of his life in that early timeline, and that was not a very pleasant though.

Within the next hour, two of history's most famous men were walking and talking as they worked their way down the cobblestone streets. They were heading from the castle into the lower flat-lands where the center of the town was located.

Nostradamus was playing tour guide, and Franklin was the very attentive tourist who actually was absorbing the many facts that his French host was throwing out at him in a rapid-fire manner. He was saying, "Our little city has a total population of about six thousand people who are concentrated in and about a five-square-mile area.

"The river, which is the life-blood of our activities, runs right down the center of the city, which has grown up on both sides of the flowing waters.

"Our city, Saint-Rémy-de-Provence, is located in the south of France, and due to the river running through it, we have become a riverside manufacturer of fine wools and silks for all of France.

"The city always has been very fortunate in breeding local talent, genius and fame. It compounded the vast amounts of money pouring into the city treasury, by building a domed Church higher that any to be found in Paris. We have more public statuaries, many sumptuous homes, and many eloquent poets. Saint-Rémy-de-Provence has always been a very nice city to live in.

"French architecture ranks high among the many accomplishments we have achieved.

"The countryside shows off our French Provincial style, which is the high second-story windows with many arches on the roof-tops.

"And there you have it, my friend Benjamin. The history of my world, as you Americans would say, 'in a nutshell.'

"And now, here we are, right in front of our little coffee shop. Come, let us go right in. I know the owner quite well, and he always has a table set for me."

CHAPTER FIFTEEN

Nostradamus was right. A special table in the rear of the small coffee shop was held for him just upon the rare chance that he might come in.

With many smiles and hugs, they were shown to their seating area, and a large and beautifully designed curtain was drawn in front of them to preserve their privacy.

Benjamin was most impressed with all of the magnificent paintings that were hung everywhere within the location. Almost all of them were done in soft pastel colors, and showed off the local countryside beautifully. Benjamin noticed one or two that had the signature of Michel Nostradamus in the lower right hand corner. It seemed that among all of his other talents, Michel was also an artist of local fame. Some other day than today, Benjamin would ask him about his art work, but for now they had other and more important things to discuss.

Benjamin left the ordering to Michel, and was pleased when coffee was served with croissants and marmalade. There were several side platters of freshly churned butter and several kinds of local cheeses. The conversation was kept very light during breakfast, and the most interesting bits were when the natural discussion between men, who were comfortable with each other, turned to women. This topic came up when Nostradamus asked

Benjamin about how passionate the American women were in the seventeen hundreds. America was known then as the thirteen British Colonies.

Benjamin, with a far-off look on his face, was smiling as he began to speak softly in response to Nostradamus's interesting question. "As I am sure you know, Michel, I was born in January of 1706 as the tenth son to my father Josiah Franklin. My father was a candle-maker in the city of Philadelphia. I was training with one of my older brothers to become a printer when I first met up with Prudence Johnston.

"Prudence was probably the most misnamed female in the entire world. She was wild and completely un-inhibited. We were both seventeen, free and unattached, and for two years we were always together as a couple.

"American girls made love in a very simple way with the guy on top and the girl beneath. It was very boring after a while if you really want the truth. Prudence was always there for me whenever the need for sex came over me, but after a while I became bored with her, and we went our separate ways. Seven years have passed since we were together in the early days, and once in a while we go out to dinner and end up in bed, but I always found things with Prudence rather dull.

"All that changed when you introduced me to your wonderful Mimi. As a gentleman, I can't go into details, but sexual relations with this special woman has turned my entire life around. I plan to ask her to return with me to the Colonies when you send me home."

A laughing Nostradamus slapped Benjamin on the shoulder in admiration for his American friend. "Let me tell you a reversal of the story you just told me, Benjamin, but this time kindly allow me to give you the steamy details. After all, you are merely an American, but I am a full-blooded French noble, and the art of sex is taken to the highest form with us. Kindly close your eyes and follow along with my little story. It is quite a sexy tale.

"I wish you to recall the day I met you outside your brothers' printing shop, and I convinced you to join me in our grand adventures. What I neglected to tell you, was that I came to your great city of Philadelphia one day earlier than the afternoon when we met. I wanted to walk around the city and get the flavor of your American Colonies.

"I didn't find much difference between the cobblestone street of Philadelphia and my own sixteenth-century village. I spent several very pleasant hours just walking around and listening to the strange way the American/British language was being spoken by the common man in the streets.

"Of course, I had my usual cup of coffee, but interestingly enough, the American pastries were really delicious, and after my breakfast, I had them give me several pastries in a bag so that I could nibble on the sweets as I walked around.

"I spent a lot of time at the harbor, and was amazed at how far advanced the ships of your day had come in the last two hundred years from my timeline. Our French fleets in the sixteenth century were made a lot simpler. They were basically wide-bodied vessels made to haul cargo back and forth, with a few cannons on board for protection.

"The ship that the loading foreman allowed me to go on board was called the *Bonhomme Richard*. I had given him one large gold coin for his trouble, and he was kind enough to let me pass up the gangplank that led to the lower deck of this huge ship of the line. I was free to walk above and below decks and I did so. I made careful notes in my head so that I could take some of the advanced logistics and organizational things that I saw back with me to improve our French fleets.

"Just as a point of interest for you, Benjamin, please try to imagine my description of this fighting ship from your timeline. It was a very large thing, this American war ship, being about one-third larger than anything we have moving about in our waters here in France at this very moment. My best guess was that it would measure at about one hundred eighty feet in length, and at least fifty feet wide. One of the sailors told me that she was built out of two thousand oak trees and had an overall weight close to two hundred tons.

"In a standard land battle where armies only are involved, two opposing fighting forces would come together against each other on a flat or semi-flat open field. When this happened, it was always the side that could fire its weapons the fastest that would win the land battle. Unlike fighting ships at sea, armies did not have to actually aim their weapons. They just pointed their guns, and fired so that their bullet was just one more among a cloud of bullets, and hopefully it would strike the enemy.

"This, of course, has never been true for the fighting ships of your day or mine. Ships involved in a sea battle had to always hit whatever it was that they were aiming at. The best target for a fighting vessel at sea was to always fire at the other ships' central mast, because with the sails going down after a direct hit, the enemy ship became helpless, and it was a sitting duck just waiting to be sunk.

"I took my leave of the ship and walked over to one of the local taverns where the sailors would go when they were off duty. I was interested in seeing what the inside of an American tavern would look like, and I needed to see what the local whores or, as they were called, 'ladies of the night' had to offer. I was looking to spend some of my time with a woman for the evening before I went to see you in the morning.

"The tavern that I chose looked a lot cleaner on the outside then did its neighbors. Each of the other locations had their outer walls gouged out in many places, and there were many suspicious brown stains scattered around the front entries. Using good judgement, I walked past these interesting but dangerous-looking locations, and approached the open door of the establishment that I had chosen.

"The doorway was completely filled up by the huge muscular figure of the guard, who carefully looked me up and down. I imagine that I passed his inspection, because he stepped aside with only one of his hands blocking my entry. I knew that he was looking for a coin of value, which would then allow me to gain entrance to the premises."

"I gave him a big smile and placed a large silver coin in his hand. This seemed to satisfy him, because he stepped aside, and I was allowed to enter.

"I took a cautious step forward and paused for a few moments until my eyes adjusted from the bright outside sunshine to the darkened illumination on the inside of this eighteenth-century tavern.

"The first thing that I noticed, was the extremely loud noise level that bounded around this large room. The room was shaped into a perfect square, perhaps fifty or sixty feet in each direction. The walls were whitewashed plaster, completely filled with many interesting paintings. Someone with a fine sense of artistic talent had done the decorating.

"There was a long bar set up across the back of the room with large stools leaning up against it, so that it could hold about thirty drinking customers, and a gigantic mirror with many glass shelves sticking out from it across the entire back of the bar. On display were perhaps thirty or forty different bottles. of various sizes and shapes. Instead of the long wooden planks and wooden tables that I was used to seeing back home in my village, I was most delighted to see many individual tables set up, and each one covered by a red, white and blue tablecloth.

"The overall view was most wonderful, but as great as it was, it was nothing in comparison to the barmaid who was busy serving drinks across the bar counter. Looking at her simply took my breath away."

CHAPTER SIXTEEN

"Her name was Lola, and she spoke with what I later found out was called a Boston accent.

"I was able to squeeze into an open bar stool between two huge American sailors who moved over a bit to allow me some sitting room. Naturally I ended up chatting with them, and when Lola finally got around to us, I ordered a beer for each of my two new sailor friends and one of the same for myself."

"After about ten minutes of small talk with my companions, the beer and Lola finally came back to us. I took out a large gold coin and put it on the counter to cover the bill. What it got me was a bit of silence from the two sailors, and a questioning look from the girl. With my warmest smile on my face, I said softly to her, 'Please keep the difference from the bill as a tip for yourself.'

"There must have been a big difference, because her response was, 'Thank you, sir. That is a most generous tip. Perhaps when I get off my turn at bar duty, we can toast each other with a bottle of wine along with a fine dinner that I can order from the kitchen?'"

"Of course, I answered in the affirmative. I had the dinner date I was looking for, and I was very excited. I must tell you Benjamin, that I was looking into the face of an angel who had the body of a goddess. The style of the day for the females of the eighteenth century was much more liberal than I was used to. I believe that this was one of those moments 'when what you see is what your get.' And I could see quite a bit.

"Lola's outfit left little if anything to the imagination, and I am known to have a great imagination. The front of her dress was so low cut that even I, Michel Nostradamus, was embarrassed. But embarrassed or not, I never took my eyes off of her breasts for a moment."

"And speaking of female breasts, a subject that healthy, lustful males do quite often, I read a most interesting paper on them, written by a famous contemporary Italian from my sixteenth century.

"It seems that this very well educated nobleman came across some documents that stated that many thousands of years ago, our planet was filled with two different types and two different species of mankind. Of course, there was our ancestors, whom we shall call *Homo sapiens* (which means 'thinking man'), and another kind of species of man called Neanderthal.

"It appears that both of these species were competing for dominance of the world and would attack each other whenever they came in contact. This situation went on for many, many thousands of years, until finally modem man eliminated the Neanderthals completely.

"A most important reason for the disappearance of the Neanderthals was that *Homo sapiens*, with their small hands and extremely mobile thumbs, invented the bow and arrow. This invention, which was almost as important as early man's discovering how to use fire, allowed them to keep a safe distance from the hand-thrown spears of the bigger and stronger Neanderthals. It is also believed, but of course unproven, that the bigger, thicker hands of the Neanderthal could not use a bow and arrow with any kind of accuracy. Humans just had to stay out of range of those deadly spears, and could shoot at the Big Guys from a far away and safe distance."

"With the bow and arrow, and other improved weapons such as the rock-throwing sling-shot, the Neanderthals never really had a chance for their survival. And so, one day many, many years ago, the Neanderthals disappeared completely from the face of the Earth. We only now are learning things about the Neanderthals from their bones and drawings that they left for us in the caves within which they lived.

"However, I must make a fantastic and most important historical point here. It is about the most wonderful gift that the wiped out Neanderthal race gave unthinkingly to *Homo sapiens*. I personally like to call this the gift that keeps on giving, and the Neanderthals have the grateful appreciation of human males throughout the world for this one. The Neanderthals gave us the gift of larger breasts for our females, and here is how that came about, according to the theory postulated by the Italian whom I have been citing.

"Over the thousands of years that the conflict between humans and non-humans went on, many female humans were captured by the Neanderthals, who kept them as slaves. Neanderthal males were no different than our human males, in that they would rape their captives. This seemed to be a normal part of the war fought by males of both species. The female children born of the union of Neanderthal males and human females acquired two very important characteristics from their fathers. They received an increased immunity to many diseases, and they received the gene that allowed breasts to grow in females.

"Up to this time, fossil remains found by our scientists show that human females were extremely flat-chested, while the female Neanderthals had well-developed chests. As time passed, the larger-breast tendency intermixed within the human population, and the human males, naturally, when given a choice, would pick the well-developed female.

"The final comment from the Italian was that he extends his thanks to the gone-but-not-forgotten Neanderthals for giving us the female figure as we know it today."

CHAPTER SEVENTEEN

Nostradamus continued in his soft voice across the breakfast table: "I am sorry, Benjamin if I strayed from my story about Lola, the barmaid.

"I spent the next few hours wandering about the Philadelphia area waiting for dinner and Lola. My mind was definitely not upon you Benjamin. Finally, the time had slipped away and I returned to the inn, and after giving the doorman another fee, I went over to the table in the comer of the tavern that had a 'RESERVED FOR LOLA' sign on it.

"I only had to wait a few minutes until the vision I was waiting for came walking over to me. She had a big bottle of wine in her hands, a grin on her face, and a definite swagger to her step. It was obvious that she had taken the time to take a bath, and to change her clothes. She smelled of fresh roses, and she now had on a less-revealing dress. I believe the see-all dress was just part of her bartender's outfit, and now, this was strictly social.

"Her smile was as bright as ever as she joined me at the table that she had set for two. Lola and I never stopped talking except to take a bite or two of our dinners, and a few sips of wine that I thought was a very poor second to what I was used to from my personal family winery. I thought to myself that one can't have everything, and I seemed to have everything I wanted in the beautiful Lola.

"Lola, by the way, was nineteen years old, and her uncle owned the tavern. She was proud to tell me that she worked at two jobs on a daily basis. First and of most importance to her, was that she worked as a trained and highly professional bartender. Her second profession is usually known as the world's oldest one, namely prostitution. She was proud of having the pick of clients, only of which a few could pay the high price she would get for her services. She was quite open and pleased about the way her life had been working out for her so far.

"I would like to add a little bit of a digression here, Benjamin. I find it quite interesting how your life and mine are similar and somehow entwined. I know that you want to take my charming Mimi back with you to your timeline, and I feel that way about Lola. I haven't told her about me, nor have I asked her to travel back in time where she could live the life of royalty with me, but if my judgement of her is correct, I am sure that I will have my life's companion soon.

"But let me continue with my narrative. I wish to tell you the special value I received for my additional spending of five large gold coins upon Lola. It was quite a night for both of us, and one that I personally will always remember.

"Please recall that even though I am only in my middle twenties, Lola is just a young lady still in her teenage years. Next to her, I am an older man, and also one who is French and knows the ways of love-making.

"When we finally were alone inside the best room in the inn, I was pleased to see that the bed was large and comfortable looking."

"There were many scattered pillows thrown around the bed,

and the only light was coming to us from many candles shining around the room. It was only a matter of moments until the two of us were completely undressed and standing there together brushing our lips against each other in the first meaningful touch."

"Very distracting," she said as she pulled her head away from his kiss. Lola relaxed and gave into the delicious feeling that was beginning to creep over her body. She in turn, planted baby kisses on his mouth.

"Very inspiring", he said as he pressed his mouth against her right breast. "Definitely that."

While he teased and sucked her breast, she ran her hand down his back, raking it lightly with her fingernails. His desire for her was already evident, as she could feel it pressing against her thighs.

"Love me, Michel," she gasped hoarsely, "I'll simply die if you don't."

"I love you, Lola," he told her, raising his head to kiss her lips. For a split second their eyes met, their mutual passion exploding as her midnight-blue eyes collided with his shining amber. Then his mouth was on hers, kissing her with a fierceness that was both surprising and thrilling.

While his tongue darted in and out, his hands found her buttocks and pressed them to his lower body. Between the force of his strong hands and the hardness on the other side, she felt as if she were in a vise, caught between the irresistible force, and the well-known immovable object. She reached down as if to guide him into the 'place that was for him alone,' but before she could manage it, he suddenly pulled away and turned her over onto her stomach. This was something new that she had never experienced before.

With one hand still cupping her breast, his powerful knees forced open her thighs while his teeth were nipping at her neck and ear as he moved with long, thrusting strokes, pinning her to the mattress as his body alone was doing all the work. The little moans of pleasure that began to escape her lips were somewhat muffled in the pillow into which her face was pressed.

Her breath came faster and faster as the thrusts became harder and harder, as the sensations caused by this new position began building up with exquisite momentum. She raised one of her arms high enough to touch his head with her hand, and she managed to tug at his soft hair like a drowning woman clutching a clump of seaweed. She was absolutely mindless now, aware only of Michel's body atop hers, stroking and thrusting with his movements building up in speed, as his own breadth fell on her neck in hot and rapid puffs.

His exuberant cry of release roared in her ear, his body collapsing in spasms against her back. In a second or two more, her own release came, throbbing and exploding, causing her to arch upward so that their union could not be destroyed.

"Michel. Oh, Michel," she cried out, as simultaneously, they collapsed against the mattress, all energy drained from their bodies. When she could speak again, her voice was a low rasp. "That was fantastic. I have never felt anything like that. You are a wonderful love-maker".

His chest was still warming her back side as he lifted a strand of her hair and softly kissed the back of her neck. "You are fantastic yourself, my love. I would call tonight a miracle for the two of us." Gently, he rolled over beside her and cupped her face in his hands. "I think I love you, Lola," he said as his eyes flashed out at her. "Kindly don't ever forget that."

She cuddled up against him as he drew her close to him, and just like that they both fell into a deep and most satisfying sleep.

CHAPTER EIGHTEEN

"And that, my dear Franklin, is what I did the night before I met up with you. I believe we are both lucky and fortunate men to have found the women of our dreams so early in our lives. And now, Benjamin Franklin, my new friend and loyal traveling companion, I must ask you to accompany me into the village square where there is a task waiting for me."

Without another word being spoken, Benjamin, followed Nostradamus out of the coffee shop and down the road. They arrived shortly at the village square where he saw a small crowd had gathered.

ॐ

Aram was one hell of a man by anyone's standards. He stood well over six foot six in his gold-sandaled feet. His sword arm was bare and swelled with muscles that rippled as he moved about the square.

Benjamin stood there staring at the big man as Nostradamus excused himself from Benjamin's side, and walked over to one of the servants from the castle, who took his jacket and handed Michel his sword.

Benjamin could not believe what his eyes and brain were telling him. He had suddenly realized that a sword fight was going to happen within the next few minutes between Nostradamus and the tall person who stood there grinning at everyone.

Nostradamus had not said a single word to him about this, and Benjamin was furious. If he had known that something like this was going to happen, he would have had Nostradamus take him back home before he was possibly stranded here some two hundred years in the past. This was unfair, unjust and beyond belief. Michel Nostradamus was not only risking his own life in a duel that was probably to the death, but he was risking Benjamin's life without telling him.

Franklin's mind was made up and it told him to get away from the brilliant but now scary Nostradamus while the getting-away was still possible. He would have the matter taken care of shortly. He knew that now was not the time to distract Michel from the upcoming fight. He only hoped that Nostradamus was as good with a sword as he was bad with promises.

Benjamin continued to stand there silently, his thoughts to himself, as he watched the goings-on as one of the many spectators.

☙

Aram, the small giant of a man, had been a problem for Nostradamus ever since he had rebuilt the Nostradamus castle within the town limits. The castle shared a property line with Aram's land holdings on the far side where the water moat was located.

It bothered Nostradamus to no end when he learned from the servants that Aram was constantly throwing his garbage and waste products into the moat's water and polluting it.

Nostradamus had known that Aram was angry with him

when he had made the purchase of the land and built his castle. Nostradamus had simply ignored Aram's suggestion that they fight a duel with the winner to get both properties. This was a legal way of solving local disputes, but Nostradamus had always refused to lower himself to Aram's level and had just ignored him.

But recently, Aram was causing small problems that Michel could no longer ignore and he had finally accepted the offer to fight for the property rights.

☜☞

Through a middleman, Nostradamus had made arrangements to meet Aram in a duel of swords, with a local judge present and to act as a professional witness. Michel always liked everything he did to be legal and proper. He had spread out many gold coins to keep everything as secret as possible.

Only one servant from Michel's castle was present; the rest of the crowd was made up of dozens of Aram's friends, who were treating the event like a holiday. They came out with large blankets to sit on, and food and drink to bring the event into a party atmosphere.

Everyone seemed to think that the fight would be very one-sided, in favor of Aram. The assumption was that the castle property would soon have a new owner. Aram and his friends had already begun making plans for the restoration as if Nostradamus were already dead and buried.

The judge was now standing between the two combatants, reading from his legal papers. Michel was standing there quietly listening to the judge, while Aram was moving about.

The judge read:

"It is hereby decreed that by force of arms, the winner of

86

*the duel between Michel Nostradamus and Ahram will become
the legal holder of both properties that are hereby in question.*

*"This contest of arms may legally be held to the death or
anything short of it.*

"The loser hereby loses all rights to his property."

The judge nodded at both men and drew himself away from
the center of the area where now only the two swordsmen were
standing.

Aram, looking huge, ferocious and angry, was busy swinging
his arms back and forth in an attempt to loosen up his muscles. He
was not wearing a shirt and his physical appearance was somewhat
overwhelming to everyone except Michel Nostradamus.

Nostradamus had just finished with his own warm-ups and
had taken a sip of the white wine that his servant had brought
him in an iced container.

Both men pulled out their swords as the taller of the two
men looked Nostradamus up and down.

Aram was saying, "You should be at home in your castle,
Nostradamus. Someone like you should not end up in the dirt
after we are done here."

Nostradamus replied, "Aram, you have been a pain in the ass
to me for a very long time. I believe that now is the right time
to personally take you down from that high perch you have been
sitting on all these years."

All eyes are now upon the combatants.

Nostradamus takes the proper *en garde* position for a left-
handed fighter. Even though he is a natural right-hander,
Nostradamus thought that Aram would have more trouble
fighting against him if he came at him from the other side.

A hush falls over the watching crowd as they collectively
find themselves holding their breath.

Aram quickly makes the first move as Nostradamus defends himself from the approaching blade.

In his left-handed defensive position, Nostradamus does not move his feet at all, and that leaves little, if any, openings for Aram to attack.

Aram steps back and brings a halt to the action. He seems to be taken aback somewhat by Nostradamus's skill level. "Finally," Aram said, "I find a swordsman worthy of my time."

Nostradamus smiles but does not reply.

Aram again lunges at Nostradamus, going for a deadly low blow to the ankles. Nostradamus easily jumps above the swinging of Aram's sword.

Aram seems stunned at the gracefulness and skilled moves being shown by someone the size of Nostradamus.

Nostradamus says, in a playful voice, "Let me know when you would like to start, Aram. I shall try to be of service to you whenever you are ready."

Angrily, Aram charges once again, and for the first time, he forces Nostradamus to step back and give up some defensive ground.

A fast and furious fight ensues, going back and forth, with Nostradamus still using only his left hand. The two men are engaged in a battle of skill that goes strong for several minutes. Aram has the greater strength, but Nostradamus has the higher skill level.

Aram steps back, which brings the action to a momentary halt. He is gasping for breath, while Nostradamus seems to be in no difficulty at all.

Nostradamus smiles as Aram goes down to one knee which signals full surrender.

"I yield to you, Nostradamus. I see that I cannot beat you at force of arms. I shall sign the papers and be gone from the property in a most timely manner."

A smiling Nostradamus turns and walks toward his nearby waiting servant.

Aram suddenly stands erect with a look of evil upon his big face. Without warning, he pulls his knife and goes after Nostradamus's turned back.

Benjamin's shout of warning gives Nostradamus the split second that he needs to swing his sword unexpectedly from the right side and with his right hand.

Nostradamus's razor-sharp sword makes contact with Aram's extended arm, and that arm is completely severed as it falls to the ground.

Aram's knife clanks as it hits the ground. The knife is still held in the clutches of the now-separated arm. Aram screams in pain and pulls another curved dagger from his hip.

Nostradamus leans forward and calmly runs his sword into Aram's heart. Aram falls down dead.

A calm Nostradamus walks over to his servant and takes a sip from the chilled wine glass that is extended to him.

CHAPTER NINETEEN

The slight breeze that touched their cheeks as they approached the river was absolutely delightful. It was just soft enough to keep both Michel and Benjamin cool and comfortable and yet was strong enough to rustle the leaves in the trees along the river banks. The two men had agreed to leave the field of battle and not to talk about what had just happened until a later date.

This was fine with Benjamin in that he was determined not to go either backward or forward in the timeline with Michel again. He was beginning to doubt the stability of the time-traveler, and as soon as it could be worked out, he planned to return to his life in the American Colonies. He decided he would withhold his desire to leave until the moment was right, and so he listened to Michel as he walked and talked at a slow pace. These were peaceful moments that Benjamin knew he would one day look back at with wonderment and fondness.

Each man was carrying his own cup of coffee and had a few sweet nibbles, forced upon them by the coffee shop owner, who had nothing but smiles for Michel. They settled onto a small, shaded bench that gave a clear view of the comings and goings on the waterway. It was a most delightful spot.

It was Michel who opened the conversation. "Benjamin, for

the past week or so, I have spent a great deal of time going over and reviewing my notes upon the things that we have done so far, and the things that we might yet want to accomplish together. I know that you will agree that what we have done, either individually or together, is to arrive at our destination as mere spectators. We appeared in each new timeline just to make our observations from a safe distance. Except when I was personally attacked by that Knight Templar, there has been no interaction between us at all in any of the time periods that we visited.

"I have to admit that I was shaken up at the time that I was attacked, but since then I have reviewed all that happened there, and I realize that all I did was defend myself from an unwarranted attack upon me by someone who was extremely paranoid. Do I have any regrets at having killed that man? The answer is absolutely none. In fact, I feel a sense of excitement in taking the life of another human being.

"I know that I have to be very careful here, because I do not want to become a murderer moving about the timelines of history. I feel an underlying and deeply submerged part of me that says to take chances and let the devil have his due. I have to keep tight control over this power that I now have acquired.

"When the French king took that splinter in the eye and died, did either of us express any sadness or remorse? I believe not. I came to the realization that we have been too remote, and far distanced from what we went to observe. I came up with a brilliant solution to these problems, even if I have to say so myself. I am hoping that you will agree with me after you hear what it is that I have done to get us more involved in the lives of those people we visit.

"While you were sleeping in late this morning, I was up and about, and I projected myself into the far future. This is something that I have never done before. Please be sure you are clear in your understanding that I actually did project myself far into the future. As I stand here, right at this moment, I am actually eleven months older than I was this morning when I went onto the roof.

"Remember please, that time spent in the past or future is still physical time spent, and our bodies age at the same pace as they always do. I was away for eleven months, and so I am eleven months older than I was when I left.

"The question to be asked here, was what did I do, and what did I accomplish in that amount of time? You have to be thinking that it should have been something very special for me to give up this significant amount of my allotted lifetime.

"Before I left, I raided my private vault which I keep in the basement of the castle. I took with me a huge bag of gold, rubies and other precious stones that were enough to ransom a king. I did this because I had a plan, and it would be expensive to bring this plan into reality.

"I directed the time-wand to take me into the far future, to the year 2308, to be exact. This was about eight hundred years in the future from where we are sitting now in my timeline of the fifteen hundreds.

"My thought process was quite simple. We both know that the human race has changed very little in the past few thousand years. We are still hunters and gatherers at heart, and we will always have the primitive deep within our soul. This seems to be nature's way of allowing us to protect ourselves against ourselves.

"Even though mankind is still a savage deep down in our basic make-up, civilization has been allowed to improve itself around us in spite of that. Cultures have changed over the last few thousand years and have made things and events easier and more civilized as the years went by. It is evident that while civilizations have improved greatly, mankind in general has not.

"I thought that eight hundred years in the future would give me a civilization so advanced that they could fulfill my desires and give me what I was looking for. Happily, I was correct and things worked out pretty much as I had hoped and planned they would.

"I stayed in France for the entire nine months, because I am, first and foremost, still a Frenchman, and I wanted to see what my country would be like. I am proud and pleased to tell you that the world that I visited in the future is at peace with itself, and is highly advanced in all the important sciences. I won't go into the many stories about the things I saw and experienced because of the time factor.

"You would be amazed how far your own country, now called the Greater United States of America/Canada and Mexico has come. Unbelievable. And, Benjamin, our Earth people are living on Mars and one of the moons of the planet Jupiter. I heard it mentioned that there has been a visitation to us from otherworldly beings. It seems that they landed on our moon, and have been working with Humanity's finest minds to eliminate all sickness and disease. My visitation to visit the future was an excellent selection on my part and I couldn't be more pleased.

"Perhaps a time-jump by the two of us would be in order at a later date. You would find the experience worth-while. You will have to excuse my wandering all over with my telling you about my time-travel experiences. It is just that I have no one else to talk to about all of this. You are very special to me, Benjamin. I want to continue sharing my thoughts and ideas with you for a few more minutes, and I promise you that I will try to focus better on the here and now.

"When I finally was able to get to see a scientist at one of the local French universities, he easily understood what I wanted, and he actually knew who both you and I were. History has been very kind to both of us.

"I was still having a little bit of a problem expressing myself in my native language of French, because over the many years, new words and phrases and even a different way of speaking had gotten into the language and changed it around a little bit. I believe my French sounded backward to them at first, and until I adjusted to the new way of speaking, they all must have thought that I was a bit different from the big city people.

"I took the liberty of looking you up in one of their mechanical devises that they called a computer. Before I go any further with my little narrative, let me tell you something about what a computer is, what it does, and why it has become so important to mankind in the future years.

"A computer is an electronic machine that was invented in the nineteen hundreds. It contains stored information, complex calculations, correlates and selects data information that can be used in multiple ways. It is like a book of knowledge that holds everything that the human race has ever done or ever plans on doing. On command, it will print out the requested information on a simple form of paperwork.

"After the invention of the computer, the world was never the same in that everyone had knowledge available to them on any and every subject that could be thought of. I am sure that you are familiar with the old saying that 'knowledge is power,' and it is so true about the computer. A computer user has a world of information about almost everything at his or her fingertips. This machine has changed everything around in the future world.; and for the better. Mankind can never have too much knowledge.

"The computer told me—and what I am allowed to tell you—is that you are headed for greatness Benjamin, and you will be one of the most important men of your time. I cannot tell you much more than this because, as you know, no man should know his own future. I firmly believe this, and that is why I did not look myself up on that computer thing.

"What I told those future scientists was that we wanted to be able to hear, see and feel everything that the subjects of interest were hearing. seeing and feeling. In other words, I asked them if they could put our consciousness and awareness into their minds so that we could share some special moments. And then, when those special moments had passed, could they take us out of the hosts' minds, and return us to ourselves once again?"

"As an example, I told them I wanted a up–close and personal experience with Julius Caesar, Mark Antony and Cleopatra, as their important lives played themselves out on the stage of history. I also threw Napoleon into the mix and got the same answer that I expected. After a few days of waiting, I received a reply from the university that said, 'No problem, Mr. Nostradamus. Please stop by our office for another conference.'

"Just as in your world and mine, Benjamin, money talked, and I had obviously brought enough valuable and precious metals with me to qualify. You see what I mean when I tell you that people don't change. Only the civilizations around them change."

Benjamin, who knew that he would soon be taking his leave of Nostradamus, nodded and listened carefully to everything being told to him. In a detached sort of way, Benjamin still found everything that he was being told absolutely fascinating.

CHAPTER TWENTY

The two friends were still sitting there quietly, just watching the river waters flow by.

Nostradamus was watching Benjamin closely, trying to read from his facial expression what he was thinking.

Finally, the silence was broken by Benjamin. "Michel, I understand everything you have told me, and I think that I am caught up to the moment. I fully realize that this is your project, and I am sure you realize how greatly honored I am that you have chosen me as your companion for what you call 'The Grand Adventure.' Of course, I have a lot of questions, but I have only one major concern—and it impacts both of us."

"It seems to me that you are getting swept up into the time-travel thing more and more, and it has taken over your everyday thinking. Before you tell me more about what happened in the future, I want you to know that I believe it is time for me to go back to my life in Philadelphia. Before you take your next leap into the time stream, I'd really like to return home."

"Here is what I am thinking about and it is important for you to understand. What if, on a remote chance, something happens to you or to the wand that makes everything happen? What if you are unable to get back here to your present where I would be waiting? I would be really stuck here for the rest of my life, and that scares me a great deal, because I could not fit into the local French lifestyle these two hundred and something years into my past."

Nostradamus was quiet for a few moments before he offered his response. "Benjamin, I agree that right now is the proper time for us to return you back to Philadelphia where your entire life is waiting for you. As per our agreement, I promise to return you home well before my next departure date.

"What you have to think about in the next few days, is whether or not you want to take Mimi with you. I offer you this wonderful possibility, and I realize that you will have some very important discussions with her as to whether or not she really wants to go. Be sure that she understands that it will be permanent once she commits. There will be no coming back.

"And now kindly let me tell you about one more thing that I am going to be doing for you. You have been my trusted and faithful companion, and I wish to honor you as such with a little gift. You will be taking back with you a special package that I will have made up for you. Its contents will make you an independent and very wealthy man. This should allow you to buy out your brother's printing house, and for you to step into the future with your head held high.

"Remember that the history I saw in the computer said that you will be very important in the formation of your soon-to-be independent country. You will be much honored by your fellow citizens, and you should have a most wonderful life ahead of you. Each success that you have will make me proud.

"An interesting side question does pop into my mind here. I shall throw it out at you and never will I mention it again. I know that you will be thinking about it for the rest of your life.

"Let us say, just for the sake of this discussion, that I never found you, and never brought you to my home to share my life and adventures with me. If this were so, then you never would have received the fortune in rare stones that I am going to give to you. Without these stones, would you have achieved the grand future that the computer said you will have? This is something for you to think about for the many years ahead of you."

Nostradamus's comments did not please Franklin at all, but he was very careful not to allow his displeasure to show upon his face or his body language. Could this be Nostradamus's way of suggesting that he refuse the offer of riches that he had just made? If Nostradamus was looking for a turn-down on his offer, then he would be very surprised. That package contained the future that he had always dreamed about, and if it was offered, he would be taking it with the biggest of smiles.

It began to worry at Franklin's mind that Nostradamus was acting more strangely than ever, and it confirmed that he was better off centuries apart from the brilliant man who now wanted to tell him about his further adventures in the year 2308.

CHAPTER TWENTY-ONE

Sundown found the two young men sitting in the back room of the local tavern. The sign out in front had a picture of a nasty-looking pirate looking up at the sign which named the location the Black Spot.

A healthy looking young barmaid brought them each a large container of the local beer, along with her best smile. As she stepped away, she drew a large decorate curtain across the opening.

Nostradamus was saying softly to a very attentive Benjamin Franklin that when he sat down with Doctor Jacque Pierre of the Institute of Advanced Studies, the year was 2308, and it also was late in the afternoon.

Michel found himself unable to tear his attention away from the windowed view of what appeared to be a timeless city of high towers and spires, sitting under a glowing golden dome of energy. It was an unbelievably beautiful sight.

The doctor pressed a button on the side of his impressive desk, and the window darkened and became a reflective mirror that showed only the inside of the interview room where they were sitting.

꩜

"Benjamin," Michel Nostradamus was saying, "I know how you like to read my notes on predictions and other things, so I took the time and wrote out the details of my interview with the Institute of The Future.

"Within my notes, I cover everything that I will be attempting to accomplish, and what I will be writing up in my predictions at a later time. I have personally signed each page, and hope that perhaps one day they might be of value to you.

"In the meantime, please sit back and enjoy the beer. I hope you really enjoy it, because it came from one of the local breweries that I have an interest in. Here is my report in detail so you can follow everything as I go along."

I clearly established the fact that I was truly a citizen of France who lived in the early fifteen hundreds. The proof of who I was came from that wonderful mechanical device that I told you about, called a computer.

He looked up my name, Michel Nostradamus and page after page of information came up on my life. There were things that I have done already in my few years of life so far, and things that the computer showed me that I was yet to do in my future back home. This was most interesting.

I easily answered all of the usual questions such as who were my parents, my aunts and uncles and the starter of the family line.

He asked the exact parcels of land that I owned and who were the people indebted to me.

I showed him the scars on my body which matched those I had received as a young man that were actually recorded in our town records. I believe the village elders kept track of the nobility that way.

After dozens of more questions, he accepted the fact that I

was who I said I was. He wanted to know how the time-travel process worked, and when I refused to tell him, and when I started to leave his office, he became easier to deal with. I believe that at first, he thought that I was just another crazy person who came in off of the streets of the city to bother him.

I established beyond a doubt that I had indeed traveled from the fifteen hundreds to his present timeline and was sitting there in front of him (I made no reference to the great Benjamin Franklin being with me at any time).

He finally accepted that I was really from the fifteen hundreds, and we spent a long time talking about how French customs had changed in some ways and stayed the same in others. It was most interesting getting each other's views on all things strictly French. Based upon my in-depth conversation with doctor Pierre, I was really pleased and proud with the way the French had developed over the centuries.

He asked me to explain why I wanted to bother with making predictions about future events.

I told him that being born to the French nobility within my timeline gave me the time to do something different, and this was the most interesting thing I could come up with. By actually seeing the events that I would later go back and write about, I would have the benefit of being one-hundred-percent accurate.

I think that I impressed him with my 'wants', but I do not think he saw a 'need' for these predictions. We definitely disagreed upon this point, but it did not matter since I was there as a paying client.

He asked about a few examples, and I gave him the easiest ones for him to understand.

I talked about my Knight Templar travel, and how I had to defend myself, and we talked for a while about the religious happenings in the holy land in the twelve hundreds.

The doctor was very weak on many historical facts, and I had him spellbound as I spoke about things I had experienced. I also went into how I had witnessed in person the famous storming of the French prison called the Bastille, which started the French revolution almost by itself. For twenty minutes, he asked question after question about the bastille, until I finally told him that I almost died in the crowd that stormed back and forth on the wild streets of Paris that day.

I finished off my time-travel stories by telling him about how the king of France in my personal lifetime had lost his life in a joust. I explained that the joust was just the king's way of showing that he was still at the peak of his physical powers. This, I said to the doctor, was well and good, until that wood splinter that went in through the eye opening, killed him. I said that in my opinion, we should all accept our aging gracefully, and not try to capture back our faded youth as the king had tried to do.

After the telling of these tales and the verification of each detail as I gave them to him, the good doctor was finally mine to command. He asked to clear up what problems I had when I was only one person within a crowd of people. I think he was looking for a personality disorder. He questioned my wanting more close-up experiences and not just being a distant observer.

He asked me to explain my desire to be in an intimate and up-close relationship with the people I wanted to observe. He thought that I might have a common medical condition called 'voyeurism'.

When I asked him to explain what that was, he said it was a person, either male or female, who has an exaggerated interest and personal need in viewing or watching sexual and closely related sexual activities of other people. He went on to say that these people do not like to be seen viewing these activities, and that they go to extremes to keep their desire to watch, secret. He asked if I thought this applied to me in anyway.

I completely ignored his question except to say that I would consider the matter and think about it another day. I asked myself at the same time if there might be some truth in what he just told me about myself. Was I one of "those"? It was something to think about.

He asked me about my fixation upon Cleopatra, Julius Caesar, and that time period. He asked if history books couldn't satisfy the many questions that I had.

I told him that they could not, and that the reason that I was talking with him was because I wanted some way to "get into" the mind of the person I visited.

I wanted to know exactly what Julius Caesar thought when he first saw the most beautiful woman in the world, Cleopatra, unrolled from within that famous carpet. What was she thinking when she first met Caesar, the most powerful man in the world? I wanted to be there, right on the spot.

I wanted to know what it felt like when Julius Caesar was stabbed to death inside of the senate by his best friends. I really wanted to know these things and I told him that I was quite willing to pay a most generous amount for his services.

I told him that money was no object and I asked him to use his advanced science to get me into the heads of the people that I wanted to visit. It was my desire that my riches would open up the world of possibilities for me.

The doctor made the right promises to me, made a firm commitment along with them, and I authorized a transfer of funds to him based upon his agreement. He said that he would be ready for me in about thirty days, and we agreed upon a date for what he said would be a simple surgery called a transplant.

When I asked him to explain what a surgical transplant was, he gave me a short pamphlet that he said would explain it all.

He said that I would be fully recovered from the transplant

surgery (whatever that was) within a few weeks from when it was done. He then said that I would have to go into a six-month training class in order to learn how to use the implant that I would be getting.

I knew that I had to master the use of this implant thing. There was no use having an implant if I could not use it in the field under real-life conditions. Obviously, one simple mistake on my part, and the guards surrounding the famous persons that I wanted to visit would kill me.

I told the doctor that I would spend the time he wanted me to spend here in my future, which was his present timeline.

Before I left his outer office, I sat down in a quiet corner and read the little pamphlet on implants. I thought it would be nice to know what was going to be put into my head. After absorbing the procedure from the pamphlet, I would find a place to stay for the night and go out and see my city of Paris in the year 2308.

I had plenty of time to play tourist.

CHAPTER TWENTY-TWO

Ah, Paris in the springtime.

As Michel walked along the Champs-Élysées, which is the main avenue for central Paris, he saw a lot of familiar things and a lot of things that had been added since his days back in the fifteen hundreds.

The trees and the flowers and the very smell of the air was as he remembered it. That had not changed.

The clothing being worn in this twenty-fourth century was very different from what he was used to.

Of course, it was the women that caught his eye as they strolled down the avenue, going into and out of the Parisian shops that filled up every available space. Very little was left to the imagination, as most of the outer clothing was pretty much see-through, and what was being displayed were the undergarments, which had not changed that much over the centuries. There were only so many ways one's undergarments could push up, pull down and tighten the female figure, as Nostradamus casually walked along taking in all of the sights.

The men were still pretty much the same, with see-through shirts with thin string ties, regular pants and shoes. There were some light-colored see-through jackets, but mostly short sleeves.

At the very end of the Champs-Élysées boulevard stood a most interesting and strangely shaped structure called the Arc de Triomphe. It was a fifty-meter-high monument which could be seen from just about everywhere in central Paris, built in 1806 to celebrate Napoleon Bonaparte's many victories.

Michel had briefly looked up Napoleon on one of the local computers, and it seemed to say that he was a most interesting character who completely dominated France and most of the known European world during the nineteenth century.

Now Napoleon Bonaparte was a Frenchman and he, Michel Nostradamus was also a Frenchman. An idea was forming in the back of his mind that it might be an excellent idea to visit Napoleon on one of Michel's timeline adventures. He was thinking that there might be a most interesting wrinkle in a future visit to Napoleon.

The computer had implied that if Napoleon had covered one of his flanks or sides better during the famous Battle of Waterloo, then he could have won that battle and gone on to more fame and fortune. Of course, history and his new friend the computer told him that he didn't, and the British general, Lord Wellington, was able to sweep around the weakened main body of French troops and catch them in a vise like containment, which spelled the end of the Napoleon forces at Waterloo.

The question bouncing around in Nostradamus's head at that moment was, what if he, Michel, would jump back in time to the Napoleon era and help Napoleon win this decisive battle that had set the stage for Bonaparte's complete downfall? What would Napoleon's life and Michel's life be like if he stayed at his side and guided him with all the correct moves during the eighteen hundreds?

Napoleon would never be defeated again if they formed an unbeatable team. Michel probably would be the number-two man under Napoleon's new worldwide empire. Michel would still be within his beloved country of France, and he saw visions of greatness flowing before his eyes.

Without getting too excited, Michel thought it was a good idea to go into one of the comer computer shops and look up the real life and times of Napoleon Bonaparte and see if there were any possibilities for all the wild thoughts rushing through his head. Michel settled himself into an open computer slot, put in the required coins, and made the following copy for himself:

Napoleon Bonaparte—born August 15, 1769 and died May 5, 1821.

On the island of Corsica, Italy, Napoleon was born to a noble but impoverished family.

Bonaparte was a French military and political leader who quickly rose to prominence during the later years of the world-shaking French revolution.

The Napoleonic wars from 1803 to 1815 were a series of wars declared by the worried European nations against the newly formed Napoleonic French empire. This group of many European nations united together in order to oppose this new aggressiveness on the part of the French under Bonaparte. These independent nations had no choice but to join together as they found the French pounding at their very borders.

Within the following campaigns, Napoleon stepped onto the world stage as a central figure of European importance. A dozen sparkling and decisive victories by Napoleon in as many months told the world that this man was definitely someone to reckon with.

After his many victories, Bonaparte overstepped his limitations and made two very major mistakes that cost him greatly.

The first of his two mistakes was his decision to invade the nearby country of Russia in the early fall with the onset of winter getting ready to arrive. He could not get his campaign moving quickly enough, and it was finally the terrible Russian winters that defeated him and not the poorly organized Russian army of the czar. After his forced retreat from Moscow where he had lost over half of his fighting force, he returned his battered army back to France where he wanted to return his forces back to full strength.

However, he was not given the time that he needed to regroup.

It was the British empire that quickly put together a large coalition of fearful European nations, who gladly joined them because they knew that Napoleon had taken a great loss of men and military equipment from the Russian campaign. The coalition put their forces together at the edge of France at a huge flat area known as Waterloo.

It was at the following great battle of Waterloo that Napoleon made his second costly mistake.

Napoleon did not provide the proper amount of man-power upon his weakened left flanks' fighting position. This allowed the British, under General Lord Wellington, to sweep around the French forces and catch them in a military vise from the rear. This caused the French to have to fight a two-front battle, instead of the usual one main frontal one. With his soldiers now divided into two weaker groups instead of the usual one powerful one that he always counted on, Napoleon's forces lost the battle, and most of the French troops were either captured or killed.

After Napoleon's defeat at Waterloo, Great Britain

became the major European power, and it allowed other smaller countries such as Germany, Spain and Italy, to unite their own countries into independent states. They all became players immediately thereafter in the affairs of Europe and the world at large.

The computer stated clearly that after France was removed as the major power of the area, all of these other countries defined and accepted each other's borders, and the outline of Europe was set for future years.

The last comment that the computer made was that it took a total of thirteen countries, acting together, to defeat Napoleon. The computer then listed the thirteen countries before it closed the report: Great Britain, Austria, Russia, Germany (called Prussia at that time), Spain, Portugal, Sicily, the Vatican, the Turkish empire, Sardine, Sweden, Netherlands and Switzerland.

CHAPTER TWENTY-THREE

Nostradamus was feeling pretty good as he now realized that it was within his power to easily turn the tide of Napoleon's defeat at Waterloo, into a victory that would make France the dominant world power that it had always wanted to be.

He would plan his actions out after he received the implant services that he had just paid a small fortune for. Once he had full control of the new ability to be within the head of the person he wished to observe, there would be no limitations as to what he would be able to achieve.

It was too bad that he could not make use of Benjamin Franklin. He had personally chosen him from a dozen other possible candidates in that he was the best choice overall. Nostradamus had at first thought that he could turn Franklin away from his extreme sense of right and wrong, and get the perfect assistant that he needed. It appeared that he was wrong, and that Franklin was too set in his ways. He would have to find a new backup after he returned Franklin to his proper timeline.

He could hardly wait to have his scheduled surgery, and get the months necessary for healing behind him. There was nothing that he could do except wait for himself to get well.

He felt that Napoleon Bonaparte, a fellow Frenchman,

inspired within himself, a form of hero worship. Nostradamus was beginning to come to grips with the realization that there was a burning desire within himself to get his own name out there on the world stage as a mover and shaker. Time, which he could now control, would be his stepping stone to greatness.

Within a fifteen-minute walk, he passed by the Museé du Louvre—the museum called the Louvre.

He knew that it was packed with masterpieces from all over the world. It specialized in galleries that showed fantastic collections of paintings and sculptures from the Thirteenth to the Nineteenth Centuries.

After his surgery, when he needed to spend time healing, he planned to spend a few days just wandering around inside the famous museum. He especially wanted to see the *Mona Lisa* that he knew was a masterpiece by the world-famous Leonardo da Vinci. It would be an interesting conversation if he decided to drop in on Leonardo by use of the timeline. They both were living in just about the same time-frame of the early fifteen hundreds, and they would have a lot to talk about.

With his mind made up to definitely stop by and see da Vinci, he took a few minutes out and stopped at another store that rented out computer time. He was becoming totaling dependent on this computer concept, and was worried that when he went back home to his own timeline, he would have to leave them behind. He asked the computer for the shortest possible readout on the great Italian and then sat back and read the brief report that the computer put together.

Factual information regarding Leonardo da Vinci:

Although not continuously, Leonardo da Vinci spent a total of eighteen years in the Florence/Milan area of Italy.

He enjoyed the stirring companionship of close friends, and filled his notebooks with subjects for treatises he would never actually write.

He preferred the enterprising spirit of the local Medici family to any other in his early years. He offered plans to the Medici family for fantastic weapons, as well as, for grand schemes including military architecture, and hydraulic engineering. Those early years were his most productive.

He was a painter, a wartime general, and a designer of background sets for many of the local court festivals. He always made the time to pursue his interests in anatomy, biology, mathematics, physics and general mechanics. His anatomical human studies, he boasted, led him to dissect some thirty corpses.

The city of Florence enlisted him as chief engineer in their war with the nearby city state of Pisa, and he did very well, as he always did in warfare.

After the Florence/Pisa war, he was personally invited by King Francis I of France to come and live in Paris. He lived the remainder of his seventy years there. In his will, he gave King Francis ownership of the *Mona Lisa* painting that he had never let out of his own possession.

That is how a world-famous Italian painting by a world-famous Italian painter ended up in a French museum.

Of all the mysteries surrounding da Vinci, none is more remarkable than the disproportion between the quality of his finished works and the grandeur of his reputation. Our awe of Leonardo da Vinci is as much for what he was as for what he actually accomplished in life.

His career was actually vagrant and unfocused. In fact, for all of his high intellect, he never really had a career. His efforts and his works were dispersed among Florence, Milan, Venice and Paris in his lifelong search for patrons of the arts. He willingly accepted commissions to perform works from the Medici family, the Duke of Milan, the French kings, and the Pope.

His vast disorderly notebooks, called codices by modern historians, were all written in his special backward handwriting style. They mystify us as much as they explain.

❧

Michel left the corner computer store and continued on his walking tour of the city.

The dominating structure from anywhere in Paris is the beautiful Eiffel Tower. He planned on spending some time there as he made his recovery from the surgery. For now, he just noted that the impressive structure was built by Engineer Eiffel in the year 1889. It stood 3,234 meters high and weighed well over ten thousand tons.

The advertisement said that from top to bottom, there were one-thousand-six-hundred and sixty-five steps if someone wanted to skip taking the elevator and decided to walk up.

I decided to walk over to the location where I had gone on one of my first time-jumps. This was during the street riots that led to the French Revolution. I was sorry to see that there was nothing but a small plaque indicating that the spot where I was standing was the location of the famous prison called the Bastille. My vivid memory of almost being crushed by the passionate crowd that day caused me to move on quickly from that well-remembered location. I recalled that the date that I had last been standing on this exact location was July 14, 1789.

There were two more nearby famous sites that I wanted to see before I ended my day and went back to where I had taken up lodging. The closest one to where I was now was the famous Notre Dame Cathedral, and so I headed in that direction.

Now this was something that I knew about personally, since I had visited it often when I was at home in my own timeline. It was started in the year 1163 and was completed in 1334. Its style was Gothic, which was the same as my castle back home.

The Cathedral held twenty-nine chapels, and had twenty-nine religious statues standing in front of each one. I had personally seen each statue. I found them to be very impressive then, and I am sure that they are still quite impressive now. Some things don't change with the passage of time.

The focal point, if someone was looking at the Notre Dame Cathedral from a distance, as I was now doing, was the huge twin towers, which were sixty-nine meters high.

My final destination for the day, a most tiring day, after all, was the famous village of Montmarte, perhaps the most famous village in all of France. This area was known for the very relaxed Bohemian lifestyle that celebrated the pleasures of the flesh, and a sample of every wine that has ever been produced in France.

Walking around the charming area, one can see acrobats and painters that take you back to France's long and historical beginnings. A lot of the paintings looked somewhat familiar to me, and one or two of them looked a bit like my own village, with our river flowing along behind it. I stood there for a long time admiring that one.

One of the sellers of paintings told me that several famous artistic movements started here in Montmarte. I had never heard of them before he mentioned them to me. He counted out five of them for me. Impressionism, Cubism, Fauvism, Futurism, and Surrealism.

I thanked him and left the area, and went back to my room for a much-needed rest.

CHAPTER TWENTY-FOUR

Several weeks had passed for Michel, but practically no time at all for Benjamin, when the two of them agreed on a departure date to return Franklin back to his own timeline.

Benjamin was simply overwhelmed when he looked through the going-away gift bag full of precious jewels and solid gold pieces that Nostradamus had given him. It turned out after all, that Michel Nostradamus was a man of his word, and the silly assumptions and guesses that Benjamin had thought about him were completely wrong.

As Michel always had told him, "Persons born to nobility must live by the highest of standards."

In this case, Benjamin was speechless and Nostradamus found it most interesting and highly amusing that the extremely verbal Benjamin Franklin was practically unable to speak to him. At least he was speechless with Michel during the last few days, but obviously not so with the adorable Mimi.

When Benjamin had asked her to marry him and go forward in time to the seventeen hundreds, where she would be the wife of a wealthy man and have many servants of her own, she practically attacked him with her consent to his proposal. She dragged him, not unwillingly, into her bed for another session of love-making, French-style.

On their last night, when Michel was helping Benjamin and Mimi consolidate all the things that they would be taking back with them, Michel reminded them that if they could keep their hands on the things they wanted to bring back with them, then that would work out. He suggested they tie ropes around some of the heavier things and loop the ropes around their necks to keep everything in contact with their bodies.

However, he warned them, anything that was not in constant contact with them at the exact moment of transfer would be left behind. He promised to hang a few items around his own neck, and help them with some of the transfer problems, but he needed to keep his hands and arms free to work the time-travel wand.

It was highly amusing that Benjamin brought to the departure only the clothes he was wearing, one picture of Michel drawn by a local artist, and the bag with all the gold and jewels in it.

On the other hand, Mimi brought her finest dresses, which she planned to update to the local styles of the day, her personal pots and pans handed down to her by her deceased parents, and lots of needles, thread and other things that she thought were absolutely necessary.

Benjamin and Michel would never tell her that almost everything that she was going to bring with her could easily be purchased when she got to where they were going. They both realized that she needed her personal things with her to help her adjust to a completely strange world whose only familiar item was her husband-to-be.

After the final packing had ended, and everything was set down on the roof ready to go when the sun came up, Michel brought them both down to the kitchen, and he personally served them fresh cups of coffee and some sweet things to nibble.

He also introduced them both to Fifi, who would be taking over Mimi's job with the household duties. Fifi came to Michel from a dear friend's household, and Michel was anxious to explain to her what her duties as housekeeper and personal mistress to the master entailed. Her education, however, would have to wait until Michel came back from returning the loving couple to the seventeen hundreds.

Fifi, by the way, was a tall, slender and extremely well-built girl of about twenty years of age. Michel's friend told him that she was exceptional in bed, and that Michel now owed him a very big favor for his gift of her. Michel wondered what he wanted in exchange for the girl, but he put that out of his mind to deal with it another time.

After Fifi had left to go about her new duties, Michel brought out several sheets of paper from one of the drawers and told them the details about having his implants done in the far future.

He also said that he had spent an hour or two in the same computer store where he had gone before, only this time it was to get information for Mimi to take with her. Michel said that she needed to know about the new civilization that she would be living in. She would need to know all of the things he had copied down for her in order to easily fit into the new life waiting out there for her.

Mimi gave Michel her utmost attention while Benjamin calmly looked on. He was thinking that this special thing was something that only Michel Nostradamus would think of doing. It was another grand gesture on Michel's part.

Michel cleared his throat and began to speak. "Benjamin, I am sure that you remember my saying that I was going to return you back to your timeline after I did the Cleopatra adventure.

"Something that you said a while back got me to thinking that I was being selfish. You said, what if something happened to me before I returned you to where you wanted to go? And this is very true. What if something did happen to me? That is the chance I take for myself, but I would also be playing with your life and my Mimi's life.

"So, in honor of my friendship to the both of you, my latest wedding present to you is my taking you to your new home together before I put myself at risk again. And Benjamin, the moisture you see in my eye is not a tear, but something that just flew into it. These damn insects are everywhere.

"Anyway, please pay attention to what I call 'Mimi's got-to-know list.'"

The average span in colonial America is short. Life expectancy at birth is thirty-five years of age.

One-half of all colonists died before age sixteen. However, if you lived to get out of your teen-age years, your chances of getting to age fifty were good.

Most people made their living by farming. Our Benjamin here, is one of the very few exceptions to the rule. Farming was back-breaking work that lasted from dawn to dusk.

Medicine in the seventeen hundreds was performed by barber-surgeons. Their knowledge of the human body was weak but it was improving rapidly.

The main room in a prosperous home was called the 'keeping room.' Why in the world they called it that, the computer and I could not figure out. The keeping room was used as a living room and dining room.

Carpets were placed on the top of tables because the carpets were too expensive to put on the floor and walk on. Chairs were a great luxury, and often only one was used per family. The rest of the family would sit on long wooden benches. Large chests were used for storage.

It was not safe to drink the water as it was always filled with dirt from the outside water wells. Beer and hard cider were substituted for water, which was only used for bathing and the livestock. For the wealthy, wine and brandy were imported for drinking. For the ordinary people, rum became a popular drink.

Corn was the main food crop. It was made into bread or mush or eaten with beans. Some rye, wheat and barley added a little bit to the corn diet. The farmers grew onions, turnips, parsnips and carrots. What they did not eat themselves they would sell at market.

They would share wooden plates and rarely had knives and forks. Most people would just use their hands while eating.

Men wore starched collars, and women wore frames of wood or whalebone under their dresses. Men wore knee-length leggings called breeches. They also wore stockings and boots. Wealthier men wore linen shirts and a jacket called a doublet, which had a short cape attached. Men wore their hair long, tied into a queue.

Women wore a linen garment called a shift. Over the shift, they wore long dresses that were in two separate parts called the skirt and the bodice. The bodice was very low cut and showed off a great deal of the female breast. The computer said that this was to keep the interest of the local men.

And the final bit of information that shocked me the most was that women in the seventeen hundreds did not wear panties.

"And now," Michel said as he handed the papers to the smiling Mimi, "I see that the sun has come up, and that means that it is time for us to get on with our travels. It would be a good moment to make our way to the roof."

CHAPTER TWENTY-FIVE

A puffing and exhausted Michel Nostradamus dropped the last of the pots and pans that he had been carrying onto the floor of the tiny room that Benjamin Franklin had been given by his father. They were back again in Colonial America.

When Mimi and Benjamin unloaded what they were carrying, the tiny room seemed filled to the brim.

A happy but very nervous Mimi started putting things away, while the two men stepped outside to take a few minutes to make their final goodbyes.

A big hug and a bigger handshake were given, and Benjamin turned and started back inside, when Michel called out his name for the very last time.

Benjamin turned and took the small envelope that Michel was holding out to him.

Michel was saying: "I thought very seriously about not giving this to you, Benjamin, but then my better judgement took over and I feel that it is the right thing for me to do in giving this to you. When I was at the Paris computer of the future, I called up one more thing just to satisfy myself about you. I feel so very close to you and to where you will be going with your life that I wanted to make sure that you stayed on the right path.

"Inside this envelope is a complete readout of just who and what you will become. Let me tell you that it is a wonderful read, but I am not sure that you want to read it now. If you will recall, we talked about this point at great length, and we both agreed that no man should know his future. This letter is just what we were talking about.

"I am going to take my leave of you now, and I am sure that we will never meet again in either of our lifetimes. I know that you and my Mimi will be very happy, and I also know that whenever you look at the beautiful Mimi, your thoughts will be drawn to me.

"Remember me well, Benjamin Franklin, and know that I am and always will be your friend.

"And in case you are curious, I am going to take a little walk down toward the harbor and see if I can find the most interesting barmaid/prostitute in all of Philadelphia. I do believe that I told you how I met her the day before I introduced myself to you. That will always be one of my most beloved of stories."

With a final wave of his hand, Michel Nostradamus walked away and completely out of Franklin's life ... except for that envelope Benjamin was now looking at.

Benjamin started to think, really think. Thanks to the generous gift of valuable stones and gold, he was now a very rich man. And maybe, again thanks to this envelope that Michel just gave him, he will find out the best way to put it all to work for himself. *Hmmmm.*

Maybe, just maybe, after he helps Mimi with whatever needs doing in the house, he will find the time to sit down and read the letter. Michel was so very serious about it and that made Benjamin want to find out why.

After all, it might just help him get through the tough times that were usually ahead of someone as young as he was, and besides all that, didn't he have a responsibility to his new bride, Mimi?

Would it not be the wise thing to know, if possible, what life had in store for him, instead of just blundering along in his usual manner? *Hmmmm.*

CHAPTER TWENTY-SIX

It was absolutely quiet in the little house after Mimi had fallen into an exhausted sleep.

Benjamin settled down in the only chair in the room and took the now crumpled-up letter out of his pocket. He looked at it for a few moments before slitting the top of the envelope open with his pocket knife. He opened the letter and placed it on his lap and just looked at it without reading it.

Should he put it aside as Nostradamus had suggested, or would that simply drive him crazy thinking about it?

He easily knew the answer to that question, and with a grim smile on his face, he began to read. An immediate big smile appeared, and he could not help himself from laughing out loud. He hoped that he didn't waken Mimi, but he just could not help himself.

At the top of the page, in large hand printed lettering that he knew to be Michel's, he read the following words:

Hello Benjamin:

If I know you, and I really do think that I do, it is not too very long since we said our final goodbye, and I handed you the following letter. I know that I suggested that you do not read it for many years, but I believe that a man with your curious nature has to know what I was referring to.

If I am right and you are reading this letter within a short time of my leaving it with you, then I win the bet that I placed with myself. However, I will never know if I am right or not since we will never meet again.

Once again, I thank you for being my trusted companion for all the things that we did together. And now, please enjoy this letter to the fullest.

Computer Readout—Benjamin Franklin

Benjamin Franklin suddenly returned to Philadelphia after a short and unexpected disappearance. When he came back with the young lady who soon became his wife, the word was that they had been away on a very secret romantic holiday.

Franklin, upon his return, began a rise that was professionally and financially astonishing. Within an amazing short time, he was able to retire, having accomplished the following:

- Started a newspaper.
- Organized a tradesmen's club called Michael's.
- Founded the first American subscription library.
- Became clerk to the Pennsylvania legislature.
- Established the first fire department.
- Became postmaster of Philadelphia.
- Established the American Philosophical Society.
- Launched *Poor Richard's Almanack*, a famous collection of wit, wisdom, and financial advice that he produced for twenty-five years.

Franklin then turned his attention to science and politics.

He performed his electrical experiments, with the most famous one being the silken kite experiment, which proved once and for all, that lightning and electricity were the same force of nature—and he then turned around and invented the lighting rod. He added to his list of inventions with bifocal eyeglasses and the wonderful Franklin stove.

He was a key mover in the Pennsylvania legislature, from which he was sent to England as the colony's agent. He emerged as the leading spokesman against the Stamp Act.

With war looming, Franklin returned to America a month before the famous battles of Lexington and Concord.

During the war, he sat in the second Continental Congress and was a member of the committee that formed the draft of the Declaration of Independence (written by his friend Thomas Jefferson), and soon afterward was sent to Paris to negotiate an alliance with the French, staying in France for a long time to make the terms of peace.

An interesting footnote to Franklin's historic visit to Paris was his putting up a marvelous statue and plaque to the famous Frenchman, Michel Nostradamus, who had died a mysterious death at the hands of others while out of his home country of France in the fifteen hundreds.

Benjamin Franklin would never explain his connection to the memory of Michel Nostradamus, who had a very mixed reputation.

End Computer Readout.

Benjamin put away the letter in a safe place, locked up the house, and went to sleep beside his beloved Mimi.

CHAPTER TWENTY-SEVEN

After handing Benjamin the letter that held the Franklin readout, Nostradamus walked rapidly away without looking back. He still had, in his jacket's inner pocket, two more special letters that he had put together from the information that he had gotten from the computer in the future. He had decided not to give these two envelopes to Benjamin because they would give him too much knowledge about the near future, and that would not be a good thing.

Nostradamus knew for sure that Benjamin would read the one letter that he had given to him. It would be a rare person who would not open a letter telling him or her about their personal future.

One of the letters that he kept told Nostradamus about six very special events that led up to the successful break-away of the thirteen colonies from the mother country of Great Britain. He planned to destroy this letter and the third one that he carried with him very shortly. They were very dangerous.

He had committed the second of the three letters to memory in case he ever wanted to add to his book of predictions. He took a moment and brought its contents into his mind's awareness just to be sure that he had them properly memorized:

Somebody will dump British tea into a place called the Boston Harbor.

Someone will hang a light in a Boston church steeple and this will refer to the British landing by land or by sea.

A person named Paul Revere will ride around the countryside announcing the arrival of the enemy British soldiers.

A famous person named Thomas Jefferson will write out the Declaration of Independence.

There will be several hard-fought battles and a very rough winter in a special place called Valley Forge.

George Washington will defeat the British forces in the final battles, and the thirteen colonies will become an independent and united country calling themselves the "United States of America."

☙☙

Knowing that he had all the facts correct, Nostradamus ripped the papers up into small pieces and placed them into a nearby trash container.

He held the last and final computer printout in his hand and read it over one more time. He had asked the computer to give him a short list of three very important people who were vital to the American victory, but did not come down through time as very famous. He would also throw these papers away in the same trash container after he looked at them one last time.

1. John Hancock—1736 to 1793—was the richest man in New England before the war broke out. He was a merchant who had inherited his wealth from an uncle who had acquired it through smuggling. Hancock's money assured him a prominent place among the Patriots, and he bankrolled the rebel causes.

John Hancock attended the Continental Congresses and

served as president of the Congress at one time. Despite a total lack of military experience, Hancock hoped to command the Continental army and was extremely annoyed when George Washington was named as commander-in-chief.

He was the first and most visible signer of the Declaration of Independence. He signed his name in triple size so that King George of England could not miss seeing it.

He was later elected the governor of Massachusetts.

2. John Paul Jones—1747 to 1792—was essentially an adventurer who became America's first naval hero. He was born with the name of John Paul (no Jones at that time) in the country of Scotland.

He began his career working as a sailor on a slave ship. He came to America under a dark cloud following the death of one of his fellow crewmen. Since he knew that people were looking for him for a possible crime, he added Jones to his name and from that point on he became known as John Paul Jones

When the American Congress commissioned a small navy, Jones volunteered and was given command of a ship called the *Providence*. Jones used this ship to raid English ships very successfully. He sailed to France and continued his raids off the English coast.

The French later gave him command of a refitted and more powerful ship called the *Bonhomme Richard*, and with it he engaged and defeated many first-class English man-of-war ships. He became a hero to the French people and later was sent to France as an emissary from the Colonies.

He received a Congressional Medal of Honor in 1787.

He finished his naval career with the Russian navy and died in Paris several years later.

And the final computer choice was of course Nostradamus's favorite because he was a Frenchman.

3. The Marquis de Lafayette—1757 to 1834—was one of the

revolution's idealists. This young Frenchman came to America at the age of nineteen to help. He was wealthy enough to pay for his own ship to make the journey from France to the Americas. After getting here, he donated the ship to the American navy.

Like other young European aristocrats for whom war was a matter of personal honor and social standing, la Fayette came in search of glory and adventure. In exchange for a major-general's rank, he offered to serve without pay, and he quickly earned George Washington's affection.

During a trip back to France, he was important in securing the French military assistance that was the key to the American victory at Yorktown.

As the British surrendered after Yorktown, the final battle of the war, Lafayette had his personal band proudly play the song "Yankee doodle dandy," which was a song thought up by the British to make fun of the rough-and-ready American soldiers.

After the war, Lafayette returned to France with a huge amount of plain American dirt. He kept it in a private cemetery until his death so that he could be buried in American soil. This was taken by all Americans at that time as a truly noble gesture by this much-beloved Frenchman.

Nostradamus cried for a few moments as he read the last entry and then ripped up these final computer papers and went on his way.

CHAPTER TWENTY-EIGHT

Michel returned to 2308 again and felt the relaxation and good feeling that being in the future gave him. He liked the calmness and relaxation that came over him when he entered the no-crime, no-poverty big-city feeling that the new Paris always gave him.

He went into the hospital for his weekly blood-work and psychological session, but this time something came up that the hospital staff brought to his attention. His physical report was excellent, and the blood work was perfect. What came up was a discussion point with one of the profiling doctors, who was not happy with what he said was an indication toward extreme aggressiveness and self-fulfillment needs on his part.

When Michel asked just what it was that they detected, it was explained that he was bringing his fifteen hundreds self-protection and "me first" attitude with him when he came to the twenty-fourth century. He and the world were out of step.

I understood exactly what they meant when they said that the worldwide civilizations had moved forward a great deal since my time, and unless I was willing to get more into just what the world of today was all about, there was a possibility that the scheduled implant surgery might be put on hold.

When I finally left the hospital after more discussions of what my mental profile was showing the doctors, I had to put several questions to myself. Here I was, Michel Nostradamus, world and time-traveler, having the time of my life, moving into and out of the life and times of people and places I admired.

I had to question myself as to where the thought of putting myself into a position where thinking about changing the world into a different kind of place came from. The ideas that came and went into my head about teaming up with someone like Napoleon and conquering everything before me now sounded all wrong. This world of the future, which was at peace with itself, where poverty and disease seemed to be in definite retreat: was that not enough for me?

I had to agree with the hospital staff that my personality profile left something to be desired, and I was more than willing to try the solutions that they offered me.

And so, I found myself sitting in a classroom as the oldest member of a high-school graduating class seminar. They were being lectured about college science courses that they would be required to take. I was there to see if I could become more socially in tune with the new world that so warmly welcomed me.

The doctors wanted me to see just what the young people of today were like, and there was no better sampling to be found than that of kids getting ready to graduate from high school, and getting themselves ready for college and on into their future.

I knew that I had a lot to learn, and so I found myself sitting in the classroom as the oldest member of the graduating class of June 2308. The young people were being lectured about a college science course that they would be required to take, and I was there to see if I could become more socially in tune with my new world.

I, of course, took my usual extremely detailed notes that I would review later. I rarely missed much by listening to the live discussions, and then reviewing my written notations and impressions.

It also did not hurt my attention span by listening to the very attractive, well-dressed, blonde female teacher going through the lecture for the benefit of myself and my fellow students.

The brochure which described the special one day class was entitled:

SPACE AND TIME AND WHAT IT MEANS TO YOU.

This was exactly what I probably needed to hear and I was looking forward to the lecture. I copied down the course information that was listed after the title. It read as follows:

"Away from daily life here on earth, the universe is a weird and truly wonderful place. Stars are born and explode. Star clusters, called galaxies, fly away from each other as time slowly passes.

Straight lines are really bent, and time can go faster or slower depending on the stresses put upon it.

Modern science can explain some of these mind-boggling events—but not all of them."

Also on the front cover were the following six questions to think about. Somewhere in the course that the college offered were the answers.

I surely had no idea about the answers. I could barely understand the questions.

I copied the six questions down, word for word:

How can a simple clock's pendulum swinging to and fro help to tell the time?
How does the sun's heat reach us through space, and how long

does it take to get here?
Radio waves come naturally from deep space, but can you
make your own here on earth?
How can you tell the time of day from a shadow?
There are times when every split second counts. How fast can
the human body react to sudden events?
Sunlight seems to be white; if so, why is a sunset red?

With a wonderful look on her pretty face, our teacher began her lecture, and I took down every word, phrase, pause and exclamation mark that she said.

Here in my condensed notes, is what I learned about the physical world through the year 2308:

In ancient times, people believed that the earth was flat, and that it was the center of everything. Gradually, scientific study and great explorations showed that the earth was not flat, but ball-shaped, and that earth's place in space is really just a small planet going around its local star, called the sun.

From our planet, the sun, moon and stars seem to travel across the sky. While it is true that the moon does orbit the earth, the movement of the other heavenly bodies is due to the movement of our planet earth.

The space age began on October 4, 1957, with the launch of the satellite Sputnik 1 by the former Soviet Union. This was a simple metal ball about twenty-three inches across and weighing one hundred-eighty-five pounds.

The earth's magnetic field curves around our planet, as if a giant bar magnet was inside the globe.

Earth is one of four planets that orbit relatively close to the sun. The other three are Mercury, Mars and Venus.

From space, our home would show some of the most exciting changes of any planet, as white clouds swirl in ever-changing daily patterns over the deep blue oceans and the green and brown land.

Along with the planets and their moons, thousands of smaller bits of rock and ice circle the sun. They range from tiny dust particles to mini-planets that are hundreds of miles across. They are asteroids, which are leftover debris of the solar system. They were fragments too small and too far apart to form into a proper planet. These asteroids lie in a wide band between Mars and Jupiter, which we call the asteroid belt.

The sun is our local star, a vast, fiery spinning ball of burning gases, made up of three-quarters hydrogen and one-quarter helium. The sun is huge. It is more than 1.3 million times the size of our earth. The sun's temperature is twenty-seven million degrees; the surface is a raging inferno.

The few hundred thousand stars we see twinkling in the night sky are just a tiny fraction of the stars (actually, each star is a sun when seen close up) scattered throughout the universe.

And finally, our galaxy or grouping of stars is something that can be seen from earth as it wanders across the night sky. The ancient Greeks, who named it the Milky Way, said that it looked as if someone had spilled milk across that part of the night sky.

There was a brief question-and-answer session, and then Dr. Goodman, the teacher, dismissed the class.

Before everyone got up to leave, she reminded them that the classes were to begin in three days, and they all needed to attend. She also asked if Student Nostradamus would please report to her office in the administration building after the lunch hour.

A curious but happy Student Nostradamus answered that he would be there, and then he joined the rest of the student body as they left the lecture hall.

CHAPTER TWENTY-NINE

The sign on the door read *Dorothy (Dot) Goodman – PhD*. Michel Nostradamus, transplanted sixteenth-century adventurer, knocked timidly upon the outer door and, hearing a clear command to "Come on in," paused only a moment before he entered.

The room was done up in soft feminine colors of pinks, light blues and soft browns.

She pointed me to a nearby couch, and continued to speak into a small cube shaped telephone of some sort that showed the picture of the person that she was talking to.

I really didn't pay close attention to Doctor Goodman, who was sitting behind a large desk, but was immediately drawn instead to looking at the collection of three watercolor pictures hanging over the far side of the couch. They looked very familiar to me since the artist's signature in the lower right hand corner was mine.

I was looking at the original paintings that I had drawn of my village just before I went off and time-traveled to the time of Benjamin Franklin.

I must have been standing there with my mouth open because she was suddenly there beside me and smiling a great smile at me. She reached out and took my hand in hers. Her grip was firm, dry and strong. She stood quite close to me as we shook hands, which allowed me to tower over her. To her credit, she did not step back nor pull her hand away.

Close up and personal, she looked even better to me than she did from where I was sitting eight rows up in the student seats. Her figure, noteworthy from across the auditorium, was even more remarkable as we stood there looking each other over.

She pulled her hand back, and said, with a light touch to her voice, "I thought you would be somewhat older. The Michel Nostradamus I know about was well into his early forties. You look like you are still in your teenage years."

Well, that broke us up, and we moved over to the couch where we both sat facing each other.

I told her that I was twenty-six years old and was enjoying myself greatly in her world. I told her I loved her 'Touch-Of-Science' class and asked her if she had asked me to come to her office for some special tutoring.

Now, I realized that females in this timeline were said to be bold and aggressive, but her response to my little joke took me completely by surprise.

She told me that she was the world's greatest Michel Nostradamus authority, and that she couldn't believe it when she heard that I was here for an implant that would further enable me to continue my time-travel studies. My comings and goings were all in the reports that had come across her desk a few days ago.

She was the one who suggested to my medical team that it would be quite beneficial to me if I sat in on her advanced science class. She thought that this would be a polite and proper way for us to meet each other.

Of course, I was very flattered by this extremely attractive young lady being interested in the happenings of my life.

She told me that it would be wonderful if we could meet for dinner, dancing and some deep conversations on her favorite studies. She was very serious about the dinner and dancing, and she said without batting an eye that she was looking forward to comparing how sexual intercourse from the fifteen hundreds compared to it in the twenty-fourth century.

She went on to say that we would have to try it out and compare notes, and she thought that it would be a lot of fun for the two of us. Naturally, I had no objections to her immediate plans. I was beginning to really like this self-assured lady from this very advanced society.

Her degrees were in Greco-Roman history, and when my surgical file told her that I was planning on paying a visit to Julius Caesar and Cleopatra, and possibly some of the other great names, she knew that she needed to somehow get involved.

There were some very secret and very secure files that she wanted to look at before we met tomorrow evening. She said that it had something very important to do with Cleopatra and Alexander the Great. She refused to answer any question about these two, famous people, who lived many hundreds of years apart.

She smiled shyly as she said that if I was as good in bed as she thought I would be, then all the secrets of Alexander and Cleopatra were mine. I had no concern about my abilities. After all I was twenty-six and a Frenchman.

I kissed her on the cheek, took the slip of paper that had her home address on it, and quietly let myself out of her office. I would listen to her suggestion and take tomorrow off and gather together my strength for what I knew would be a wonderful evening of fun, games and important information.

CHAPTER THIRTY

I had hired the twenty-fourth century's version of a limo, and the driver would be on standby for me for the entire day and evening. After all, money was not a problem, and if I couldn't enjoy myself with wine, a woman and a little bit of modern sex, then who could?

I was getting a little nervous, as the date for my scheduled implant was getting closer.

On my way to Dot's house for the start of my evening out, I had my driver, Pierre, stop at one of the fine jewelry stores located just off the main boulevard.

Thirty minutes later, I was back in the limo and on my way to pick up my date for the evening. In my pocket and wrapped wonderfully was an outstandingly beautiful ladies' diamond bracelet. I had spared no expense and I knew that my gift would be a big hit with my number-one fan.

I was looking forward to a lot of things this evening. Good French food, some dancing, female companionship, and most interesting of all, some special information that I obviously had missed regarding my time-travel adventures.

Dot Goodman should be the perfect lady for me to visit whenever I moved around in the timeline. I have heard the statement that a sailor should have a girl in every port, and for me a girl in every time-period would be just perfect.

About an hour later, we were seated in a tiny restaurant located at the very top of the Eiffel Tower.

The restaurant was enclosed in clear glass and the entire dining room moved around slowly, showing off Paris, the City of Light, in a wonderful way. The view on this clear night was good for many miles, and I could just imagine my village off there to the eastern part of the city.

Dot allowed me to do the ordering, and I in turn had our waiter suggest what he thought was the best that the kitchen had to offer.

The wine that kept flowing throughout the evening was a product of the local grape, and both the red and the white that we had were probably the finest that I had ever experienced.

We were dancing another slow dance to the wonderfully soft and elegant music, where her body was pressed intimately against mine, when I made a great show of giving her my present. I never thought that I would experience the moment when this product of France's perfect female breeding would run out of words, but at that moment she was speechless. If she pressed herself against me any harder on the dance floor, I would have been squished to death.

It wasn't long before we were back in the limo and on our way to Dot's place. Along the way, she was pointing out the special sights that she wanted me to see. Everything in this fabulous City of Light was lit up, and I marveled at familiar things I knew and new things that I didn't know. Paris was constantly improving upon itself. I was most impressed with my new girl, my city, and my country of France.

Dot's two-bedroom home was about six blocks from the river area that I loved so very much. After a quick conference with Dot, I had the driver drop us off at one of the dock areas where we could watch the big ships as they drifted by. I told Pierre that I would not be needing him for the rest of the evening, and that he could pick me up around noon tomorrow at Dot's house.

It was in our plans to walk the six blocks back to Dot's house. Like two love-struck teenagers, we sat quietly on the park bench and watched other lovers glance at us and walk quietly by. It was a most pleasant feeling just sitting there quietly.

As we strolled slowly on our way back, I remarked that I had not seen any beggars or poor people in the streets of Paris.

Dot told me that the government found a job for everyone who needed help. It made for a peaceful and comfortable society where almost everyone was sort of content.

After about a two-hour slow walk through the amazing streets of Paris after dark, we arrived back at Dot's home.

Dot asked me if I would please excuse her for a few minutes. She wanted to shower and change clothes.

She sat me down at her formal dining room table, made sure that I had a glass of sherry and lots of overhead light to read by. She then told me that she had taken most of this morning off from any of her normal chores, and spent the day at the University's private library. She said that she found what she was looking for, and that something most interesting and noteworthy in the life of Alexander the Great would affect my seeing Cleopatra on my proposed time-jump.

Dot would not tell me what it was that I should be looking for, but she promised me that at the end of the reading, it would simply jump out at me.

She said that my understanding of the time period would be much greater and easier for me to get into with this new knowledge. And she said that my reward for reading the boring text that she had prepared for me, was to be given the privilege of coming into her bed, where untold sexual delights would be mine for the taking. With a wink and a wiggle, she left the room to me and the neatly typed manuscript that waited upon my attention.

CHAPTER THIRTY-ONE

As I turned to the first page of the thin manuscript, I discovered a little note to me from my soon-to-be lover. *Michel, I know you well enough to know that you believe that there could not be a connection of any sort between Alexander the Great, who lived in Greece and was born two hundred and eighty-seven years earlier, and the wonderful Cleopatra of Egypt.*

Kindly believe me that there is a direct connection and I have enclosed the answer within this manuscript for you. I believe that you will have a good laugh when you figure it out. I am not the head of the History Department without having learned a little bit about history.

Enjoy this boring manuscript first and then the exciting me second.

Kisses
Dot

Dot's printout began:

At the battle of the Granius river in northwestern Eurasia, during the first military engagement of Alexander the Great's invasion of the Persian empire, young King Alexander came very close to sudden death

At the Granius river, Alexander's Greeks encountered the

enemy Persians on the opposite banks. The enemy was massed in a defensive formation and did not seem ready for a fight.

The young King Alexander, age twenty-two, obviously had much to learn, and he did not listen to his senior commanders, who cautioned him to stand down and wait for his reinforcements that were due to arrive the next day.

Ignoring their sensible advice, Alexander mounted his great horse Bucephalus. He was wearing a white-plumed helmet which made him stand out from everyone else, as he was quite conspicuous wearing white when everyone else was in dark colors.

The young king led his shock cavalry troops in an audacious charge across the river and up the opposite bank. The Persian forces fell back before the attacking Greeks, and Alexander, who did not stop his charge, suddenly found himself in the middle of the enemy lines. This was probably exactly what the Persian tacticians had planned from the beginning.

Due to the suddenness of his charge right into the middle of the enemy lines, he only had with him a small number of men, momentarily cut off from the main body of the Greek mounted cavalry, who were trying to catch up. At this critical moment in the battle, young Alexander was completely surrounded by enemies, including one Spithridates, an ax-wielding Persian noble who managed to deal Alexander a heavy blow to the head.

Alexander's helmet was severely damaged and the king was disoriented and unable to defend himself. A second strike would certainly kill him, and with the young king would die the hopes of the entire expedition and all the Greek imperial aspirations.

Greece would never have risen to greatness as it did if Alexander had died, and the entire world as we know it would have been changed forever. In those next few seconds, the future of the great Persian empire and the entire course of Western history would be decided.

Did Alexander's brief life flash before him as he awaited imminent extinction? How had he come to arrive at this place, at this terrible fate that was only seconds away? How could so much have come to depend on a single blow to the head?

༄༅

Alexander was born in Macedon (a northeastern region of modern Greece) in the year 356 BCE. He was the first and only son of King Phillip II of Macedon. Philip had seized control of Macedon just three years before his son's birth. By the time Alexander was ten years old, Macedon was the most powerful state on the entire Greek peninsula.

Alexander was being groomed to help govern the kingdom and eventually assume the throne of his father. Alexander was well trained. His tutor in intellectual and cultural matters was the famous and brilliant Greek philosopher, Aristotle. His mentor in military and diplomatic affairs was his own father, who was probably the best military mind of his generation.

And in the corridors of the royal palace, Alexander learned the dark arts of political intrigue. The Greek court was always full of rumor and arguing factions.

In Alexander's twentieth year, Philip was cut down by an assassin. The killer, a Greek named Pausanias, was in turn butchered by Philip's bodyguards as he ran for his horse. Although Pausanias may well have held a personal grudge against the king, there was suspicion that he had not acted alone.

One obvious candidate for the mastermind behind the killing was Darrius III, the great king of Persia.

In the mid-fourth century, Persia was a mighty empire that stretched from the Aegean coast of Turkey to Egypt in the south, and east as far as modern Pakistan.

In the years before his assassination, King Philip had been

making open preparations for a Persian expedition. A few months prior to his death, his generals had established a beachhead on Persian-held territory.

King Darrius of Persia was famous for his statement of always wanting to cut off the head of primary enemies whenever possible. This made him the prime and most hated of enemies. Alexander himself stated in public that he personally blamed King Darrius as the primary suspect.

Other fingers pointed at Phillip's jealous wife, Olympias (Alexander's mother), while others spoke about the young Prince Alexander himself being involved.

The kingdom was full of speculation as Alexander took over the reins of government. He quickly assumed the full title of king of all Greece and no one opposed him.

Alexander had definitely proven himself ready and more than worthy of rightfully taking the throne, but his one problem was that his treasury was seriously depleted. He had no choice but to follow through with the planned invasion of the western provinces of the Persian empire. The prospect of great war treasure fired up the imagination of his Greek troops.

And that now brings us to where the ax of the Persian was getting ready to strike the shattered helmet of young King Alexander for the second time.

It appeared as if the glorious expedition would end right here before it really got started. Yet the deadly blow never landed. Just as the Persian Spithridates prepared to finish off his opponent, one of Alexander's personal bodyguards, Cleitus the Black, appeared at his king's side and speared the Persian axman dead on the spot.

Alexander quickly rallied, and the wild charge that might have ended in disaster spurred on his troops. Most of the enemy forces crumpled. Alexander was spectacularly victorious.

He lost only thirty-four men and killed over twenty

thousand of the enemy. Treasure and spoils of war were sent back to Greece to be displayed in places of honor. Alexander was now on his way up, and it seemed that nothing could stop him.

In the course of the next ten years, Alexander and his Greek army repeatedly demonstrated their capacity to overcome tremendous odds. They went on to conquer the entire Persian empire and more. Alexander's conquest of the Persian empire is among the most remarkable military campaigns of all time.

By 323 BCE, Alexander had laid the foundation for a successful empire that might have included one-half of the known world at that time (and here is where you, Michel, must pay the most attention if you are going to pick up on the point I want to make.) However, most unfortunately, Alexander did not live long enough to see his hard-fought new empire get started.

In the year 323 BCE, Alexander the great, king of Greece, ruled a domain that stretched from Egypt to the distant Caspian Sea. Historians call him the most brilliant soldier of all time. Sadly enough, he did not die a warrior's death in battle, but expired as helpless as a baby in his own bed.

On the night of June 1, 323 BC, within the royal bedchambers of his palace in Babylon, Alexander was holding a memorial feast to honor a personal friend. Suddenly, around mid-evening, he was seized with intense pain and collapsed. He was taken to his bed chambers where he tried to fight off a raging fever. He came back and forth to awareness but finally passed on after ten days of suffering.

The passing on of Alexander the Great is one of history's most enduring mysteries. What caused the strong and healthy young ruler to so quickly and unexpectedly die at the very height of his power?

Historians have proposed malaria, typhoid, and alcohol poisoning as possible causes of death. There have also been those who have suggested outright murder as a possibility. There has never been an investigation into any of these possibilities.

And now, Michel Nostradamus, here is the link that connects your Cleopatra to the dying Alexander the Great. This is your reward for patiently reading all of this.

Please recall that in the last few days of his life, Alexander came in and out of his fever. In one of his few moments of clarity, he had his doctors send for his four most senior generals.

When they finally all appeared before him, in one of those moments when he was alert and clear-thinking, he told them that he had not prepared for his own death at so young an age. He told them that he had not thought about who should step into his shoes and become the next leader of the world that he created. He was sorry, but no young man ever thinks about his death.

Rather than have the four of them fight against each other and tear the new empire apart, he divided the empire into four parts. Each of his loyal generals was to get one part of the empire as his very own to rule as he saw fit. They had to each take an oath before him now to support each other in their new positions and come to the aid of each other if needed.

Alexander then had one of his loyal servants bring in a map of the newly formed empire. In bright red, there were four large sections drawn. One was Europe, one was Asia, one was Greece and the last was Egypt.

Alexander said that in his opinion, all the areas were worthy of any of them, but he ranked the greatest prizes to be best in this order: Greece, Asia, Europe, Egypt. He said it would become clear in a few moments which part of the empire would belong to them.

Again, the servant came in, but this time he was carrying a large wooden box that had wooden walls build up on three sides. The servant set down a pair of large dice in the center of the wooden three-sided box.

Alexander said that each of the generals would roll the pair of dice one time, and the highest number rolled would get the best area, and so on down to the fourth choice. He again told them that any of the four would be extremely valuable and not to feel badly with what the luck of the dice gave them.

They would roll alphabetically according to their last names: General Cassandra, General Lysimachus, General Ptolemy, and finally General Seleucus.

After much mumbling and complaining, the four generals got down on their knees and prepared to roll the dice that would divide up the known world. The servant wrote each name on a scroll, and was prepared to write down the number rolled by the dice. Alexander had himself placed in a soft chair next to the kneeling generals so that he could watch this most unusual event.

General Cassandra rolled a six and a three for a total of nine. The number nine was entered next to his name.

General Lysimachus rolled a six and a five for a total of eleven. The number eleven was entered by the servant next to his name.

General Ptolemy rolled a three and a one for a total of four. The number four was entered next to his name.

General Seleucus rolled a six and a five for a total of eleven. The number eleven was entered by the servant next to his name.

The servant cleared his throat and read the following: "General Lysimachus and General Seleucus will have to roll the dice one more time. They have both tied with the number eleven, and since they are the two top numbers, they will get the top two selections."

The servant continued, "General Cassandra rolled a nine, which makes him the third highest number, and he receives Europe. Congratulations, General.

"General Ptolemy rolled a number four, which makes

him the fourth highest number, and he receives Egypt. Congratulations, general.

"And now, Generals Lysimachus and Seleucus, kindly roll the dice one more time. Alphabetically if you please; allow General Lysimachus to roll first."

The general's dice rolled a pair of fives for a total of ten.

General Seleucus's dice rolled a six and a one for a total of seven.

The servant announced, "General Lysimachus rolled the high number, and he receives Greece. Congratulations, General.

"General Seleucus comes in second, and he receives Asia. Congratulations, General."

The four generals were now gathered around the seated Alexander who was absolutely exhausted.

Alexander said, "You have all been with me from the very beginning. Words are not adequate for what I feel in my heart for each of you. The best gift that I can give each of you is one-quarter of the empire that we all worked so hard to create. I wish you all the best of everything that life can give you. Please remember me as I was, and not as I am at this moment."

He waved his hand and each general bowed and quietly left the room.

Alexander passed away quietly in the night, and the great man was gone for all eternity.

Dot's final note to Michel:

Here is the kicker that I promised you.

General Ptolemy loses at dice but becomes the real winner, because each of the other three generals were overthrown by the countries that they were given. Only the fourth-place winner, Ptolemy, established a dynasty that lasted. His family ruled Egypt for thirteen generations until Ptolemy XIII and Cleopatra, his sister, took over as co-pharaohs.

The funny line for me in all of this, will be that you will be going back in time to see the people who ruled a country that was won or, actually, lost on the roll of a pair of dice.

Okay, Michel Nostradamus—how about you 'rolling' yourself into my bedroom? I do hope that you will be able to find it.

CHAPTER THIRTY-TWO

A soft glow emanated from inside Dot's bedroom as Michel stepped through the door. He realized that there were candles all around the room, lighting it softly.

What he saw was a lovely large bedroom area with a couch, two matching chairs, a cabinet, and an extremely large bed. Beyond the bed and on the far wall was a large picture window that overlooked the river, with a beautiful view of the Eiffel Tower in the distance. Everything glittered outside in the light of the full moon.

"I've missed you, Michel."

He turned at the sound of her soft voice and saw her standing there, framed in the candlelight that was shining behind her. The glowing candlelight accentuated the outline of her exceptional figure.

Michel's heart filled with joy at the sight of her. "I've missed you too. I have been kind of busy catching up on some interesting reading material."

Dot looked at Michel, and he looked absolutely fabulous, wearing a long-sleeved dressy black shirt made from some soft-looking fabric, and he had unbuttoned the top two buttons. Her gaze returned to his face, his square jaw, his well–sculpted cheekbones, and his inviting eyes.

She smiled, hoping that she didn't look too ridiculous as she stared at him with the longing she felt deep inside her. After all, standing right there in front of her, and actually here in her bedroom, was the Michel Nostradamus, right out of the history book.

She slipped off her sandals, then stepped toward him. He drew her into his arms and pulled her close, his lips meeting hers, with a hunger that matched her own. Oh, God, his hard, muscular body felt so good. His strong arms were around her and his lips were caressing hers.

His tongue slipped between her lips as she touched it gently with her own, loving the instant intimacy suddenly between the two of them. Her breathing accelerated and she wanted to tear off her clothes right after she tore off his.

His arms stroked her back and his kisses heated up. Her breasts pressed hard into his chest, her nipples beading to incredible tightness.

She felt her sexual organs tightening and pulsating. She wanted to wrap her legs around him, ready for his hot, hard erection to spear her. She could feel it growing against her stomach.

Michel felt that it was heavenly, feeling her warm, feminine body pressed over the length of him.

She nodded at the implication that his shy smile suggested to her. His fingers caressed along the neckline of her blouse, then dipped into the fabric to release the first of the buttons. His touch was as light as the brush of a butterfly's wing, as he undid the next button, and then the next, thrilling her senses with his soft and delicate touch.

Finally, her blouse gaped open, and he simply threw it away from them over her shoulders. It dropped to the floor in a heap. He stroked along the lace edging of her bra, then between her aching breasts. He released the front clasp that was holding everything together, and then also threw the bra aside.

His look of awe as he gazed at her nearly melted her heart. She, of course, was already deeply in love with this man who came to her from out of the ages.

"You are exquisite, Dorothy Goodman, PhD."

As his heated gaze looked at her exposed breasts, her nipples puckered shamelessly. She longed for him to touch them, but he did not, at least not yet. He merely took in the sight of them. Finally, he unzipped the trousers of the pantsuit that she wore to dinner, and slid them down her slender hips.

She was unable to help him or stop him. She was completely his, and whatever he wanted to do with her would be fine with her. She helped him with her trousers by stepping out of them, now wearing only a skimpy black panty.

He hooked his fingers under the lacy elastic, and drew them down, then off.

Even though she stood before him completely naked, his desire for her which was evident, made her feel alluring, but somehow innocent, like the young schoolgirl she once was, only a few years before.

He gazed down at the panties and smiled, as though he was having the same 'schoolgirl' thoughts as she had.

She had to be careful here, she thought. Michel was very sensitive to thoughts and body language. He was a master at reading both. She hoped that the language that her body was giving him was the one he wanted.

She laughed to herself, knowing that even though he was Michel Nostradamus, he was still a man. And that man was here with her in her bedroom, and that man was hopefully, about to have his way with her in the style that she was planning on becoming very much accustomed to.

He broke into her thoughts by taking her hand and leading her across the room to where the king-sized bed waited for them both. It was a big bed, she thought, but it seemed appropriate for Michel. A broad, tall man like him, needed a big bed.

It took him but a minute to rid himself of shoes, socks and his other clothing. Unlike her things, which were scattered all around the room, he folded and neatly piled up his things in a corner.

Leave it to a Frenchman, she thought. With a naked and passionate lady waiting for him, he still took the time to set his clothing aside so as not to cause them to wrinkle. Dot sat down, and the high-quality cotton sheets felt like smooth silk against her skin. He tossed aside two of the pillows and moved the remaining two to the center of the bed.

"Why don't you lie on your stomach," he suggested.

She settled onto her stomach, tucking one of the two remaining pillows under her chin, and pushing the other one aside.

He sat down beside her, and his hands began moving over her back in long, soothing strokes. His fingertips feathered out from her spine with a gentle pressure. Then he stroked over her shoulders and down her arms, his fingers moving back and forth, kneading her muscles. Dot's cares drifted away as he paid careful attention to her arms, then her wrists and hands.

He shifted to her thighs, then kneaded his way down her legs to her ankles. He followed this with long, light strokes up and down. Her limbs grew limp. Every part of her tingled under the expert pressure of his fingertips and as he moved up her legs again, she felt a prickly awareness of his masculinity, of his nudity, and of her own.

He caressed her bare buttocks, his palms stroking and soothing but at the same time, exhilarating her naked flesh. His hands moved round and round. She was aware of his squeezing her buttocks together and the separating of them slightly with each circular stroke.

Her vagina pulsed with internal heat as she longed for him to slip his finger between her legs and stroke her there. His fingers slid down the slope of her buttocks to her thighs and she moaned softly.

Michel felt his penis harden as he became aware of the soft sounds that she was making. He wanted her to get used to his touch, and for her to associate it with being in a completely relaxed state. At the same time, he wanted to enter her and sexually stimulate her to a frantic frenzy, then flip her over and thrust into her until they both screamed in passion.

"Why don't you roll over onto your back," he said in a raspy, strained voice. He didn't know how much longer he could hold back on his need to enter her willing body.

As she rolled onto her back, he grasped the pillow and repositioned it under her head. She lay there staring up at him, her body beautiful in its nakedness. Her breasts pointed straight up at the ceiling, the nipples fully erect. Her soft pubic hair curled daintily between her thighs, as her long, shapely legs lay parted in a relaxed state. The lady was ready for him.

His penis twitched. He dearly wanted to capture those nipples in his mouth, to feel them rise and fall as he kneaded them until she wailed in her orgasm. He loved bringing a woman to orgasm by touching her breasts alone.

He stroked those lovely mounds as if they were just any other part of her body. Of course, they were a special part of her, as breasts were an erotic and most tempting treat for him or for any other man. Her erect nipples pushed themselves into his hands every time he stroked them.

He eased her legs apart and leaned toward her intimate flesh. He drew the folds apart with his thumbs, and dabbed his tongue against the little points of flesh. Her body was quivering beneath him as her fingers tangled in his hair, and she began to moan in pleasure.

He looked at her from beneath her thighs, over the tops of her breasts. His eyes blazed at her, his face like the face of one possessed. Then he suddenly lowered her legs and positioned himself on top of her.

She felt his hardness probing at her, his hands helping to open her as he finally invaded her. He was pushing hard inside her, and then thrusting with long deliberate strokes, slowly measured, and yet determined and with breath-taking ferocity.

Dot met his strokes with determined thrusts of her own, each one of them fanning the flames that threatened to erupt in an all-out explosion at any moment. The strokes came faster and harder, and Dot could feel herself an instant away from the blazing climax she was craving, and yet she tried to hold herself back.

Suddenly, the most glorious sensation of all—her body was no longer her body. It was a series of shooting stars all going off in different directions like a huge firework display. She said his name again and again, as the spasm of joyous release washed over her.

But before she had even caught her breath, she felt him enter her deeper than before, and once again there was another buildup of imminent explosions inside her. She gasped as he rode her, faster and faster, ruthlessly, not caring that she had not recovered from that first powerful climax. Mindlessly, she moved with his moves, her energy equal to his, her thrusts as strong and determined as his.

Their final passion exploded simultaneously. Dot gasping and clutching him desperately, and Michel collapsing in an exhausted heap atop her body.

CHAPTER THIRTY-THREE

The doctor led Michel down a long, white corridor whose floor bore the scuff marks of rubber-wheeled gurneys.

This path had been used before by many others before him. He was moving at a fast pace, and Michel was hard-pressed to keep up with him. They were heading for his office in the surgery department, where they were going to continue their discussion of implants and DNA.

The last time Michel was here, he felt extremely uneducated on what they were talking about, and so he did a lot of research at his local rent-a-computer store. Between the computer and Dot Goodman, who was now his constant companion, he had a pretty good idea of what it was all about.

It must be remembered that Michel Nostradamus, was born in the early fifteen hundreds, and all they really knew about surgery in those days was a clean knife and some string. Michel was feeling pretty good with his new knowledge, and when they finally were sitting quietly in Doctor Tirsch's office, Michel was able to talk intelligently about what was about to happen to him.

Doctor T. as he was called, was the actual surgeon who would be doing my surgery.

Michel reviewed in his mind just what it was that the computer had told him about surgery in the most general of terms. Doctor T. would go into the specifics in a few minutes. Doctor T. was busy bringing up the Michel Nostradamus records from his in-house computer, and it was interesting to watch as perhaps dozens of printed papers kept corning out.

It was probably giving him what Dot had told him that she had found when she had researched him earlier. There probably was lots of stuff about his predictions, their accuracy, and most likely some recent entries about his time-travel movements.

While he waited for Doctor T. to organize the many papers that he had now spread out on his desk, Michel continued to review in his mind, what the computer told him about the art of the surgeon.

Surgery, was an ancient medical specialty that used operative or manual techniques on a patient in order to investigate or treat an internal condition. What that meant was that surgery went way back in history, and the cutting that was associated with it was to correct an internal problem that had occurred within the body.

That seemed to be easy enough to understand. The computer went on to say that after the surgery, depending upon what was done, the patient was usually down for a few days or possibly a few weeks. Dot had told him that her best educated guess for what he was going to have done would be for him to recover enough to move about within a week's time. This also seemed reasonable.

A miniature micro-receiver was going to be attached internally above his left ear. This would allow his visual and hearing systems to receive signals from the outer world, and translate them into meaningful terms that he could understand internally. The highly-advanced study of DNA made all of this possible.

DNA was a separate field that stood alone in the scientific community. DNA meant deoxyribonucleic acid, which Michel had great trouble pronouncing. It is the hereditary material in all living organisms, including humans.

The two scientists who discovered DNA in the twentieth century were Doctor James D. Watson and Doctor Francis Crick. They proved that DNA is a nucleic acid that contains the genetic instructions out of which all life follows. They specifically said that there are no two DNA samples that can ever be alike. They showed the entire world how to read and code DNA so that it can be easily used to identify one human from another and that there could be no doubt of the accuracy. This process was given the name of genetic coding.

This led Michel to believe that there was something good and something not so good that would specifically effect his plans. It appeared that there was no doubt that he could recline comfortably here in the future, and receive the factual information that he needed by getting a readout on the person that he wanted to study.

All that was well and good for someone presently alive, but how would he get a blood sample from someone in the past? Michel knew that he just couldn't walk up to them and ask them for some of their blood so that he could get into their head. And without that blood sample, all the greatest machinery in the world, would not be able to send him back in time, so that he could do what he wanted to do. Another way to say this was that without a blood sample, it all would be a big waste of time and money.

When Michel expressed these thoughts to Doty, saying that maybe he should not go forward with the surgery since the machines would not have the blood sample that was needed, and that he was looking at a dead end, the response that he got from her worried him at the same time as it gave him great encouragement.

She said that he should trust her. She said she absolutely guaranteed that she could solve his blood problem. She said that she needed some time to figure it all out. She was very strong when she said she could do it.

Michel simply hated it when someone told him to trust them. He had learned in life, that the best person to trust with anything important was himself.

However, in this special case, I had nothing to lose if I gave her the opportunity she wanted. I knew that she was looking to impress me and I was hoping that she could deliver even though I could not see how she could give me the blood I needed.

I could see in my mind's eye how it would end if I time-traveled back in time to, let us say, Julius Caesar. Could I ask him for a small sample of his blood? I would be dead before the words were out of my mouth.

When I repeated my thoughts to Doty, all she said was that she would definitely deliver what I wanted, if I could deliver on something that she wanted.

Obviously, it was easier for me to do that special something for her then for her to do what I thought of as impossible for me. Does this make any sense? All I had to do was let her "have her way with me" which is what I planned to do the day before my surgery anyway.

So, I told her, with as much sincerity as I could come up with in my voice, that I trusted her and I would go forward with the surgery. I told her to be ready to deliver the blood samples when I was up and about, and she promised that she would.

With all of these thoughts rumbling through my head, I turned my immediate attention back to Doctor T., who was now ready to talk to me about my upcoming surgery.

CHAPTER THIRTY-FOUR

Time is a very strange and yet wonderful thing. It moved along at its regular slow but steady pace when Michel was back in the fifteen hundreds. He woke up in the mornings, did whatever he had to do during the day or evening, and then he would go back to sleep and do the very same things over again the next day and the next. In this case, time was not really something Michel thought about, or paid attention to, as he went about his normal life.

However, when he was able to time-travel, his awareness sharpened and he became very conscious of how time meant different things to different people.

After Michel's three-hour implant surgery with Doctor Tirsch, and the four-week recovery period that he spent getting his strength back, he was most eager to get on with his plans. Time was now moving much too slowly for him.

Doty came to visit him daily, and his relationship with her was becoming very strong.

She told him, that as she promised, she had figured out a solution to the Julius Caesar/Cleopatra problem.

This was something that Michel thought would be impossible to do, but she said she had done it, so, he took a wait-and-see attitude.

She would just smile at him each time she told him that he had to wait for all the answers. She was like a cat playing with a mouse. Michel was smart enough to know that he was the mouse, but what else could he do except wait for his full recovery?

Doty wanted to be sure that he had mastered the skills he needed before he was turned loose. She had rounded up several local volunteers who would work with them and the DNA specialists that they had hired to perfect his skill level.

She also made it perfectly clear that she wanted to be the final person whose head Michel would enter. He gave her his word that she would be there with him all the way.

Doty was proving to him that she was very concerned for his well-being, and that she would like to be his help-mate for the rest of their lives. However, since he had never committed himself to just one woman, this was a completely new concept for him. He promised that I would give it some deep thought when things calmed down a bit. Right now, there was too much going on around him. He needed to concentrate upon his immediate needs.

It was just good to know that this special lady was there for him at all times. This was a wonderful feeling, and it was something that Michel had never experienced before.

❧

Michel finally mastered the ability to give a mental command to the specially constructed door that opened and closed off his new work room/lab area, located in one of the old buildings at the University. The cubicle was completely independent of the outside world and it was set up this way in case an emergency would arise from one of his time-travel adventures.

Nostradamus planned to take advantage of this future world that he was now living in. It had all the advanced scientific hardware that he needed, and it all was incorporated into the computer that he alone controlled. No longer would he need to bend the light rays of the sun and focus them on his hand-held wand. By comparison, the old way of time-traveling was way out of date, and the simplicity of the new system made it highly desirable.

His new office/workshop had power, air, and a special filtration system of its own. It even had its own food synthesizer. Michel was simply amazed as each and every program that was available to him was explained.

The controlling computer now only recognized him, and would be lethally resistant to any attempt by anyone else trying to enter his private kingdom.

Michel was feeling very secure within the little world that he had created for himself. If he thought of something that he wanted or perhaps needed, his wealth made all things possible.

Michel was now sitting in absorbed silence, listening to the various discussions coming at him from micro-tapes that were transmitting their sounds directly into his head.

Most interestingly, when Michel was under Doctor Tirsch's surgical knife a few weeks ago, he had them add a few things to his body that would bring him up to being the equal of the present-day, perfect male. A few nips here and a few tucks there, and his twenty-eight-year-old body was much the same as his fellow humans in this much-advanced century.

From the viewpoint of his earlier timeline of the fifteenth century, he was now a walking superman. This was called genetic repairing and the advanced engineering made it possible. Since every man and woman walking around in this timeline were also at the very peak of perfection, Nostradamus was merely an average-looking young man with jet black hair and blue-gray eyes.

But Michel Nostradamus was anything but just another

human being. Inside his head was a brain that set him apart from his fellow humans, and that was why, at this moment, he was sitting there looking at Dot and one of her friends inside the waiting room to his private cubicle.

He mentally ordered the computer to lower the small probes which he carefully placed on his head. He then ordered the master computer to administer the blood sample of the DNA taken from Doty's friend into his own arm. If things went well, he should shortly be able to mentally find himself inside the head of Jackie, the pert little lady in the lightly colored clothing.

For a few moments, he felt somewhat disoriented, but it seemed to pass in a semi-hypnotic fog, from which he emerged with a clear head to find himself looking out of Jackie's eyes at himself, who was reclining in the special chair that he was using. This looked kind of strange to him, and he knew that it would take time to get used to.

It was obvious that the drugs and the small neural probes had done their jobs of allowing him to see and hear whatever his female host was hearing and seeing. A great excitement was starting to build up within Michel Nostradamus as he thought about all the possibilities that now seemed to be opening up for him.

CHAPTER THIRTY-FIVE

It was quiet in the area after the visiting friend of Doty's had left. Michel had expressed his appreciation for her great help. He told her that he and Dot would like to take her and her husband out for a nice evening of dining at a fine restaurant of their choice. He said that it might be some time until this could happen, but Dot would make all of the arrangements.

And now, a very quiet and serious Dot had many questions for him about what it was like being inside the head of another human being. She just had to know all about it. She wanted to know if his range of sight was clear, and if the sounds coming into him were sharp and easy to understand. Was there any pain or discomfort involved, etc., etc.

When she finally ran out of questions, they agreed it was time for Michel to honor his promise of performing the transfer of his mind into her head. He had promised her that she would be the last person that he would practice upon before he entered into the final preparation for the big leap back to the timeline of Cleopatra.

Doty's blood sample, inclusive of the all-important DNA, was already entered into and cleared by the master computer. A trip into Doty's head was ready to go.

To satisfy Dot that he really could see and hear everything

perfectly from his host, Michel asked her to leave the cubicle and settle down outside by the table and chairs. He asked her to write him a note on the writing pad that was there, and to place it on the table, along with several other objects that she should pick up from around the room. She was to put everything in a scrambled order on the table and then return to the sealed cubicle with him, and Michel would then recite all the things he saw and heard while she was outside.

Once he satisfied her that he could perform perfectly in another human's head, he would ask her about Julius Caesar and Cleopatra. There was no doubt in his mind that when Dot said not to worry, then it was a done deal. This was one very organized and super smart lady. She seemed to have all the answers to making his life so much easier than it would be if he had to do all the little details himself Maybe, just maybe, it was time that he put this special young lady into his life on a full-time basis.

It was only a matter of a few minutes later that Dot was once again sitting comfortably in one of the cubicle's overstuffed chairs across from Michel. She was looking at him with a soft look on her face. She just sat there waiting for him to convince her that he saw what she saw outside in the other room.

"My dearest Doty," Michel began. "I have been doing some very serious thinking about the two of us. This is probably not the right time or place, but I strongly believe that when I am with you, I am much happier and more relaxed than I am with anyone else. This is not a proposal nor is it a proposition, but a commitment from me to you. When I get all of the things I want to accomplish done, and I am finally finished with all this foolishness, then I want you to know that I believe we should talk about our future together. I know that this might sound kind of silly coming from a time-traveler like myself, but I wish to spend whatever real time that is left to me just being with you."

Once again in recent days, the outgoing and very verbal Dot was speechless. She got up from her chair, met the now-standing Michel, and the two of them hugged.

"Yes," was all that she said as she walked back to her chair and looked across the room at Michel Nostradamus, who had in his own quiet way, just proposed to her. What it was that he proposed was not clear, but it was a step in the right direction. She was excited inside but calm as a shiny blue lake with no breeze blowing across it on the outside.

Michel was saying, "I wrote down on my writing pad what I heard you say out loud, and I saw what you were looking at. I also noted what you put onto the table, and the order that you put them there. I have to add Doty, that you are the sweetest and strangest woman I have ever come across in all my travels."

He paused, smiled at her, and then said, "But let us get on with all this. I saw you turn and close the cubicle door behind you, and watched *through your eyes*, as you took the pen and paper from the table and wrote me the following note:

Hello Michel Nostradamus,
I know that this is part of our experiment, but I feel very silly at this moment.

If you can read this note, and I hope you can, then please know that I love you very much and can't wait for you to get out of this place so that we can go home again and make our wild and passionate love again and again. I am sorry about writing this one huge paragraph and running on with all the words but I am very nervous.

Kisses and wild things

Dot

Michel continued to look at his writing pad. "You then placed the following items on the table, in this order—one writing pencil, one red and one black pen, yesterday's newspaper, one couch pillow and one empty coffee cup. I closed the DNA contact as I saw you approach the door and I waited for you to come in. And here we are again. So, please tell me: how do you think I did?"

"How do I think you did? I think you did everything perfectly. You not only saw and heard all that I did, but as your host for those moments, I had no awareness that you were there. I believe that the experiments with Jackie and myself are one hundred percent perfect, and I also believe that you will be very successful in your travels once I explain to you what it is that I found that will make it all work."

"I also spoke with Doctor Tirsch, and he told me that everything you see and hear will have another benefit attached to it, and it was nothing that he had planned when he worked out the program that he implanted in your head. You will hear the spoken word, and the computer will translate all languages into French for you, so that you will understand everything. You will see whatever your host will see, just as they see it. If they are nearsighted or farsighted, you will see things the same way, and so on.

"But here is the bonus that the good Doctor did not see coming, and one that will have to excite you beyond your wildest dreams. You will feel the same surge of emotions that your host will feel. This means if they feel pain, you will feel pain. If they are making love, it will seem as if you are making all the moves personally, but here is what has the scientific world all talking.

"The second stop on your agenda is to spend some time with Julius Caesar, the dictator of ancient Rome. If things go as planned, you will be with him on the ides of March, or March fifteenth. This will be a week or two after his return from fooling around with his mistress Cleopatra in Egypt.

"History tells us that a dozen or more daggers will be plunged into this helpless man, and you, Michel, will be there to experience dying with him. Actually, he will be the one to die, and you will be just sort of passing through the timeline moment. You see, your computer, within a few seconds of his death, will sense that something is wrong, and will instantly whisk you away from that moment and bring you back home to us.

"Think about this for a moment. You will be the first person in known history to actually die and live to talk about it. You will be the most sought-after speaker that the world has ever known. You will be able to speak personally as to whether there is something that follows a person's death. You will have had those few moments before you are called back home to actually know what happens moments after our human body dies. You can tell us if death is the end of all things or the beginning of something else.

"You can possibly tell us if there is that famous proverbial bright light at the end of the tunnel, where a being, greater than all of us, is holding out its hands to receive us, or is a trick that our brain plays upon us when it is in the shock of death or the possibility of death. You will have been there for a moment or two after the Great Caesar dies.

"You will have those few moments before the computer snatches you back home to us. But in those few moments, what will your senses be telling you, if anything at all? Will it just be darkness as in the end of all things, or something else?

"Our entire world, and I mean absolutely everyone, will be following you with some type of special hook-up. The realm of possibilities is limitless, and you will be in full control while everything you do will be recorded for all of mankind to share. It is kind of overwhelming, isn't it?"

CHAPTER THIRTY-SIX

Doty sat there quietly for the few minutes that Michel needed to absorb everything that she had just told him. It was a tremendous amount of new information that he had to deal with.

Michel was very serious as he finally broke the silence. "Doty, I understand all that you have just told me. It all sounds wonderful and scientifically most interesting. However, there is still a fatal flaw in the plan, and unless you can explain to me how to solve it, I'm afraid all of these wonderful thoughts will be for nothing.

Michel continued, "Yes, it is true that I want to go back and see Cleopatra and Julius Caesar. The problem seems to be that Doctor T.'s computer will work for me only if we have a blood sample of the intended host. This blood sample will allow us, of course, to extract the needed DNA sample that we need. We had your blood and we had Jackie's blood, and that gave us the required DNA for both of you. However, I seem to recall that several thousand years have passed, and both Cleopatra and Julius Caesar are long gone, and their DNA is buried with them. I just can't jump back in time and ask them for some blood so that I can re-appear at the right time later on in their lives."

Doty reached down and pulled out her huge carry-all purse

that was top-of-the-line in women's luxury wear. She pulled out a blue file folder and removed a small batch of letter sized papers that were held together by a paper clip.

Nostradamus enjoyed watching her walk over to him, turn around and walk back as she returned to her seat. Neither of them said anything as he removed the paper clip and read the cover sheet.

✆

My dearest Michel:

I am so very pleased that I am able to deliver upon my promise to you.

I have found out a way to allow you to pinpoint a day and date for two important events that you wish to personally observe. This is my gift to you.

The problem, as you constantly pointed out to me, was that you needed the DNA of each of these individuals so that you could have your computer pinpoint their location within the exact time you wanted. In that both bodies were immediately buried after their deaths, there was no way to withdraw the necessary blood that was needed to provide us with the vital DNA for Cleopatra and Julius Caesar.

However, as you know, I am a professional historian, and as such I have access to things that mere mortals cannot get at. Before you read the very important background that I have put together on each of the two subjects, let me tell you how I recovered their DNA and delivered the two packages to your computer operator.

Frederick, the operator, has assured me that he

has enough of the DNA from the two samples I gave him to satisfy the computer requirements, and he said the only thing that he is waiting on is your personal authorization and codes.

You see, my love, I remembered reading somewhere in some dust-covered file that when Cleopatra killed herself by allowing that snake to bite her, she had been buried naked as was required of someone like her, who after giving up her life was now considered a goddess.

Well, any clothing worn by gods' and goddess' on the last day of their human life, were sacred and they were sealed in a lead lined vase and buried in the main temple in Egypt. All I had to do was fly down to Egypt, and talk them into opening up the sealed goddess vase and give me a piece of the still-bloody gown that was in that sealed bottle.

The curator of the temple gave me a choice of my either sleeping with him, or giving him a valuable artifact from my personal collection. It was a tough choice, but I chose to keep my virtue for you, and I sent him a six-shooter pistol from the 1880s American collection. This was the gun that was used by a famous American cowboy called "Billy the Kid." I knew that Billy the Kid wouldn't care one way or the other what happened to his pistol, so I swapped the gun for a piece of the cloth that I wanted.

You owe me big-time for that six-shooter. I figure that when we have the time, a little shopping trip to one of the cute little shops near the Eiffel Tower would be a good thank-you.

Anyway, I got you the DNA that you wanted for Cleopatra, and you are good to go anytime you want after you read the background of the timeline she lived and died in. Her story by the way, is a fascinating one.

It is also an interesting story on how I got Julius Caesar's DNA for you. But this story will have to wait until you get back from the Cleopatra adventure. I don't wish to clutter up your brain with too many facts at any one time.

After Caesar, could you please pick someone easier if you are going to continue to time-jump.

Love you

Dot

෨෨

Be sure to read Cleopatra's background extremely carefully so that what you will be seeing and hearing will make sense to you.

XXX

CHAPTER THIRTY-SEVEN

WRITTEN BY DOT GOODMAN,
HISTORIAN TO THE PARIS HISTORICAL SOCIETY

The story of Cleopatra, the last queen of Egypt, does not start and end with her. The story of Egypt itself is worth noting because it was so very important to the ancient world. Please remember that we are talking about civilizations that were at the very top of their game over twenty-four hundred years ago.

The importance of Egypt has ever been due to the overflowing Nile river, which always gave a great abundance of food crops to the world. In these ancient times, whoever controlled Egypt, controlled the "breadbasket" of the world, and as a result the land of Egypt was always a desirable and wealthy land.

The story of Egypt has to begin with the story of the life and death of Alexander the Great of Greece. Alexander lived some twelve generations before our Cleopatra, but his life had a direct impact on her.

Alexander, of course, was one of the world's greatest military minds. He was the equal of a later great leader called Napoleon, but that is another story for another time. Alexander, in a very short life time, conquered almost all of Asia, Europe and the Egyptian area.

He was born on July 19, 356 BCE, and he died thirty-three years later on a stopover in the city of Babylonia, where he became suddenly ill and died within a few days of his coming down with an extremely high fever.

History tells us two tales of his death. One said that he caught a fast-moving illness that killed him, and one said that he was poisoned. My personal belief is that poison did the job.

Here is the point that ties Alexander the Great to Cleopatra. As he lay on his death bed, he called in these four senior generals. Being such a young man, only thirty-three years old, Alexander had never thought about naming someone to take over and rule the kingdom that he had carved out of the known world. He divided his conquests into four parts, and had the four generals roll a pair of dice for them.

The interesting part and the point that I wish to make here, Michel, is that Cleopatra's direct ancestor, General Ptolemy (later called Ptolemy the first) rolled the lowest number of the four generals and as a result had to settle for the least of the four parts that the world was divided into, which of course was Egypt. Ptolemy's family kept control over Egypt for twelve generations, until the country was taken away from the dead Cleopatra.

As you were told before, the other three generals who won Greece, Asia and Europe lasted as kings for less than fifty years each until they were overthrown.

And so now we have found out that the kings and queens of Egypt (called *pharaoh,* which means "ruler") were not Egyptian at all. They were Greeks, as was the founding general of the Ptolemy line.

๛

BRIEF HISTORY OF CLEOPATRA
PREPARED BY DOT GOODMAN FOR MICHEL NOSTRADAMUS

Cleopatra was born in the year 69 BC, and died in the year 30 BC at the age of thirty-nine.

She was the eldest child of Ptolemy XII, who died in a hunting accident. He left two children to inherited his throne. Cleopatra was nineteen and her brother was twelve. As was the custom, they married each other, but were extremely unhappy.

Cleopatra, with her strong personality, set herself up as the main ruler and just pushed her younger brother aside. The twelve-year-old brother, Ptolemy XII, was unhappy at being ignored, and with the help of his advisors, declared Cleopatra an outlaw and forced her to flee from the palace with all of her loyal followers.

Cleopatra fled to the countryside, where she was able to hold off the army of her brother, and they finally settled into an uneasy truce with Ptolemy staying inside the royal palace and Cleopatra moving about in the open countryside.

Now entering into this picture came Julius Caesar of Rome. He came to Egypt to personally set up an agreement to buy all the food supplies that he needed for his huge army that was expanding its influence throughout the area. When Caesar learned of the split in the royal family, he declared himself neutral and said that he would only deal with whoever had the power to sell him the supplies he needed. This was Ptolemy who was living in the palace.

And here is the interesting point of this reading: Cleopatra, at this point in time, had never met Caesar. It was always one of his officers who handed all the details when food arrangements were made.

Now let us talk about Cleopatra herself. Not only was she said to be a beautiful young woman, who was now nineteen and extremely intelligent, she was said to be able to speak nine different languages with no accent at all. She would have come in contact with languages from all over the known world when buyers of food products came to Egypt to make their purchases.

Now, Cleopatra was smart enough to know that she could not win the civil war that she was involved in with her brother Ptolemy, and so she came up with a desperate plan that would allow her to meet with Julius Caesar.

She was aware that Caesar had stationed, outside the city, his standing army, which was about double her small number of soldiers and those of her brother's (husband, if you wish). She came up with the pretense of having a group of local merchants deliver and install carpets into the rooms at the palace. The palace rooms were known to be cold and drafty, and no one questioned the carpet installers. After a few days, when the installers were now well known to the guards who were always present around Caesar, she got ready to put her plan in action.

Cleopatra dressed herself in one of her most seductive outfits, and she had herself rolled up inside one of the rugs that were coming into the palace each day. It took two workers to carry the heavy rug with the queen rolled up inside it. The workers passed security with no problems and they found the room where Caesar was sitting and writing out some order for the troops.

The history books were not very specific but the general impression was that the rug was unrolled in front of the amazed Caesar, and the beautiful and very sexy Cleopatra rolled out.

This is the part of the story that you, Michel Nostradamus, will be able to fill in for all the historians like myself, who are eager to hear the conversation that went on between a startled Caesar and the sultry Cleopatra. What did she say to the ruler of Rome, and what was his reaction to her?

You will be able to witness this exciting "roll-out" first hand and prove us right or wrong about whether or not they went to bed that very same night.

It goes without saying that Caesar decided to restore Cleopatra to the throne of Egypt, and he declared war upon her brother, who immediately gave himself up to Caesar. It was Ptolemy's loving sister who had him put to death a few days later.

Cleopatra's life and the life of Julius Caesar became entwined thereafter, and I will give you only the highlights in the following notes.

❧

Cleopatra had a son with Julius Caesar, whom they named Caesarian. Cleopatra had a hard time delivering the new baby, and the doctors had to use a new method of delivery for those days. They had to make a special incision to help deliver the baby. This medical process is called a caesarian delivery and it is still in use today.

After Julius Caesar was killed on the Ides of March, in the stabbing to which you will be a witness, Cleopatra married the new commander of the army that shortly came and occupied Egypt in the name of Rome. His name was Mark Antony, and Cleopatra's recovered personal notes said that Mark Antony was her one and only true love. Julius Caesar, she wrote, was only someone whom she could use to help her reclaim the Egyptian throne from her brother/husband.

Cleopatra had twin boys with Mark Antony, but not one of Cleopatra's children survived her death due to the new ruler of Rome, who was Julius Caesar's nephew, Octavius Caesar, having any and all persons who might have had a claim to his throne put to death.

Cleopatra's title was Cleopatra VII, and she was the last pharaoh/queen of Egypt.

Another most interesting historical note is what led up to the death of Mark Antony and Cleopatra, and it must be noted here. It seems that Mark Antony, like Julius Caesar, fell in love with Cleopatra when he was stationed in Egypt. Cleopatra, clever woman that she was, married him and convinced him to help her win back Egypt's freedom from Rome.

The troops who were stationed in Egypt were loyal to their general, Mark Antony. So, when their general declared Egypt to be a free state once again and not part of the Roman empire, the soldiers stayed loyal to him and staged a mutiny against Rome and its ruler Octavius Caesar.

Normally Octavius Caesar would have ignored a small piece of real estate like Egypt and moved on to bigger and better things. But Egypt was his breadbasket, and he knew that he needed it to feed his hungry army. And so, the new Caesar declared war against his former general and his queen, Cleopatra.

Now, Mark Antony was definitely the better military man and won most of the battles against the forces of Rome.

But, in the end, Rome had too many ships, and too many soldiers, and in a final sea battle, Mark Antony lost his life and without his leadership, the forces of Rome won the conflict.

Again, history is somewhat clouded here. Did Mark Antony actually kill himself (very doubtful) or was he helped to his death by someone loyal to Rome and Caesar?

With Mark Antony confirmed as dead and the soldiers of Rome getting ready to march against her city, Cleopatra decided to end her own life with a bite from the famous snake.

Michel—This Brief Historical Note Should Bring You Up to Date.

Love and stuff—Dot

CHAPTER THIRTY-EIGHT

Michel was reviewing the current events that were happening all around him. People were trying to pull him this way and that, and he was not too happy about it. He was thinking that time had passed since he had read Doty's historical briefs, and he felt that he had a pretty good feel for the ins and outs of the local politics of the Cleopatra timeline.

I was very confident that the computer and I were in perfect harmony, and it pleased me to no end to know that I now had two distinctly separate ways of time-traveling.

If I wanted to make a physical appearance anywhere in a timeline, I simply had to return to my sixteenth-century castle and transport my physical self with my sun-wand and mirrors to where I wanted to go.

This was only if I wanted my physical self to be present.

If I wanted to enter into the mind only of someone that I wanted to visit, I could do so now by means of my computer and the DNA blood work.

Michel found himself lately just sitting around and thinking about the advantages and disadvantages of each form of time-travel option.

There was no downside to the computer-aided concept. I could go where I wanted, whenever I wanted, and return to home base at any time.

Of course, I did not have a physical body of my own to move around in, and that was sort of limiting.

The downside to putting my physical body into the various locations was an obvious one.

If I physically was injured or killed, it was a permanent condition, and I was locked into it.

I made a final decision. No longer would I physically transport myself through time. I would play it safe and remain an observer only, and then I should be able to live through whatever adventures I was involved in.

I liked the idea that Dot had floated at me. What if I stayed as long as I could in the head of Julius Caesar as he was being stabbed to death. What if I could delay for a few vital seconds, the computer's sensing that death was happening and transport me away?

What if I could take those extra moments to experience life after death, if there was such a thing? I decided that I would really do this after I visited Cleopatra, and then visited the soon to die Julius Caesar. I really wanted to share the moment of his death, and see where it took me. That should be the ultimate voyage, and I wanted to play that role.

∂∽

Several more weeks have passed, and Michel is completely healed. It was time to move on.

An outwardly calm Michel Nostradamus was speaking to his standby medical team, the computer expert, and one extremely attractive Dot Goodman. They were all sitting in the comfortable room adjacent to the computer cubicle. Another month had flown by, and finally everything was in a ready-to-go-mode, as they once more went over the various details.

This was to be the first real time-travel live-recorded adventure that was not being done under controlled laboratory conditions. For the world news media, who were all gathered in a different section of the huge hospital's assembly hall, an unusual silence was being observed. Michel Nostradamus, whose name was on the lips of almost everyone in the known world, would soon be sent off into the past by the master computer.

Nostradamus had one hundred percent, full control of the computer functions, unless it sensed that something was going wrong and if that happened, the master computer would have the ability to put him out and return him to home base. Nostradamus and the computer expert had programed the system to follow the trail of the DNA of Cleopatra, Queen of The Nile. The required DNA sampling was cleverly uncovered by the project spokesperson, Doctor D. Goodman.

The master computer, with only a five-second delay, would record and pass on whatever sights, sounds and emotions that Nostradamus was experiencing when he relocated within the mind of the nineteen-year-old Cleopatra.

An additional—and probably the most fascinating—special feature of the project was that not only would they all see, hear and feel everything that was going on around Cleopatra, but Nostradamus would be able to mentally speak freely and his words and thoughts would go on a one-way transmission to the home computer. The host, Cleopatra, and anyone else in her presence would not be able to hear or sense that he was there.

They were trying to time his arrival in Egypt early in the morning, so that they could hear the instructions that the Queen was giving to the workmen who were going to make the delivery. Two of the men would carefully be carrying the wrapped-up

Queen, and another man would lead them on their route to the room where they expected to find Caesar alone in one of the sitting rooms located off of the main corridor of the huge palace.

The sendoff moment had arrived, and hugs and handshakes had been given all around as Michel issued the mental command to the computer to open the door leading into the cubicle. Another command from Michel, and the walls turned clear on both sides so that he could be observed at all times from the outside.

Michel had given full computer access to Doty, so that in case of a physical problem, entry would be possible. With a wave of his hand and a serious look on his face, he adjusted the necessary headphones and lay back comfortably in the overstuffed chair. The observers all knew that the computer would tell them when his mental being had fled the shell of his body, which would just lie there in complete comfort, waiting for the mind of its owner to return and reactivate it.

The countdown started and the next thing Michel knew was that he had the usual few seconds of discomfort, and then a sense of well-being flooded over him as he arrived.

CHAPTER THIRTY-NINE

There was no feeling of being disoriented or uncomfortable. There was just the usual flash of bright light, and then a feeling that everything was normal. He had to fight off the urge to stand for a moment and look around to see where he was, but he was able to resist doing anything at all, and he just concentrated on looking out of the eyes of his host.

Cleopatra was standing quietly in the middle of a large room and looking into a full-length mirror that was being held up for her by a young girl who was obviously one of her special handmaidens. Behind the mirror, he could see two other young girls moving about. Since this was the first time that he saw what his host looked like, he paid strict attention. He could only see whatever Cleopatra was looking at. If she looked left, he saw left. If she looked down, he saw down. He could only see what she was seeing, no more and no less.

Reflected in the hand-held mirror was a long-legged, cute teenage girl who was just looking at herself like any other teen-ager would.

He sent back a thought to his computer for a direct line to Doty. "Hey, Doty. Here is the answer you were looking for about what Cleopatra looked like. I would say that she looks just like a regular teen-ager would look if she was dressed very scantily and standing looking at herself in front of a mirror while she was getting dressed.

"From my point of view, it is difficult for me to judge her height, but I would estimate that she stands about five foot two and is generally rather slender. Her body, and believe me, the full-length mirror in front of me (her or us) is showing me all of her figure, is slim, with long legs that taper upward into a slender waist, and a great set of breasts that would drive any normal male into a frenzy if they could see them as I am seeing them.

"What is interesting, and I want the medical team to make a note on this, is that if I was standing here in my own male body, the testosterone would be shooting through me, telling me to ravage this young, beautiful girl. However, in that I am merely an observer, I note the ripe young body being reflected back at me from the mirror as just another observation. This is an unusual personal feeling for me, where I feel no reaction whatsoever to a practically naked, perfectly beautiful female body.

"Her hair is black, and she is wearing it up in what I would call a bun. I note what looks like clips of some sort holding it in place. I am assuming that she is wearing it up so that when she is rolled up in the large rug that I can see out of the corner of her eye, her hair won't get in her way.

"I personally don't like the extreme amount of makeup that I see on her face. Probably this is normal for this time period. I am used to my Dot wearing an absolute minimum of anything on her face, but here I am seeing a lot of purple and black shading around Cleopatra's eyes. I must admit that the coloring does seem to set off the color of her blue/gray eyes quite well. I cannot tell if those eyelashes are hers or not, but they are quite long and shaded purple like her eye makeup."

"Let me take a moment here and talk about Cleopatra's nose. Doty's historians said that they thought she had a hooked nose with a funny look about it. I have to disagree with them. Right now, I am looking at what would be called a pug nose, which to my understanding is a small nose that is a bit wide but is rather cute. She has no make-up covering up the many tiny freckles that are all over her face. These are there because she is so young, and they will probably disappear in the next few years. I can see the possibility of her tiny but wide nose, growing a little wider and probably a little bit longer. I hope this answers Doty's nose question.

"Her speaking voice is what we could call husky. It is somewhat deep and yet sweet and melodic as she calls out her instructions to her maids. She is speaking to them in what I know to be Egyptian, but if I remember what Dot told me, she has full command of nine languages and that she would probably speak to Julius Caesar in Latin. What I am hearing is the computer translation of all speech into my native French. I am having no problem understanding the words spoken around me. My compliments to our brilliant computer controllers.

"I cannot help but notice the ease and smoothness of her movements as she carefully puts on her earrings. Her ears are pierced just like the girls have them back home. This seems to be one of the universal things that tie females together in one big 'girls club' since the earliest of civilized times. The actual earrings look like twisted brooches made out of silver, and are in the form of flowers. They are quite attractive on her.

"One of the girls just came up behind Cleopatra and secured a fine, well-made, tiny golden crown. This was probably being put in place so as not to leave any doubt in Caesar's mind that he was in the presence of a queen of the royal bloodline. Around her soft throat was a lovely diamond necklace. She was now wearing more jewelry than clothing.

"I could not help notice that her eyes would dance behind her lashes as she fluttered them, and I must admit that the stories about her remarkable beauty were not overly stated. This is one beautiful young woman.

"One of the maids helped her on with a splendid robe which shown with the brightness of fire. It was basically golden with all styles of needlework woven into it, and it shimmered like the moon on a bright night. Cleopatra was just about ready for her performance. To me, and I am sure she will also be to Julius Caesar, an exotic female, full of grace and beauty who had plans.

"I almost forgot and Dot would never forgive me. Her fingernails and toes were painted in royal blue matching colors. She said to the maid who had by now set down the full-length mirror, to step outside and ask the three work-men to enter.

"There followed a few minutes of conversation before the three men acknowledged that they understood Cleopatra's plan. Each man had a very large smile on his face when she handed each of them a large-sized money pouch packed with gold pieces. Cleopatra was a smart one. She overpaid the three workers to be sure that they would do what they were supposed to do."

"She was trying to make sure there were no mistakes. She had only this one opportunity to get at Julius Caesar and everything had to work perfectly. She had previously dismissed her maids so that they would not be able to listen to her conversation with the workmen. All was in readiness as the workers started to lay out the rug."

CHAPTER FORTY

It was an absolute wonder of advanced science in the way that I could feel and share every emotion of my host, Cleopatra. I saw, heard and felt, every thought and emotion that raced through her mind as she was being carried down the main hallway on her way to the sleeping quarters of Caesar. She was unhappy about the roughness with which she was being carried. She felt that they were carrying her along as if she was a well-paid-for sack of potatoes.

I personally think that the Queen was way off base here. The men were handling her as carefully as they could. It was not every day that they carried a queen in a carpet into a gentleman's bedroom.

The leader of the workers knocked heavily on the door, and a booming voice answered, 'Come in.' The unseen voice was speaking Egyptian with a heavy accent, and everyone knew that this was the voice of Julius Caesar."

The lead man led the men in and quickly took a look around the room. Within a few moments, he felt assured that the great Caesar was completely alone. He pointed to the ground, and the two big workers carefully set their burden down and walked rapidly out of the room. Caesar had not yet looked up from whatever it was that he was working on.

The lead worker stepped over to the carpet, took a firm hold of it, and said the nine famous words that he had been taught to say: "Great Caesar, here is something very special for you. Without a moment's hesitation, he carefully unrolled the carpet, which caused Cleopatra to spin twice, until the carpet finally lay flat on the floor.

It was only a few moments until Cleopatra was helped to her feet by the worker, who quickly bowed at the General and then again at his queen before he flew from the room and snapped the door shut behind him.

Cleopatra and I were dizzy for a moment from the spin, but the spunky nineteen-year-old took just a moment to recover. She took a few small steps forward toward the open-mouthed Caesar and dropped her covering gown on the floor behind her. There was still not one word spoken between the two of them as she did a deep bow of respect before Caesar, and then straightened up to her full height, and stood there defiantly, with her snow-white breasts stretching out before her.

From where we (Cleopatra and I) stood, I could see quite clearly that Julius Caesar, ruler of the greatest empire that the world had known up to that time, had fallen under Cleopatra's spell the moment he put his eyes on her. Remember, great leader that he was, Caesar was still a man.

I promised to give Dot a moment by moment and word by word report of what followed next, because if I did not see it with my own eyes, I would never have believed it. As the old saying goes, the room was so quiet that you could hear a pin drop.

Well, that pin would have been thunderous if it had fallen, because without a word, Caesar, the man, put down his papers and walked over to the standing Cleopatra, where he slowly made a complete circle around her. It was as if he was buying a horse at an auction, and he was just checking her out.

Still not a word was spoken as he came around to the front once again, bowed deeply, reached for and gently took her left arm in his right, and slowly led her over to the far end of the room where he had his small sleeping room. She smiled at him, and he smiled at her, as he slowly and gently removed the few bits of clothing that she had on. He did it quite slowly, and by the smile I saw on his face, seemed to be really enjoying himself.

He touched as little of her body as he could while removing the bits of clothing. It was only a few moments later, that Cleopatra, still not having said a word in any of the nine languages that she knew, was lying flat on her back where the two of us (Cleopatra and I, of course) were looking up at him. Her eyes followed him as he slowly walked across the room and secured the lock on the door. Obviously, he realized that this was not a good time to be interrupted.

Her eyes continued to watch him as he rapidly removed his sword belt, and the three or four other weapons that he had secured about his body. Obviously once again, he was pretty sure that Cleopatra had no concealed weapons on her. What next happened was very fast, and the French lover in me was very disappointed with the known ruler of the world. I had been expecting a long and drawn-out passionate love affair that would give me stories to tell and emotions to share. But no, it was not to be.

I remembered Dot telling me one late evening after we had made wild and passionate love for most of the evening hours, that one of her early research projects had told her that over one half of the world still makes love in the position called the Missionary Position. She said that this was with the man on top, and the woman underneath, and they would grunt and groan for a few minutes and then it was over. This was hardly the French way, and we had both laughed and made love once more that night, and I do remember distinctly, that it was not the Missionary Position.

There I was, waiting along with the beautiful and highly desirable Cleopatra, Queen of the Nile, waiting for some great sex, but it never happened.

The Queen seemed to be well-trained in her movements, which I could tell by the body moves she put on when Caesar finally entered her. The problem was that Caesar had such a firm hold on one of her breasts and shoulders that she could hardly move at all, so all she did was lie there and quietly satisfy the puffing Caesar.

I was the one who was the most disappointed of all. I was the one who always had made love to women in the past as a man. After all I was born a man and it was natural for me to love a woman. Here was my chance, I thought, to see, hear and feel the joy of making love from the viewpoint of a female.

Sadly, it was denied me when Caesar, with a loud growl, threw himself off of the complacent but unhappy Queen. Both of us were quite unhappy with the performance of the great Caesar. I had enough of this experience and could not wait to get out of Cleopatra's head. I did stay long enough to listen to them finally talk.

He had quickly figured out that she was the Queen. I wondered if the crown she was wearing gave her away? And he took her body offering first and decided to talk later. I believe that it was a good choice if you thought about it. It is not every day that an almost naked young lady, without any chattering, offered up her fantastic body for the taking. Caesar was a lousy lover, but the man was no fool."

They were talking about Caesar helping her regain her throne, and she in return would offer her standing army to him and all of her country's food supply. This went on for thirty minutes, but then when he rolled over on top of her once again, I could take it no more and I sent a signal to my computer to take me home. I was terribly sad and disappointed in the Great Caesar.

Cleopatra would get everything she wanted from him, and she would rule her country uninterrupted until she took her own life many years later. For her, the meeting that I had just witnessed was a great success. Now I understood why, a few years later after Julius Caesar was assassinated, she took a young Mark Antony to her bed and kept him there as her lover and co-ruler for years and years.

It also brought home an interesting message to me. Young people should be with young people and older people with older people. This rule became crystal-clear to me when gorgeous and nineteen met up with chunky and fifty-something Julius Caesar.

And my last comment for this recording of my thoughts and feeling on this timeline adventure was that after a little bit of relaxation time passes for me, I still plan on watching Caesar die on the ides of March. But I do not think that it will bother me as much as I originally thought it would. Julius Caesar, as a man among men, did not measure up to be what I expected him to be.

What I hope to get out of the experience of dying with Caesar was to see what, if anything, follows our human experiences here on earth.

Is there really an afterlife? I will know shortly, won't I.

End Report
Michel Nostradamus

CHAPTER FORTY-ONE

Styles may come and styles may go. Hemlines go up and hemlines go down. Hair may be worn long or short. But there is one truth about women that never changes. They never have enough shoes.

This fact of life pushed itself into my awareness as I walked along next to Doty, carrying three pairs of shoes that were packed carefully into three shoeboxes. I had just made good on my promise of taking her shopping in return for some research that she did for me on one of my projects.

I got smarter at the fourth shoe store and had her latest "had to have them" shoes sent to her house by special delivery along with the other boxes that I was carrying. I made grumpy sounds about shopping with her, but the truth of the matter was that I was having a wonderful time, and there was no one else that I would rather spend time with then Doty-the-shopper.

Several days had passed since I had come back from the Cleopatra adventure, and I was pleased when Dot insisted that we spend the day together walking around Paris. Just being in my city immediately picked up my spirits, and holding Doty's hand made everything perfect. I put all my thoughts of time travel far away from where we were, and smiled and swapped stories with Dot as we walked along.

The windows along the boulevard were full of wonders and the happy couple continued to window-shop.

In one window, rivulets of diamonds and avalanches of pearls poured onto dark velvet holdings as Michel quickly moved her along past those windows.

Next door to that shop was one that Michel lingered at for a moment until he was pulled along. It had fake female models showing off sexy lingerie of every shade from lime to raspberry. It was very different-looking.

The one thing that they both could definitely agree on as they watched the walkers, who were on parade all around them, was that all the female tourists who poured into the city were outclassed by the local Parisian ladies. The Parisians were completely coiffed and creamed, toned and taloned, and carried themselves like the royalty that they thought they were. In all the world, there is no woman like a Parisian woman.

The two of them sat together in the Jardin d'Hiver (the Winter Garden) of Paris. It was located just beyond the lobby of the newly refurbished Rotes Meurice De Rivoli. (Hotel of the Old Revolution). Palm trees in tubs and many other exotic plants helped to create the garden effects so prevalent in this charming and comfortable spot where lunch and tea were so beautifully served. The waiters were magnificent in black jackets and white ties. They patrolled the aisles with stiff deportment and the smooth inhuman speed of robots on wheels. It was the nicest restaurant that Dot had ever been in.

Michel had decided that it would be a good idea to take Dot to a special lunch before he told her what he had in mind regarding the time-travel situation and how he saw their life together. In the past two days, he had done much soul-searching and reviewing all the pros and cons of his travels, and the truth was that there were a lot of negatives and not too many positives in his present lifestyle.

He had to admit that all his plans to see and meet special people within their own surroundings were beginning to depress him. He was almost killed by a crowd at the Bastille, attacked by a knight, saw a king die in front of his eyes and watched one of his all-time heroes turn out to be a bore.

He could only think of two things that made all of this worthwhile. He had developed a friendship with Benjamin Franklin that had been wonderful while it lasted, and of course his special Doty, who had come into his life at the perfect moment.

It was interesting, when he got around to thinking about it, but whenever his thoughts turned to her, a smile always came to his lips. He was now old enough and smart enough to realize that she was the best thing in his life. It didn't seem to matter what century he was in, Dot was always there with him, somewhere in the back of his mind. He knew that he had to do something to get things straightened out, and today was the perfect time to do it.

Michel simply ignored the background sounds of glasses pinging off zinc counters. He ignored the sizzle of cooking meats that gave unbelievable smells to the air, did not pay any attention to the clinks of spoons stirring coffee all around him, and above all, ignored the soft fever of conversations at other nearby tables.

There were lots of gestures and hand-waving going on around him, many cigarettes being smoked, and lots of noise being generated by the well-dressed, multiracial, good-looking crowd. In other words, everything here was very French and also very wonderful, and Michel simply loved it.

He took another good look at Doty, who was poring over the many-paged menu. This was one attractive lady, whom he knew would always be true to him. Not only was she well-dressed, as always; he knew that she was his intellectual equal, and that excited him more than anything else. He could talk to her about the change in the weather, or in women's clothes, or about anything else.

She was there for him and probably ahead of him on what he was doing with the time-travel thing. She gave him all the freedom he needed in the pursuit of his interests and was his researcher for all the impossible little things that he needed. She seemed to realize that he was running down on his ambitions with his new hobby, and it was just a matter of time until he would have had enough, and would settle down and write his predictions.

Dot's major at college and her professional career were just perfect for him. Her studies into historical oddities would be very helpful with insights into the events he wanted to predict, and with her help he could avoid actually having to go to the locations. This last part was one that he was not sure about, but today was not the day to think about something like that.

And so, with a nervousness that was not usual for him, in front of the amused waiters and all the patrons at that exclusive French restaurant, Michel Nostradamus got down on one knee, held out the five-diamond engagement ring, and asked Dot Goodman, woman of the twenty-fourth century, to marry him, a mere nobleman from the French countryside.

Amid the cheers and other noises that surrounded his proposal, Doty, with tears in her eyes, helped him up, nodded yes, and hugged him so hard that he could not catch his breath for a few moments.

They were now officially engaged and would later work out their lives and schedule, traveling between the sixteenth century (where he would have to go back every so often, since this was the source of his great income), and living in the luxury of the good times offered by the modem lifestyle of their present surroundings.

They would talk about all these things at a more convenient time, but for right now, the food was starting to be served, and then Michel wanted to get them home as soon as possible after their meal and jump into bed for wonderful sex with his new life partner.

CHAPTER FORTY-TWO

Doty was thinking to herself how wonderful her Michel was. He was like a dream come true for her. He was everything she had ever wanted in a man: intelligent, adventurous, wealthy beyond her wildest dreams, someone who listened to her, and now, as he was going to prove once again, the world's greatest lover (at least in her mind).

It wasn't long until Michel's fingers slid carefully around her soft neck, as he tenderly kissed her with a slow, sexy, lingering kiss.

Doty could taste the wine from his last drink, as well as taste his obvious desire for her. Dot sighed deeply and returned his kiss as she wrapped her arms around this great hunk of masculinity.

She felt herself unable to resist the sweet, hot warmth of his tongue against hers. The feel of his hands running over her back as he held her close, seemed so right. It felt wonderful to have him touch her as she felt the heat of his body coming through to her.

Suddenly, they were deeply kissing each other, drinking in each other with a deep intensity that seemed so special. Her tongue stroked his in return.

He twined his fingers into her hair, tugging away the band holding it at the nape of her neck. He continued to angle her mouth to his, taking more of her and still it was not enough for him. She leaned firmly into him and felt the thick ridge of his erection melding to her moving hips.

"You feel good," he murmured, "so darned good." Michel wrapped his arms around her and pulled her closer, twining his fingers in her silky hair. He inhaled the familiar scent of roses that was so Doty, so much this woman who was now his.

With his mouth held gently over hers, his tongue continued to caress her, in long languid strokes that had them both moaning with the contact, with the connection, with the sudden burning between them. Seconds ticked by and they were still satisfied just kissing, softly and tenderly.

Michel barely remembered how his shirt, pants and shoes came off, but he remembered everything about undressing Doty. He roughly shoved her top upward and over her head and quickly unhooked her overflowing bra and unzipped her skirt.

Doty tossed her clothing aside as Michel quickly filled his hands with her high, full breasts and stroked her plump pink nipples. He gently pressed her back against the nearest wall, his gaze devouring her almost-naked body while she helped remove whatever jewelry she had on. She left on her dark stockings, garter belt and panties.

She kicked aside her accumulated clothing as he went down to his knees in front of her. His hands went to her hips and his lips slid down to her sexy tummy. "Finally," he breathed out. "I have been looking forward to this all evening."

He slid his hands delicately to her backside while he bent his head, brushing his lips over her hips, trailing kisses over her midsection, widening the space between her thighs and kissing her very slowly. He explored the intimate V of her body, his fingers teasing the slick wet heat of her sexual arousal that he felt coming.

He suddenly stood up and scooped her off of her feet, as

easily as if she were a mere child, and headed to the far end of the house toward the bedroom. Moonlight was spilling into the large master room as Michel carefully deposited Dot on her back in the center of the huge bed. He thoughtfully placed an oversized pillow underneath her head to ensure her comfort.

Michel pressed his lips to hers, slid his tongue into her mouth once again as the sweetness of her filled his senses. He tasted her with his eyes, seeking the flavor of her openness, her willingness, and definitely her love. His hands roamed freely over her willing body, and she shivered with pleasant chills running up and down her spine. He palmed her breasts once again, teasing her nipples and plucking them into tight little peaks.

Doty gently wrapped her hand around the base of his erection, and Michel could feel himself thicken with her touch and the anticipation of what was yet to come. She guided him to the wet slick center of her body, and she felt him shaking with his urgent need. He seemed to be trying to resist pushing into her on his own, rather than waiting for her to take him there.

She easily pressed his throbbing shaft inside her, as she slid down the length of him, taking him in all at once.

Michel was thinking about how hot and tight she was, and how she was so wet for him, and she felt ever so good. Raw hunger rose inside him as he moaned softly while pressing her down deeply into the forgiving softness of the bed, as he lifted her hips to allow him to smoothly get on thrusting inside of her.

Her body tightened around his throbbing erection as she took him hard and deep inside her. Her fingers were in his hair, and their soft touches sent shivers down his spine. He loved her kisses, those delicate, sweet kisses that could be so wild and wicked and yet so soft and feminine.

Doty was everything that he wanted her to be. She was the one that he had been searching for all these years.

He was still hungry for her as she seemed to be for him.

It was in their every move, in their every touch, in their every groan of pleasure. If they could melt into each other and become one, they would have done just that at that moment.

Doty leaned back as Michel settled on her flat stomach, pumping himself into her, as she allowed him to ride her in their erotic dance. Her beautiful breasts swayed with the rhythm of their bodies, and her nipples seemed to call for his mouth once again. She spiked her fingers again through his hair, with her moans turning into sexy little pants of pleasure that were driving him wild.

Michel knew that he was coming to the end of his ability to hold back from the final bursting of his manhood into her welcoming body, and he pushed and thrust with the final moments of the glorious pleasure that she was giving him.

"Yes, Michel," she moaned burying her face in his neck. "So … good … Michel."

With his name on her lips, asking him to pleasure her for the last time, he was driven over the edge. He could not hold himself back any longer. For the two of them, almost in perfect timing, the room disappeared and what was left was the flush of completion to the wonderful sex act that they had just shared.

As they both completed the act, the two of them just collapsed into each other's arms and lay there, unable to move. For long seconds, they clung to one another, skin damp and breathing heavy.

"I love you, Michel, I really and truly do."

And with those words bouncing around inside his head, he held her closely and softly kissed her lips once again as they both fell into a deep and most pleasant sleep.

CHAPTER FORTY-THREE

Several more weeks passed. The newly engaged couple had made all the rounds and met all of Doty's family and friends. Doty was hard at work upon some urgent new project that had come up recently at the Historical University. She didn't say much to Michel about it but hinted that it was something big, and something that promised her a huge promotion if she could bring it (whatever "it" was) off.

All he could get out of her was that an archaeological dig in Central China had come up with new information about Genghis Khan and the early Mongols who had swept out of Asia in the thirteenth century and conquered almost all of early Europe. Dot was excited when she learned that she had been chosen to work on the opening study. Michel knew that when she was ready to talk to him about Genghis Khan and the Mongols, then he would hear all about it.

He put it out of his mind for the moment and went to look over the special report papers that she had left for him on the kitchen table. The paperwork immediately got his complete attention. It was the advance report on the death of Julius Caesar that he had talked to Dot about.

Michel was not quite clear if the playwright William Shakespeare had gotten it correctly when he made Caesar the tragic and heroic figure that he immortalized forever in one of his plays. Ever since Michel's one and only encounter with the Great Caesar, Michel had turned away from being a fan of his.

He removed the cover sheet and read it over carefully.

My dearest Michel:

Once again, I am so very happy that I am able to help you with your next adventure. It pleases me to no end to do so because I know that you are now doing your time-travels mentally and not physically. This makes all the difference in the world to me, in that I know that you will not be injured in any way since you will be inside your hosts mind.

The problem that you have pointed out to me was the same one that you had with Cleopatra. You needed DNA from blood taken from the body of Julius Caesar. As usual, I am the answer to your wants and desires, and this one was no more difficult than usual for me to get the desired sample.

Here is how I did it. After Caesar was slain by all the senators who hated him so much, he was finally buried and given all the honors of royalty. All the honors of royalty, Roman style, means that his body was entombed and the bloody clothing that he wore was given to the local keeper of historical artifacts of early Rome. His clothing was sealed up, blood and all, and it was carefully preserved with items from all the other descendants of Julius Caesar who ended up ruling Rome and calling themselves "Caesar."

Again, I was able to trade something of value from our university archives for a scrap of his bloody shirt.

I know that you will wish to thank me in person,

and I will be pleased when you do so. I believe another grand shopping spree will be in order, and I know that it will have to wait until you return from Rome on your next time-jump.

You do know, don't you, that you will be center-stage once again for the world press when you try and figure out whether or not there is life after death by means of your visit to your good friend Julius?

Please know that I have already delivered the bloody samples to your computer guy. He told me that he will be ready to go whenever you let him know the timing.

In conclusion:

In your whole lifetime, Michel Nostradamus, has anyone but me, made you promises that were so difficult to fulfill, and then turned around and delivered them? I just want to remind you that you have an amazing young lady here who is madly in love with you.

I'll see you tonight and I think I will have something that might perk you up about Genghis Khan.

Kisses and stuff until I see you tonight.

XXX DOTY

૭૪૭

Michel set the cover sheet down and prepared to look over the detailed text Dot had left him with all the details he needed to time-jump over to see Julius.

Doty never let him down, and he knew that he would be

taking her to Italy on a vacation with him in the near future.

It would be fun to see the ruins of Rome and compare them in his mind as to what they looked like when he saw them just after they had just been completed.

He was starting to look forward to the Ides of March trip and to find out something about the life after death thing.

After another cup of coffee to wake him up, Michel sat down again, and began to read Doty's research paper on Julius Caesar and the Ides of March.

JULIUS CAESAR AND THE IDES OF MARCH

*Written by Dot Goodman, Historian to the Paris Historical Society:

General background for the eyes only of Michel Nostradamus.

The ides of March is the name of the fifteenth day of March in the early Roman calendar.

The was the actual day in the year 44 BCE that Julius Caesar, self-proclaimed dictator of Rome, was assassinated in the Roman senate chambers.

There is a historical rumor that has been around for centuries that a fortune teller (called a soothsayer in those days) had said to Caesar, as he left on his way to the Senate, that something terrible was going to happen to him if he left the security of the military camp where he was staying with the troops.

I, Doty, personally doubt, as do many of my fellow historians, that this soothsayer ever spoke with the leader of all of Rome. We all believe that it was William Shakespeare, in one of his famous plays, who made up those lines and gave the soothsayer credit for having said, "Great Caesar, beware the ides of March."

Either way, it does not really matter, so please continue to read on, Michel. No matter how the ides of March got into the public awareness, it is there, and it stands for bad times. Since the time of Caesar's violent death, March fifteenth has forever been marked as a day of infamy. It has fascinated scholars and writers of history ever since.

SIDEBAR NOTE TO MICHEL:

On the day of your time-jump, see if you can get to Caesar early enough in the morning, when he will still be within his armed camp. The army, of course, would still be all around him, and it would be interesting to know if a soothsayer had any access to him at all.

We would like to put this idea of a conversation having happened to rest for once and for all. Your recording by the computer of what you are going to be seeing and hearing about Caesar will clear up lots of things for us.

END OF SIDE BAR ENTRY. NOTES CONTINUED AS FOLLOWS:

The assassination of Julius Caesar set off major changes within the city of Rome, and that in turn had a rippling effect throughout the entire known world. Rome controlled by force three-quarters of the continent of Europe, and when something this major happened to one of its leaders, the whole civilized world felt its effects.

Before Caesar declared himself to be dictator of Rome, the city had a republican form of government that was headed by two consuls, or heads of their respective political parties. It was Caesar's removing the old form of government that directly led to his being killed. In those days, if you disliked something a politician did to you or said about you, you had him killed in a violent way so as to make a statement to your enemies.

Julius Caesar made a huge personal mistake when he publicly turned down the offer of becoming king through all the proper channels. He was quoted as saying that it would take too long for it to happen, and so he declared himself dictator, which took effect immediately. The strength behind Caesar's move to declare himself dictator for life was his large standing army stationed just outside the city of Rome.

His terrible error in judgement that led to his death was when, for whatever reason, he did not take his personal bodyguards with him as he normally did when he entered the grounds of the Senate, where his enemies waited for him.

Had Caesar taken proper precautions to protect himself, then his friend Mark Antony would not have left Rome, since Julius Caesar would have still been alive. But Mark Antony did leave Rome after Caesar's death, and he did fall in love with the beautiful Cleopatra, and he did become her full-time lover, and he did live in Egypt. Mark Antony later died in a huge sea battle against Julius Caesar's nephew, Octavian, who took control of the Roman dictatorship.

Octavian is known to us as Augustus Caesar. He had the month of August named after himself, just because he could. After the defeat of Mark Antony, Augustus Caesar had no more major enemies, and he declared himself dictator for life just as his uncle Julius had.

Only, Augustus went about becoming dictator-for-life in a more efficient way. He had all of his enemies in the Senate killed or outlawed first, and then he declared himself dictator. There was no opposition left, and he became the first of many Caesars to hold the lifetime office. Augustus, who was a bit wiser than his uncle Julius, always took bodyguards with him whenever he left the palace.

And finally, you need to know that there were many other Caesars in the family line, but perhaps the most in-famous of them who came down from these interesting times was Nero Caesar, who was supposed to have fiddled while Rome burned. History tell us that this was just another made-up story about another hated Caesar.

CHAPTER FORTY-FOUR

Personal question to Michel. I have a question here that I would appreciate your opinion upon: I never did ask you the personal question that was on my mind about the nineteen-year-old Cleopatra whom you visited: If you could have convinced her to time-travel back here with you to our timeline, and we dressed her up like any other nineteen-year-old girl, would she have looked better or worse than the kids of today? This is a good dinner conversation for us to have when you get back from the ides of March thing.

I also know that you never really got to see Cleopatra do her stuff in bed, since all she had to do was lie there like a piece of dead meat and let Caesar get off with no effort on her part. Kind of boring, if you ask me. We will never know anything more about that famous meeting, since you took off right after that bedroom scene.

ANOTHER VIEWPOINT ON THE DEATH OF JULIUS CAESAR

Julius Caesar had really offended the common citizens of Rome in another very important way: religiously. Religion has always had a major role in our world's history, and Caesar's screw-up was another case of bad judgement made by Caesar.

All Rome's gold and silver coins for the entire empire had stamped on them the likenesses of gods and goddesses. When Caesar had his own face stamped on everyday coins, the public was greatly offended because they thought that he was telling everyone that he was greater than the gods themselves. This was another big mistake, in that he lost most of his public support and had to depend on his standing army more and more.

The actual killers of Julius Caesar were officials called senators. It was the senators who voted on laws that affected the daily lives of the Roman citizens. When Caesar declared that he wanted to be dictator, the senators knew that they would be removed from office, and they reacted by all agreeing to kill Caesar in a single group effort so that no one individual would stand out.

The best friend Caesar had in the senate was Marcus Brutus. Brutus was a former general in the army who had lost a small battle to Julius Caesar over a problem that they could not settle by discussion, so they both brought their personal armies with them and fought a battle. After much loss of life on both sides, the brilliant Caesar smashed Brutus's forces and was the victor, but he spared his life.

Of course, Caesar had no way of knowing that within three years after having his life spared, the traitor Brutus would lead the senators on that killing day.

I need to tell you Michel, about this very bloody murder so that you won't overreact again and run away.

The killing of Julius Caesar happened as he took his regular seat, which was at the top of the senate chamber (from where it was said, by unhappy senators, that he could look down on them) from where he could see everything that was going on below him.

One of the conspirators, with the others right behind him, came over to where Caesar was sitting and said loudly that he had a request to make of Caesar. Caesar, who was seated, had turned to the senator as if to ask him what it was that he wanted to say, when the lead senator and all the others suddenly rushed up to Caesar and without hesitation began to stab him. A shocked Caesar tried to cover himself up by falling to the ground and rolling himself up into a ball. But it was no use.

Thirty stab wounds would later be counted by the examining doctor who looked at Caesar's body. It was interesting that the doctor was reported to have said that only one of the thirty stab wounds was fatal. It was the one that went directly into his back and punctured the heart.

Before Caesar died, he recognized one of his attackers. It was the man he had granted his life back to; it was Marcus Brutus.

It was later reported that he cried out in his fear and anger, "Et tu, Brute", which translated from the Latin means, "Even you, Brutus?"

Note to Michel

The lesson here is to never forgive an enemy. Never give him a chance to come back at you. You must never forget someone who hates you—and destroy him before he destroys you.... Doty

To continue and conclude

All of Caesar's killers ran off. Justice would catch up with them later, and they were eventually all killed.

And finally, it was reported that as they carried Caesar's body through the streets of Rome, one of his hands was hanging down and dragging in the dirt.

Final facts on Julius Caesar

Born Gaius Julius Caesar on July 13th of the year 100 BCE. Died March 15th of the year 44 AD.

Age at death: 56.

Roman statesman, general, and author.

Famous for conquests of Gaul (now called France and Belgium).

He changed the Roman republic into a Roman dictatorship and as a result changed the world.

CHAPTER FORTY-FIVE

Before the sun came up that morning, everyone who was supposed to be in the sitting room outside the computer cubicle was there. Michel was very pleased with his hand-picked group of experts. Since this was becoming an old routine, nothing unusual had to be brought up at the pre-send-off meeting.

The computer programmer verified that the sample he received from Dot was perfect, and the computer had accepted it and routed out the DNA program for Julius Caesar during the early morning hours of the fifteenth of march, the dreaded ides of March. The entire world was once again on standby, and they would be getting their information from the reporters who were all gathered in the much larger and nearby assembly hall.

The previous program that had sent Michel Nostradamus back to visit Cleopatra at the time of her unrolling herself in front of Julius Caesar was such a great success world-wide that money was pouring into the University/Hospital accounts. Management was very pleased.

Everyone wanted a copy of the sights and sounds of those moments between Cleopatra and Julius Caesar. The events as recorded by the computer through Michel's eyes were causing sky-high computer sales. As a positive result, Doty, who was the person who made sure that everything was in the right place at the right time and working perfectly, was given a big step up in the Institute's Ladder of Success Program.

She was very proud of her new title and working position as Director of Time-Travel Affairs. She had dragged a willing Michel along with her as she chose her new office furniture, carpeting and colors. Michel could not have been happier for his lover. Dot even had a personal secretary to do most of the busywork that her new position required.

Michel laughed when he found out that Dot had picked the oldest lady in the secretary's pool to be her aide. She loved and trusted Michel, but she wanted to limit any temptations. She really knew him well. Michel's smiles on this issue were only to himself.

And now they were all gathered together in the pre-send-off room. The doctor had done a last-minute check on Michel and everything was ready to go. Dot had done her usual detailed printout of what unanswered questions from the history books the team was hoping Michel's mission would solve for them. Dot passed the printed sheet of paper with the questions on it to everyone who was present. She had already given the information to the master computer, and the world press would pick up their copies at their convenience.

When Caesar left the army base to go to the senate, why did he not take his usual three-man security team with him?

When Caesar was driven in his usual chariot by his usual driver to the senate building, why didn't the driver go in with him?

Why did Caesar completely forgive Brutus? It was not in Caesar's character to overlook a former enemy's hatred and let him move about so freely.

When Caesar made his way up to the special section that he

had to himself at the top of the senate, why did he not notice that the guards that always encircled the entire senate floor were missing.

What answers was Michel going to get in regard to the life-after-death issue. The computer allowed him only a five-second gap before it would pull him back when it picked up the death of the host, Julius Caesar.

The answers to these questions and more would hopefully be answered shortly.

೫౩

The hugs, the kisses, the handshakes and the well-wishes were all given as Nostradamus asked the computer to open the door for him and to make the walls see-through once again. He confirmed with the computer that it would allow Dot to override the pre-set commands if she saw something that she didn't like.

With a serious look on his face, Michel sat down once again in the now-familiar chair that adjusted itself to him. He put on the computer headphones and rubbed his arm where the DNA had been injected a few moments ago. It itched terribly, but he completely ignored it as he listened to the computer go through its countdown.

Again, there was a flash of bright light, a moment or two of pain, and then Michel was seeing the inside of a well-worn tent bristling with soldiers moving in and out of the open tent flap. Outside, soldiers could be seen moving about in the distance.

Nostradamus knew that he had safely arrived in the early morning hours as he watched Julius Caesar giving his officers instructions. He thought that something of importance might be learned, as everyone seemed to be a bit on edge, which usually meant that an army was getting their marching orders.

Michel knew enough to stay quiet and listen to what it was that was going on around him. He did send a quick message back to the computer, advising it that he was hearing the translation from Latin to French in good order, and that his hearing and seeing senses were working well. He settled down mentally and paid attention.

CHAPTER FORTY-SIX

It was quiet in the tent for a few minutes as Caesar waited for his officers to assemble. During the lull in the activity, Michel took the opportunity to review some recently learned facts about Caesar and the Roman legions. He recalled that a Roman legion, which was Latin for Roman Army, was at full strength when it was made up of no less than five thousand and no more than six thousand men.

The entire army was made up of only Roman citizens. However, many soldiers enlisted from other countries, so that upon finishing up their required years in the army, they could automatically become full citizens of Rome with all the many opportunities that would give them. The legions would accept volunteers from only three surrounding countries: France, Germany and Belgium. The Romans gave one name, Gaul, to all three countries. These foreign enlistees had to stay in the army for five years before moving up to full citizenship. Roman civilians only had to serve three years.

The dozens of existing legions were completely separate from one another, but they were all united under General Julius Caesar, who paid their wages from out of his own pocket. He therefore had their absolute loyalty. In this way, Caesar had one-hundred-percent control of the armed forces. It also goes without saying that Julius Caesar was a very rich man and could easily afford the huge expense.

History tell us that Caesar kept fifty percent of all valuable items such as gold, silver and fine jewelry looted from areas that his Roman legions overran. When his forces conquered Gaul, it was said that the riches he kept were beyond belief.

It has also been said that Caesar had no mercy in his soul. He was reputed to have slaughtered conquered armies down to the last man so that they could not rise up again. He was ruthless and had a killer instinct, but his way of doing things was very successful for himself and for the City of Rome, which received the other fifty percent of his captured wealth.

All Roman soldiers had to provide their own weapons, which consisted of long knives, large broadswords, regular swords, heavy metal armor, light metal armor, and armored helmets. Caesar would advance the soldiers the money to buy the weapons and then take the cost out of the monthly money they earned. It was said that he did not make a profit out of the sale of military equipment to his men, but what he got in return was the strength and loyalty of the fighting forces of the powerful Roman legions.

To keep track of who owed money to him, Caesar had full-time bookkeepers, as well as medical staff, engineers, and other specialty occupations such as priests and musicians who would play marching songs when the men went into battle. When a full legion of five thousand or more men were sent out to do battle, or to clean up the remains of a battlefield fight, no enemy could stand up to them.

The weapon that stood out in Nostradamus's mind was the broadsword, which was a two-handed, five-foot-long double-edged blade with a pointed tip. The two-handed broadsword was the ultimate weapon that made the difference in Caesar's conquests.

Caesar, out of his own pocket, provided the Legions with another weapon that again and again proved to be unstoppable against the enemy. It was an oversized, lightweight long spear, about two feet longer than the standard spear the enemy would have. The Roman soldiers would march up to the enemy spearmen and, with the extra length of their spears, hold them back from attacking while Caesar's bow-men stood behind the Roman spearmen and shot thousands of arrows at the enemy without ever having to put themselves in danger.

If the Roman legions ever took the field to fight a pitched battle, they rarely, if ever, would lose a battle, due to having overwhelming force in their favor.

All men in battle were required to have fifteen days of food on them at all times. This was always a problem for a marching army, and that was why Caesar went to Egypt (Cleopatra) to personally secure his supply of food for his legions.

Female camp followers and servants were always allowed to follow and service their masters and others who were putting in their years of service in the Legions. Caesar paid all expenses for the female camp followers who moved around with the army.

Michel also knew that the Great Caesar supported a large naval fleet of war ships. It was bigger, stronger and better-trained than that of any other fleet in the civilized world at that time. After the death of Julius Caesar, it was his nephew Augustus Caesar who used the always-ready fleet of war ships to defeat Mark Antony and Cleopatra. This major defeat led to the ultimate death of both Antony and Cleopatra.

Nostradamus was jolted out of his inner thoughts when he suddenly heard Caesar starting to speak to his now-completely assembled general staff. He summarized Caesar's speech into a few short sentences for the computer to pick up. Otherwise Michel knew that hours of computer time would be wasted keeping track of the rambling Caesar.

Caesar, earlier that morning, had decided that the three legions that were in camp would march into the countryside surrounding Rome and take up positions covering the access points on three sides of the huge city. They did not have to worry about the river's fourth side of the city, since the fleet was sitting there quietly on alert.

He dispatched each one of his three bodyguards to accompany the generals to their appointed positions, and when the army was in place, each of his bodyguards would catch up with him at the Senate, where he would wait for their confirmation that everyone was in place. Then he was going to announce his formal takeover of Rome as the new dictator. With his legions controlling the key routes into and out of the city, there would be no way that he could be opposed.

Michel sent a special message to Dot by the computer. He knew that she would be listening carefully to all the things that were going on.

Hello Doty:

When Caesar sent his bodyguards along with the three generals, it should have answered your questions as to why they were not with him in the senate when he was attacked and killed. I believe that this answers the first of several questions you asked me to clear up for you.

I think I will know shortly why the chariot driver also was not around when needed, because I see out of the corner of Caesar's eye that his ride is just pulling up to the tented area.

Following the chariot-driver question, I believe the next one was why Caesar forgave his killer Brutus, when he had the opportunity to remove him.

Caesar was known to always kill his enemies in the past, and this question of why he let Brutus live also bothers me. I promise to clean this up as rapidly as I can.

After the tent had cleared of all of the staff members, Caesar picked up an apple from the few that were sitting on his desk and stepped outside for his ride to the Senate. Nostradamus was able to follow his thoughts as he stepped outside and signaled for the chariot to pull up for him.

Caesar was thinking that after he finished securing his final appointment as dictator, he would be ready to move on his next campaign, still in the planning stage. Even though he had come to an understanding with Cleopatra about the supply of food, he did not feel comfortable trusting her without any control over the supply situation. He would move out one of his three standing legions to the outskirts of her Egyptian city, and in that way, keep the pressure on her to deliver what she had promised in the way of food supplies.

This would also give him a reason to take a few days off every so often to visit with her. She was a beautiful young lady and she seemed more than willing to be his eager bed partner.

With these happy thoughts in mind, Caesar stepped into the now-waiting chariot, and held onto the support rail as they took off at a fast pace. Caesar knew that this chariot was a backup, because his regular and more stylish one needed to have a broken wheel repaired. His driver planned to go and pick it up after he dropped Caesar off at the Senate building.

Michel sent off another personal message to Doty:

Hello Doty:

OK, now we know that the driver will drop off
Caesar and then go on to get the repaired chariot.
This explains another question. I hope to soon
have the Brutus answer for you.

The ride through the bumpy streets of Rome was uneventful,
and Michel, who was trying to follow Caesar's thoughts, was
getting nothing of any special interest. The ride from the army
camp outside the city to the Senate building took about an hour.

Caesar got off, waved goodbye to his driver and walked up
the many stairs that led to his reserved location at the top of the
Senate seats.

CHAPTER FORTY-SEVEN

Caesar hated to admit it, but the climb to the top of the Senate was getting harder and harder. He had to stop twice before he finally arrived and was able to sit down. He always promised himself at these moments that he would work out with the troops and get himself back in proper condition. He had good intentions, but something always came up and needed his attention at that moment.

He was just sitting there quietly, waiting for the Senate to be called to order, when he noted several of the senators climbing up toward him.

They were probably going to ask him for his opinion on one of the bills that the Senate was going to talk about this morning.

He smiled to himself as he saw that one of the approaching senators was his old enemy—or should he be calling him his new friend—Marcus Brutus.

Caesar had let Brutus stay alive after defeating him in a little fight over something he had forgotten about. Brutus had sworn allegiance to Caesar and allowed Caesar to buy him a Senate seat, since he promised to always vote for anything Caesar wanted him to. Caesar could always count on his vote, since he had bought it in advance. Caesar liked to have an inside man in the rule-making of the Senate, and Brutus was his to command.

Michel sent one of his short notes to Doty:

Hey Doty:

Here is your answer on the Brutus question. The reason Caesar did not have Brutus killed when he had the opportunity to do so after their little war was because he knew that he could get Brutus into the Senate easily enough. If he spared his life, he knew that he would always have an inside man who would always vote as instructed.

Caesar's logic was good, but the long-term result would be terrible for him, as he watched Brutus and the others make their way slowly up the steep stairs.

And Doty, since the boys of doom will be here in a few moments, I am getting myself mentally ready for the five seconds that I will have within dead Caesar's body until the computer pulls me out. I hope something interesting and meaningful comes from this life-after-death thing. Bye for now.

It all happened so fast that Michel felt himself overwhelmed for a moment. Knives flashed up and down, and Caesar's body took every blow. It was interesting that Michel felt the stabbing personally and as if it were his own body taking the plunging knives into it. Michel tried to keep track of the stab wounds but lost count at fourteen, when that wound came in from Caesar's back and must have penetrated his heart, as the computer report had said.

Michel knew that he had only five seconds until the computer pulled him out, but something strange suddenly happened. He felt himself as being free, completely free from the body of Caesar, who was lying there slumped over with all the senators surrounding him. But that was not what Michel meant when he said he felt himself being free.

He felt himself totally free of all restraints either from Caesar's body or from the computer—which seemed to have lost him. He felt himself rising up but he suddenly was not sure just who he was anymore. *Who was he and what was he?* His mind was in a major state of confusion.

He knew that he was no longer part of a physical body and he also knew that it was his essence or mind that was floating away from the physical form that had once been Julius Caesar. He knew that he had no eyes, but he could see that he was hovering at ceiling height within the Roman Senate building. His personal senses were far more than the usual physical perceptions that he was used to receiving from himself or Caesar. His body— Caesar's body was dead, but he was not.

He felt that he now was much more than what he was when he was encased within that mortal enclosure. He was no longer limited to what a physical body could perceive. His essence survived, and that was the infinitely greater part of him. It was that part of him that had existed before he was born, and then had been trapped by human birth. But now there was no entrapment. He had completely freed his soul with the death of Julius Caesar.

He gazed down from the height that he had achieved, and saw the flesh and bones of what he had inhabited in the physical world he had just left. He had abandoned that body without any regrets as easily as he had once cast off an unwanted pair of shoes. There was no longer any connection between his temporary human form and what he had now become, which he believed was his true substance.

He decided to move on up, and he willed himself to pass through the arched ceiling, higher up than the tops of the nearby trees, and on into the open sky. The magnificent city of Rome lay below him. It was like toy blocks and forests, villages, and rivers. It seemed to be all laid out like a living map.

Far below he could see hundred, perhaps thousands of tiny points of movement. These were people, as he had once been a person.

Free from his earthly bonds, he continued to ascend, rising faster and faster as his spirit soared in the freedom he now was feeling. He watched the entire landscape recede as he continued to rise.

And finally, he was alone, completely alone, and he was beginning to feel uncomfortable, as the solitude was not to his liking. His personality was built on interacting with others of his kind, and not on solitude. He was not happy being alone with just himself.

He began to fight against this total nothingness. Beyond forever, further than the infinite, he suddenly found himself. He realized that he was Michel Nostradamus, a Frenchman who had a life and a love to go back to. And he realized that he did want to go back to his own kind. Back to the interaction with other human beings that made him feel alive and hopeful.

He felt himself being drawn back toward that glint of light that was the earth, and from there back to hovering a moment or two beneath the Senate ceiling, from where he still could see the fallen body of Caesar and the crowd of people fleeing the scene.

He could not stop himself, even if he had wanted to, from entering into the lifeless head of Caesar, and from there he felt the wonderful feeling of dizziness that told him the five seconds must have passed, and the computer had grabbed hold of his mind and was pulling him back to where he wanted to be.

His last though upon awakening within his own body, in the comfortable chair he had used for the sendoff, was that it was good to be back, and whatever waited for the departed was not a heavenly event.

And then Michel Nostradamus, time-traveler extraordinary, fainted.

CHAPTER FORTY-EIGHT

To mortal eyes gazing from the very top of the Eiffel Tower, the city might have looked like an impressionist's painting of Mount Olympus or Valhalla, or the Heaven that Christians prayed to reach.

Paris was in all her glory and showing herself off to my love and I, as we sat holding hands and relaxing while looking out at the vastness below us. There were no visible limits to it: soft clouds and calm, sweet-blue sky extended toward infinity in every direction. Straight overhead the sky was dark enough to show a few scattered stars, unblinking pinpoints of light that never seemed to move.

Time itself was meaningless here.

As we sat here in this place of love and quiet, we realized that we were sitting in a domain far beyond the world of ephemeral mortals, who are born in pain, struggle all their brief years, and then are snuffed out like the flickering flame of a candle.

I was a happy man. And my life's companion, whose hand I held, told me that she was a happy woman. Was this not the best of all things? I thought so but it was not to be. The news was delivered to me by my Doty, whose lovely head rested on my shoulder.

It was a few hours after our wonderful dinner at the Eiffel Tower, and we were just lying together in our bed, talking about nothing in particular, until she brought up the subject that was to get me back to my time-traveling ways once again.

I only had one hero left on my list of must-see people before I closed everything down. My plan was to appear live and in person before I closed down the entire operation permanently. I wanted to appear in my own body just before the Battle of Waterloo, to see if I could straighten a few things out that needed working on.

I had expressed my desire about retiring to Doty, and she was all for closing everything down, so when she opened up this particular discussion, I was somewhat taken aback. We had agreed that we would only keep active the sixteenth-century sun-controlled wand's physical way of travel, so that we could go back and forth from here to there, like changing one's location when taking a few vacation days.

Doty loved the idea of both being part of sixteenth-century nobility and having the ability to visit family and friends here in her present timeline and my future.

She was also comfortable with my retiring after my visiting with Napoleon, and she promised to help me as usual with the needed background information.

All of this was completely blown away when she quietly said, "Michel, have I ever asked you for a favor in all the time that we have known each other?"

I knew that something was up, and it wasn't any personal body parts.

It was not more than thirty days later that I found myself sitting in the pleasant room outside the computer cubicle. There were some familiar faces and a few new ones looking at Dot and myself as we went over the usual review session before I made a time-jump. I had agreed to leave my physical body behind me once again as the computer sent my mind out to find my newly agreed-upon DNA host.

Doty had never asked for anything before this, and it was impossible for me to turn her down for this one timeline adventure.

I looked around the room while listening to Dot address the small group of people here within the room, and the world at large. Everyone was tuned in to everything going on by means of the worldwide press covering the event once again. My computer guy was here, as were Dot and myself. My personal doctor and my security man made up the known cast of characters. New to me were the President of the French Republic and His Honor the recently elected Mayor of Paris.

I reviewed the project in my mind once again. I was confident that I understood my assignment.

I would be going back in time to the year 1241, and I would be visiting then–Paris in the late springtime, either April or May of that year. Paris, which is always lovely in the spring, was not this way at that time.

Paris was under attack. Without a miracle, it would fall to the attacking Mongol hordes who were pounding at the tall city gates that surrounded the entire city in those years.

Every European city that stood east of Paris had fallen to the forces of Genghis Khan with only a small token of resistance. It was less than a month since Poland and Hungary had been overrun. It was now Paris's turn to face the unstoppable Mongol attack.

When Dot had told me about the project that she called the Miracle of 1241, I had no ideas what she was talking about. I have since that moment, gained a great deal of understanding about the subject.

I had a few minutes, and I took them to quickly run down Doty's detailed note summary. I found them fascinating.

The Dark Ages were pure light compared to what could have happened to the whole of Europe in the year 1241.

The Mongol conquerors had reached eastern Europe earlier that year. They had destroyed one Christian army in Poland and another huge army that was sent out to defend Hungary. They were in the process of establishing the largest connected land empire in the history of the entire world.

These warrior horse-soldiers out of the central plains of Asia, with small wooden bows, formed the most disciplined and quick-moving fighting force of their time. A noted modern-day historian said that they were "strikingly like a modern army, set down in a medieval world." No one was able to stand up to them.

The Mongols despised city dwellers, city culture, and elite persons of any kind. They rampaged through an entire continent and were about to swallow it up, as they left nothing but death and destruction behind them. Never was the Western world and the historical phenomenon it represented in so much danger.

At the last moment, merely days before the fall and total destruction of Paris was about to happen, something which to this day is completely unknown stopped the Mongol horde in their tracks and made them turn around and leave the Parisian area. They just backed up and returned to Asia, never to return.

What stopped them just as they were knocking on the crumbling walls of Paris? What compelled them to turn away when this great city was defenseless before them? Nobody knows why Paris and the rest of western Europe were suddenly left alone and allowed to flower into the world as we know it today.

My assignment, the one Dot asked me to undertake, was to go back to the important year of 1241 and get into the mind of the general leading the attack. The question was, why did he suddenly end the pounding of Paris and stop all operations completely? They left as quickly as they had arrived, and it was my assignment to find out why.

This was a major undertaking and I could not say no to my Doty. And besides, I was curious about all of this, and what was one more adventure for me? I always loved playing the hero.

Michel knew that he was a thrill-seeker. Someone who needed action. He knew he was someone who liked to choose the path of *most* resistance, and he knew that he was doing these things to test his skills. He did it because it was in his personality to show that he was somewhat better than others He constantly needed to prove to himself and to others, that he was "king of the jungle."

CHAPTER FORTY-NINE

A note from Doty:

Hi Michel:

As follows, please find the usual work-up on the non-invasion of Paris. It is important that you read up on this, so things will be clear, when you send us your thoughts and the sights and sounds of what you are experiencing.

It goes without saying that you and I are writing our names into the history books of Paris, and you know that I truly appreciate all the time you are putting into the project on my behalf.

I also understand that after this timeline adventure, that there will be just one more, which will be Napoleon Bonaparte. This is the one you have spoken about so often.

Please digest the following notes and also know that I love you.

XXX Doty

On April 9, 1241, a sizable army of German, Poles, Templars and Teutonic knights marched out of Poland to attack a slightly smaller force of Mongols who were advancing westward across the open fields of Poland.

The knights in the thirteenth century were very good at their tournaments, their fine armor, and the emblems they carried telling about their ancestry. They truly believed that they were the best warriors in the world. This belief was completely shattered when they went up against the small, puny-looking army of the Mongols.

The Mongol horses were small, where the European knights' horses were large and slow. The Mongols wore no armor, where the knight wore heavy armor and moved slowly at a relaxed pace. The Mongols shot arrows and killed from a distance, while the knights had to get close enough to use their swords. The knights did not realize that they were coming up against the finest field fighters that the world had ever known up to that time.

The two armies met on the flat field of Wahlstatt, just outside of the Polish capital.

The first charge of the heavily armored Christian knights appeared to break the Mongol line, which turned around and fled before the oncoming knights of Europe. Duke Henry's men rushed after the fleeing Mongols with joy on their faces. They rushed happily into a perfectly laid Mongol ambush. Duke Henry's army died almost to the very last man.

The Mongol army that delivered this major defeat was only a small part of the Mongol force. The main part of the war party was elsewhere. The plan was thought up by General Subutai, one of four favorite generals of the great Genghis Khan, ruler of all the Mongols.

Note to Michel:

Hello again, Michel. It is into the head of the Mongol General Subutai that you will be placed.

The Mongols always treated their great warrior chiefs with the greatest of respect and buried them in specially sealed burial vaults.

I used my great influence, now that we are famous—actually, I capitalized on your fame— and exchanged something they wanted for DNA from General Subutai.

The computer accepted the blood sample as perfect and you are good to go.

Love you, Doty

❧

To continue—subject—Mongol invasion-Paris:

General Subutai was an old man in 1241, one of history's unsung military geniuses. His long and brilliant career ranged from northern China to the current campaign he was undertaking in Europe. He carried off his campaign in Europe, a complete change of location for him, in a flawless manner.

General Subutai and the main part of his army had marched into the Hungarian part of Europe after covering 270 miles in three days.

Subutai split his force into two parts and attacked the Hungarians in a frontal and rear attack. The Europeans were used to fighting a headlong frontal fight; having the enemy in front and in back of them proved to be their undoing.

After Subutai had defeated both armies the Europeans had set against him, he went into summer-campaign mode, and settled his forces upon the fields of central Europe, where he could find grass and feed for the many animals that they had brought with them.

The mighty armies of Europe were gone, and all that the Europeans could do was to run and hide within the walls of their cities. Western Europe awaited the Mongols' next series of attacks in a stunned and helpless condition. The Christian community was at a moment of critical weakness.

The city of Paris was overcrowded and under-protected. They sent several nobles to try and buy off the Mongols, but Subutai had them hanged on the spot. There was nothing for the people of Paris to do but to wait to die.

The impact of the Mongol conquests can hardly be overestimated, although the quick arc of their ascendancy spanned little more than one hundred years.

Until the rise of Temujin, the remarkable man who changed his name to Genghis Khan, the name Mongol denoted only one of a number of wandering nomadic peoples who hunted, herded and fought minor wars over the central steppes of Asia and the surrounding Gobi Desert. Temujin (Genghis Khan) changed all of that. He stoked up the central Mongol belief that they were born to rule the world, and he led his people off on a conquest that ultimately stretched from the East China Sea to Europe's Mediterranean.

His chief targets were the Chinese empires to the east of Mongolia, the Islamic states to the west and south, and the Russian cities beyond the river Volga. What he did to them changed the world forever.

And then, in the summer of 1241, after a summer's fattening on the great plains of southern Russia, the Mongols turned their attention to Europe and Paris once again.

CHAPTER FIFTY

The destruction of Paris would be disastrous. Paris was the intellectual center of the High Middle Ages. At the university, the intense study of Aristotelian logic was laying the groundwork for a fundamentally new world view. Scholars were already insisting on finding the reality of the material world. Teachers at the University of Paris were just beginning to develop the sciences as study courses. From their ideas, would come the Renaissance, and the rise of great individuals like Galileo, Kepler and Newton. By destroying Paris, the Mongols would destroy European society's strongest link to the past and to the future.

Without Paris to inspire them, there would be no Dante, no Michelangelo, no Leonardo da Vinci. Even if their ancestors survived the terrible Mongol massacre that was coming, the desolation of Paris and the countryside would have been completed, and the people that were left would have only a bleak struggle for day-to-day survival. There would have been an absolute lack of any time for poetry or the fine arts as we know them today.

Waiting out there on the flat plains surrounding Paris was a terror that would destroy any advancement of European energies and resources and crush all possible intelligent thought and aspirations.

Special note to Michel:

> You should now understand the danger and the high stakes involved, with Paris and the world about to fall. But ... something stopped the death and destruction from happening. The world went on to become what it is today; some say that this

is good, and others will take up arguments against it.

Mankind had escaped the terrible faith that the Mongols had in store for them. Why? What saved Paris?

Your assignment, as you know, Michel, is to find out the usual answers to the usual questions for us.

Love you,

Doty—xxx

৩৩

Time had passed and Michel was sitting by himself after everyone had left the outer chamber of the cubicle. He had said his goodbyes to everyone and gotten his hug from Doty. He had reviewed with her, everything she had written for him in her notes and they were both satisfied that he had digested all the important parts.

He asked everyone to please go out and have a coffee break. He said he wanted at least two hours by himself for some computer time and deep thinking. There were still a few things that he wanted to spend some time considering. He knew that whatever conversation he had with the computer would later be entered as part of the project, but he would worry about what was in the records another time. Right now, he needed some answers and he hoped he knew the right questions.

Computer entry—Michel Nostradamus—random thinking on the project called "MONGOL."

Something was missing and he could not put his finger on it. It was probably something small but very important. So, he just sat there in the peace and quiet offered to him by the empty room and the hum of the master computer in the background.

Here was the problem: why did Paris survive when every other major city in the area was destroyed? Was it something special or unique that General Subutai saw that made him pull out his overwhelming force?

There was nothing that Michel could think of that made Paris any different than any other city that the Mongols looked at. It had to be something else.

He sat and thought about this problem and finally it just came to him. The issue could not be about the physical city itself. It had to have something to do with the human element. There could be no other explanation.

He suddenly felt confident that he was on the right track, and what he needed was a better understanding about what was happening away from Paris and away from the European scene.

He needed to know more about what was happening in Asia or, more specifically, in the area around China, where the Mongol horde originated.

He spoke out loud to the master computer, which immediately acknowledged his requests. It replied that it would need a few minutes before he would have the requested printouts.

Michel had requested highlights only on the lives of General Subutai, the field leader of the Mongol horde in Europe, and then on the supreme leader of all the Mongols, Genghis Khan.

He requested that Subutai be first and Genghis Khan to follow.

CHAPTER FIFTY-ONE

Computer readout—part one of two parts

General Subutai was one of four generals that had the total confidence of the leader called Genghis Khan. Subutai was senior in years of service, and was closer to the Khan in family relationship than any of the other generals.

Subutai was a Mongol warrior, and perhaps the greatest wartime general that the ancient world had ever known. He commanded armies whose size and scope of operations surpassed those led by any other Mongol commander. Under General Subutai's direction, Mongol armies moved faster, over much greater distances and with a greater scope of movement than any army had ever done before.

When General Subutai died at age seventy-three, he had conquered more than thirty-two nations, and won over sixty-five pitched battles. This was according to Muslim historians.

If General Subutai had not pulled his forces back and away from the walls of Paris, the rest of western Europe would have fallen.

There was no reason given in any of the records searched by this computer at your command to determine why the Mongols turned around and returned to China without harming the city of Paris.

Note from Michel Nostradamus for the official record★★★

I have found nothing of any help from the above computer readout of the military genius called General Subutai. I am hopeful that the readout on the ultimate leader, Genghis Khan, might offer a glimmer of insight into our problem.

If not, I do feel confident that I shall be able to determine the reasoning once I am safely installed into the mind of the General. It was General Subutai's direct order that reversed the army's direction, and I am sure that I will find out why he gave such an order.

Computer readout—part two of two parts.

Genghis Khan was a minor tribal leader who, through personality and shown ability, rose to the leadership of other clans who joined him. At age thirty-eight, he had put together a large confederacy of warrior families, and one by one they conquered neighboring tribes of other clans who joined together under his leadership.

At age forty-two, he took the title of universal

ruler (Genghis Khan) and was known as such thereafter.

He taught his people that they were the very center of the universe. And being at the center of the universe, they were a chosen people and were favored by the gods. It was their role in life to spread out and conquer the rest of the world and bring them all into the Mongol empire.

He created a series of laws and regulations for all his subjects to live by, and the Mongols, for the first time, lived under the rule of law. The Mongols up to that time could not read nor write (illiterate), and had to bring in Chinese scholars to help them until they trained their young children to be literate.

When Genghis Khan sent his armies out to conquer the world, their entire population numbered only about seven hundred thousand. The Khan had organized his army into a highly disciplined, superbly coordinated and brilliantly tactical group that simply overran the rest of the immediate world around them.

Michel's note—again I do not see anything from the computer readout, that helps us with the solution to our problem.

Michel asked the computer for a third and final readout, but on this one he asked for specific details on the Great Khan. It was only a few more minutes until he had the report in his hands and began to read about something in the Great Khan's life that would give him the answer he was looking for.

Michel was hoping that it would not be necessary to get into the head of General Subutai.

He felt he was getting a little bit closer to solving the puzzle, if only he had a better understanding of Temujin, the man, who started it all, and not so much about Genghis Khan, the legend, that he had become.

He began his final read:

Computer notes upon the individual accomplishments and details of the life of Temujin—also known as Genghis Khan—requested and delivered to Michel Nostradamus.

> The Mongol army, led by Genghis Khan, subjugated more lands and people in twenty-five years than the great Roman legions did in four hundred.
>
> In nearly every country the Mongols conquered, they brought an unprecedented rise in cultural communication, expanded trade, and a blossoming of the local civilizations.
>
> Vastly more progressive than his European or Asian counterparts, Genghis Khan abolished torture, granted universal religious freedom, and smashed feudal systems of aristocratic privileges.
>
> Temujin always remembered himself as being strong-willed and very lucky. It was his determination to succeed that would never allow him to give up, even when things were not going his way. From the first thirty-eight years of his life, all he remembered was warfare, killing and tears.
>
> Finally, he gathered, from all of the various tribes, enough strong leaders to expand his ideas outward. Outward expansion was the main plan that Temujin had.

For thousands of years, the Mongols had fought against each other. One tribe would wage war against another tribe. Then another tribe would go after those tribes, and so on. He had finally put all the tribes together with the understanding that they would all share the profits and the great wealth to be had, if only they stayed completely united.

Temujnin had a vivid memory of being crowned as the Mongols' universal ruler at age forty-two. He was given the title of universal ruler, and was thereafter known as the Great Khan, or Genghis Khan.

The key to his success was to keep all the tribes working together and to stop making war upon each other. This was only possible if he kept expanding the empire.

Michel was beginning to get a glimmer of an idea that might give him the answer. He continued reading the computer readout with mounting excitement.

It was easy for Temijin to divide his growing manpower into several groups. He gave his generals unlimited power and complete independent decision-making.

As long as the armies could look outward and conquer enemies on the other side of the Mongolian borders, things became quiet at home.

The conquest of China and most of Russia was not difficult. All his armies had to do was defeat the rigid and non-creative armies that they put into the field against him. Once their armies were defeated, it was just a matter of time until they knocked down the walls of any city they encountered.

Temujin insisted on mercy for any city that surrendered and would pay tribute in gold. But he demanded absolute destruction of any city that resisted them. Their reputation of being fair to the people they conquered if they opened up their city and gave riches to them was what he wanted. Terrible killers of every man, woman and child in cities that would not surrender to him was important because more conquests were made by fear and by their terrible reputation then by war and arrows.

When China and Asia offered little more of interest to him, the Great Khan ordered his generals to turn their attention westward. His fear was always that once they ran out of enemies, his generals would turn on each other as they had been doing for thousands of years.

And now, Michel was thinking, this might be the key to the puzzle that he had wanted to find. One of the most important things to the Great Khan was the matter of succession. What would happen to the Mongol expansion after his death?

The Great Khan knew that even though he had achieved success beyond belief, he himself was merely a man. Men die and empires crumble. He therefore carefully made a plan for his empire to continue under one of his sons.

Three strong warrior sons called him father. Each of them was capable of leading his empire, and each of them wanted to do so. A civil war between the three of them would definitely follow his death.

From each of his generals and other high-ranking officials and from each of his sons, he demanded that they follow the procedure he now set up for the next Great Khan to be elected.

He gave every leader an equal voice in the succession. But behind the scenes he spoke to each of his sons and each leader in a one-on-one meeting. He abstracted a blood-oath from each of them to vote on a compromise future leader whom they would all be comfortable with.

Two of his three sons had no bend in them. They would declare a war upon each other no matter who won the vote on succession. Civil war within the empire would be the end result, and the Great Khan wanted to avoid this at all costs. The third brother was softer, easier and got along with everyone.

Even the two brothers agreed that they could vote for him at the time of the Great Khan's death, which would happen one day into the future.

Michel saw clearly now in his readings that the election of the new Great Khan was pretty set, as Temujin took one final step to ensure the United Kingdom that he created would continue. And here was the key:

He had required each leader who had a vote to agree that no matter where they were or what they were doing, they would return to their new capital city and take part in the vote for the new Great Khan.

With this agreement in hand, he sent everyone out into the

world to do what they did best. They could pillage, and plunder to their heart's content.

And here was the best part of all for Michel. Now he knew why Paris was saved. He knew why the city did not fall to General Subutai when he was getting ready to attack. He knew why the rest of Europe never had to go through the terror of the Mongols.

The answer to the question was simplicity itself. While the Mongols were getting ready to knock on the doors of Paris, word was received that the Great Khan had died.

It seems that the empire had developed a wonderful system of communication called the 'yam.' This was a horse-post system very similar to the Pony Express famous in the Wild West days of the United States of America during the eighteen hundreds. Barbarians the Mongols might have been, but their post system was the most efficient communications network the world had ever seen up to that time.

And it was the safest. The law of the Mongols, the Yassa, ruled the empire with a grip of steel. It was said that a virgin carrying a bag of gold could ride from one end of the empire to the other without being molested. Michel thought to himself that based upon his reading so far, he could believe this fact to be true.

So when general Subutai received the word that the Great Khan had died, he had probably stopped all preparations for the attack on Paris and turned his armies around and headed for home.

They had turned around and gone straight back to China so that the general could fulfil his promise to the Great Khan with his vote for the successor.

It is a known historical fact that, once the new Great Khan was elected, the Mongol empire continued expanding just as it had always done. Only, this time, Europe seemed very far away from China, and retracing the great distance involved must have discouraged them from returning. The generals probably put the conquest of Europe off to another time, and fortunately that time never came, and Europe was left alone to develop into whatever it was to become.

General Subutai retired shortly thereafter and led a quiet life for the few years remaining to him. The armies were now under younger and more ambitious generals who directed their forces to finishing up the complete conquest of the rest of the Orient.

At the end of the active expansion years, there was only one great power in the entire area. That power was the Mongolian empire, which eventually became known as China.

Special note from Michel Nostradamus:

> To anyone who is interested, I am coming home.
>
> I believe that I have fulfilled my promise to my Dot and to the Historical Society and figured out why Paris never fell to the Mongols.
>
> I hope that the listening world agrees with my conclusion because for better or worse, that is it.
>
> And, Doty, when you see this note, I wish you to understand that I need a vacation and I know just the place we should go.
>
> See you soon....
>
> Michel Nostradamus

I was tired. Mentally and physically tired. Dot knew me well enough to insist that we run away from everyone and completely disappear for a while. She had me do my magic once again and within moments, we had left her world behind us and reappeared back to my roots in the early fifteenth century.

For days on end we just walked and talked our way around the rustic village that always seemed to call to me. My village was the best village in all of France, as it offered us its charm of the old world in its sights, pleasures and wonderful wines.

I introduced Dot as the new lady of the castle. Everyone knew that we had gone off elsewhere and gotten married, and now returned here for our honeymoon. Everyone in the village found her charming and most interesting. She was like a breath of fresh air as she talked to me about a few things that she thought would be helpful to everyone.

I explained to her that we could not introduce any new technology because that would change the future and she understood what I meant. I gave her permission to make some minor changes around the castle, but I soon found out what was minor to me was something different for Doty. She went out and hired dozens of local workers to do some changes that she had in mind.

I watched in amazement as we ended up with glass in every window and new doors that opened within the castle. She had screens made out of local wire-like materials, so that the insects would be kept out and the breezes would be allowed to blow their cooling air in. Other workers dug deep pits and trenches in the kitchen gardens and buried clay pipe in them. She ran the connecting pipelines into the kitchen, where she had hot and cold running water coming into a big copper stove. The final touch was that she had installed a huge porcelain bathtub large enough for two people. We used up most of the hot water splashing around in it together.

One day we were out walking in the sunshine, and Dot asked about the funny smell that was in the air.

I explained that it was from the natural spring water that ran behind the hills that separated the Castle from the village. I told her that the village elders would come down and sit in the water for hours. They claimed that the waters somehow seemed to restore them to better health.

Well, that was all I had to say and pretty soon we had a hotel built beside the spring that called people from all over Paris to come and spend some time in our beautiful village. They would come and take advantage of the mineral waters and the lovely new hotel that would take care of their every need.

Before I knew it, our village was a very prosperous place, with all the houses completely restored and painted back to the original white with gold trim. Shops from the big city set up branches in our village, and my people were suddenly wealthy shopkeepers who paid rent to the family Nostradamus. They were happy, we were happy and everything seemed to be going well.

☙☙

However, one fine afternoon while we were sitting quietly having dinner at our favorite restaurant, Dot brought up a few discussion points that, as soon as I heard them, I knew that my quiet life was soon to be over. The easy and comfortable country lifestyle that I always loved so much was soon to end and at best, be put on hold.

Doty said she loved me, and that she really loved this life that I had opened up for her. But she said that she was lonely, and that she missed many of her friends and the few relatives that were still around back home.

She suggested that perhaps we could take some time away from the village and go back to the twenty-fourth century for a few weeks.

She also thought that since I was now so well rested, it

might be a good time for me to think about my final time-jump adventure with Napoleon Bonaparte.

What I found most interesting was that I thought that she was absolutely right. She was correct in that we were both getting bored with the good and easy lifestyle.

I knew that I was getting excited about my Napoleon Bonaparte adventure.

CHAPTER FIFTY-TWO

I like to think that I am an intelligent man. I like to think that I can recognize a logical point of view when I hear one. I like to think that when the only woman in my life tells me that there is something that I should be doing, the logical and intelligent part of me always knows how to respond.

"Yes, dear," was the response I gave to Dot when she pointed out that I had some unfinished business to attend to. She was right and I told her so.

I also told her that it would take a day or two to close things down here at the castle. We would need to appoint someone to watch over the many new things that were going on all around us.

๑๑

Ten days later, we were back in Doty's home in Paris, and in a frame that seemed to make both of us happy at the same time.

When I woke up in the morning, I found a note she had left for me on the kitchen table, telling me that she was going to have lunch with a few friends and then go on to the University.

We had been back to the fifteen hundreds for about three months, but only seven days had passed here. No matter how hard I tried, I could not figure out how the time difference worked itself out. I gave up thinking about it and pondered upon my new problems.

My thoughts immediately went to Napoleon Bonaparte. This was a topic that I had been looking forward to since the first time I had time-jumped.

It was very interesting to me, to analyze myself, and take apart the things that at one time had seemed so logical and simple to me. I am a Frenchman and I know that I think like a Frenchman, even though I always like to believe that I am a man of the entire world. I have always thought that logic, and not emotion made the difference in who we are and what we do as a people.

At that moment, I was in the middle of a major dilemma. France, of course, is a first-class country, and it is considered to be one of the finest countries in all of Europe and the rest of the world. And I agreed with myself upon this completely.

I knew that I could take France from where she was today, an equal among nations, and make her into such a powerhouse nation that there would be no equal to her anywhere. The question that was really bothering me was whether or not I should do that.

Before I met the beautiful Doty, and before I saw how pleasant and wonderful life in the future with her could be, I knew where I was going and what I was going to do. Life seemed so simple then, but not any longer.

Having arrived at no conclusion whatsoever, I thought that it would be a good idea to once again head over to my favorite computer store and look up a few things that I needed to clarify in my head.

Within the hour, I was settled into my usual corner with the high-speed rental computer in front of me. I had brought with me a large cup of coffee and a few sweet things to nibble upon.

This time, I had decided to print out the research paper that

I wanted from the computer. I knew what I wanted to say to Doty, but sometimes it was easier to write it out with her because I rarely, if ever, won a discussion with her.

I decided to begin with some basic background on Great Britain (England). France and Great Britain have been fighting each other for years and years and I thought that a few insights into the British state of mind in the Napoleonic years of the early eighteen hundreds might be helpful to me as a good starting point.

☜☞

Computer readout on Kingdom of Great Britain—for Michel Nostradamus

Great Britain is an island situated in the northwestern corner of continental Europe.

It is the ninth largest island in the world.

It is the largest European island and the largest in the combined British islands.

The current population is sixty million plus people.

Great Britain is currently made up of three independent countries. England, Ireland and Scotland.

Great Britain was created by the political union of the above three independent states on May 1, 1707.

The land area is 88,745 square miles.

☜☞

Computer readout on Kingdom of Great Britain—part 2

History of the war between France and Great Britain during the eighteen hundreds:

At the threshold of the nineteenth century, Britain was challenged by France, then under Napoleon Bonaparte, in a struggle that represented a contest of ideologies or ideas between the two neighboring nations. It was not only Britain's position on the world stage that was threatened by Napoleon Bonaparte, but it was a matter of defending itself from the complete control that France wanted to put on Britain, as it had on most of the other European countries that it had conquered.

In these wars of the early eighteen hundreds, called the Napoleonic wars, Britain had to invest large amounts of capital resources in order to resist the French forces. Britain had to commit its entire naval fleet of merchant and war ships to the war effort. At the time, Britain was the dominant sea power in the world.

The British empire had interests in other parts of the world that were also threatened by France. A loss to France in Europe would have meant a loss of their colonies.

After defeating Napoleon at the famous land battle of Waterloo, Britain went on to become the world's most dominant power.

One closely held secret at the time, which was said to account for much of Great Britain's many successes against France, was a special agreement made between the king of England and the merchant class. They became virtual partners in all ventures, and they shared equally in the great wealth that flowed to the British islands from all of their newly acquired French possessions.

End computer readout on Kingdom of Great Britain for Michel Nostradamus

CHAPTER FIFTY-THREE

Michel typed out the following upon the computer.

Special note for Doty's eyes only.

Over Napoleon's extraordinary career, which lasted some twenty exciting years, there were definitely various times and situations where the history of the world might have turned out quite differently with only a little push in the right direction.

I personally see, Doty, some unusual options that Napoleon or his opponents could have taken and some special moments when, if he had made several different choices, Bonaparte might just have remained on top of the world that he was turning around. This is what I wish to have further discussions with you about, as soon as we can possibly sit down and do so.

Napoleon, as this wonderful computer that I am using shows me, was a great man of action who was capable of making rapid on-the-spot decisions. Yet he was also a poet who could have made a living at it if he was so inclined. What he ended up being was a dreamer who came very close to being a real-world conqueror. He had the good fortune to come onto the scene in a period of revolutionary exhaustion, and it is hardly surprising to me, that he became the dominant personality of his time. I believe that a character as strong as his would have to have gone after the control of Europe one way or another.

Here are my thoughts on making Bonaparte the winner at the final battle of Waterloo.

You must understand that if he had won that battle, then he would have nothing standing in his way as he took over control of everyone and everything. There is no doubt in my mind that I know how to make him a winner in that decisive battle. I know how and why he lost that crucial battle, and at that critical moment I can make him win that fight, which would make him, "king of the mountain."

Doing this will be easy for me. But do I *want* to do this? Everything would be different from what we know now of the world we live in. Could you and I be as happy as we are now, if France was the only superpower of the earlier centuries? If they were in control then, logic tells us that they would still be in full control now. Do we want a different world from the one we have now?

At present, we can go back and forth to the very best of your world and mine and not have to answer to anyone. I am having serious reservations about being the one to cause a change in things.

I really think that I like our life together just the way it is.

Your important comments upon this matter would be greatly appreciated.

I probably should just pay a visit to Napoleon as an interested visitor, making no changes whatsoever, so that everything could stay just the way they are, and then go home to you, where we will spend the rest of our lives together.

And so, Doty, kindly prepare for me the advance readout notations upon Napoleon Bonaparte, as you do for all of my interesting visitations. It is also so helpful having your advance knowledge as to what I should be looking out for.

Please plan on having a serious discussion with me upon all of the above at your earliest convenience.

Please know that I love you, and that I always will,

Michel Nostradamus

CHAPTER FIFTY-FOUR

Doty and I had our serious conversation earlier today, and even though she was satisfied and tried to convince me that I should leave things alone, I was not yet completely convinced.

On the other side of the discussion was the possibility in my mind that, under the rule of Napoleon and his informed and liberal French government, would not the world be a much better place? Would there be less violence and crime and corruption? Would people throughout the world be happier than I see them now, under his type of enlightened dictatorship?

What has put me on this road of playing devil's advocate and talking to myself about the pros and cons of this matter are the following points:

Bonaparte would have been exhausted by the endless wars he had been involved in over the past twenty years. It would definitely be in his interest to see to it that war was a thing of the past. He would also have been hearing cries for peace from the rank and file of his armed forces.

Based on this, he would have proposed an agreement among all nations that would be based on logic, mercy, and unexpected clemency or forgiveness for his former enemies.

Napoleon, no doubt, would throw Russia out of their small

part of Europe. He would probably move their boundaries back to the edges of Asia. Europe without a Russia in it would be a far better place.

France would be the master of Europe, and the absolute dominant power. They would probably take the Germans into a limited partnership with them to rule the world. Napoleon had great respect for the Germans.

France, of course, would completely take over the British Empire's colonies, such as India and other productive locations. They would continue to send France raw materials in return for France's finished products. The French economy would be booming.

If all of the above things were true, and a new way of life under Napoleon was created, was I doing the world an injustice by not trying to work things out?

I had so many doubts.

❧

So, what I decided to do was to go back to the computer shop and rent some more time. I was still amazed at all the information available to me on the computer.

I settled in with my usual coffee and snacks and just sat there quietly for a little while trying to think. I had pretty much decided that I would make the time-jump back to the Battle of Waterloo. I needed to make sure that Napoleon was the kind of man that I was giving him credit for being.

If it turned out that he was the idealistic planner that I thought he was, then he and I would sit down and talk things out. I could tell him what his future would be without my changes, and discuss what he would do if I helped him win at Waterloo. Would he do the things I believed were the proper things for him to do if he became emperor of the world?

Or, on the other hand, was he just another adventurer who did not deserve my help? If this were so, I would just leave him alone, and let him lose the battle and get sent into exile, where he would die a sad and lonely death.

Doty promised me that she would spend some time in the files getting the details about Napoleon and Waterloo for me. With her handling that, all I had left to do was to get a little more information about Napoleon the man, and not so much about Napoleon the general.

I gave the computer its instructions and drank a little coffee while I waited for the readouts.

⚮

General information on Napoleon Bonaparte—overview for Michel Nostradamus

There was nothing more annoying to Napoleon Bonaparte than the name given to him by his enemies. That name was "The Little Corsican."

He personally did not attach much importance to his origins and family lineage. He claimed to be a self-made man, whose titles rested only upon his sword and on the votes of the French nation.

He was born on August 15, 1769, and died in exile on May 5, 1821, at the age of fifty-two. He was born in a small village in the city of Ajaccio, in Corsica, to parents of Genoese ancestry.

He was smaller than the average male of his time, and stood five foot six inches tall. The average male height then was five foot eight inches. It has been stated that he had an inferiority complex due to his being smaller than most men of his day.

He became overly aggressive in dealing with his lack of height. This inspired the commonly used expression called a "Napoleon complex."

He was often portrayed as wearing a large and very wide black hat. He would pose for pictures with his hand inside his waist coat.

His early military training was as an artillery officer in central France, where he was commissioned as an army officer.

His religion was Roman Catholicism.

His claim to fame came on October 5, 1795, when as a twenty-six-year-old officer stationed in Paris, he held back a rioting crowd trying to storm the government building. He ended up killing fourteen hundred of them while protecting the capital building of the city. His professional use of cannon and a limited number of troops soon were well known throughout Paris.

He became known as "Officer Bonaparte," the man who "with a whiff of grape shot" saved the French nation from being overthrown. He soon had wealth, fame and the full support of the government in Paris. He was quickly promoted to commander of the interior armed forces, and a large part of the army was placed under his control.

What helped Napoleon the most toward his success in the many battles he fought was two-fold.

First, there was an increase in the firepower of weapons being used by the French army. An improved flintlock musket with a bayonet attached had appeared at about the same time as the rise of Napoleon. This gave Napoleon's men the ability to rapidly fire their weapons before having to stop and reload.

Second, the art of using cannons before sending in the army came into being. Cannon fire would open up the enemy lines for the soldiers, who would come upon the enemy moments after the cannons had fired a barrage.

A dozen victories in as many months were announced around the world in highly dramatic and highly slanted bulletins. Most bulletins came out in strong support of Napoleon, and the nation was reading about him on a daily basis.

Napoleon was already an extraordinary man at the time when he began his rapid rise to power. There were certain basic aggressive elements in his nature and outlook that were already showing up in how he reacted to the fame and glory that was being showered upon him.

From the very start of his career, it was quite clear that he was as much interested in political and literary matters as he was in military happenings around the world.

History tells us that he was a Romantic at heart. His Romantic sensibilities were marked in his writings and letters. Most of his personal letters did not survive him because his wife, Josephine would never keep any of them.

Napoleon and Josephine did not get along for most of their married years. The issue standing between them was that Josephine seemed unable to produce a male heir. Napoleon was most conscious of passing on his empire to a royal son, which he never had.

Writers of the early eighteen hundreds always quoted the words written by Napoleon to describe himself: "The sweep and vigor of his imagination was perfectly matched and balanced by the brightness and precision of his intelligence." Napoleon delighted in writing his own press releases as he played out his many years in front of the French nation.

Napoleon appeared to display a dazzling combination of qualities that were difficult to resist, especially for the men of his own age, who had been brought up under the same influences as Napoleon. His strongest successes came with using his strong personality when it came to his men in the field. He was always out there walking around and talking with "his men," and the troops loved him for it, and considered him as one of them.

Napoleon's legal reforms, called the Napoleonic Code, were a major influence on many civil law jurisdictions worldwide.

Napoleon is best remembered for his large role in the many wars that he led against other countries of Europe, who had to join together in order to defeat him. Through military conquest, he soon controlled most of continental Europe. He said that he was trying to spread the wonderful ideals of the French Revolution worldwide. He became king of France, but wanted to be called Emperor or Imperial Majesty.

Due to his success in battle after battle against numerically superior enemies, he is generally regarded as one of the greatest military commanders of all time. His military campaigns are studied at military academies throughout the world.

End report on Napoleon Bonaparte prepared for Michel Nostradamus

❧

Michel had the printout made by the computer, paid his bill and left the location.

He had more than enough to think about as he slowly walked home. He thought he would surprise Dot and take her out for a nice dinner.

CHAPTER FIFTY-FIVE

For the last time, Michel took his seat inside the sealed cubicle and watched as the walls changed their colors from a solid, light tint into clear see-through glass.

The preparations, as always, had been smooth and flawless. There was however, one major change in the plan—and it was a major one.

It was originally planned for Michel to physically appear on the scene, live and physically present. But there were two objections to this plan going forward.

The first being that there would be a war going on at that moment when he would suddenly appear. He would not be able to fit in anywhere, since there would be no crowd to mingle in. It was thought that the soldiers with whom he would have to be among would see him as a stranger and probably shoot him as a spy.

And secondly, even if he could mingle with the soldiers moving about, he would never be able to get near Napoleon, since he would be surrounded by his officers and staff, who would be waiting for their orders. They also would identify him as a stranger, and most likely have him taken out and shot.

Since his own death was the most likely outcome of either possibility, Michel agreed with the advisors, Dot specifically, that he would have to go the safest way, which was by computer inducement directly into the mind of Napoleon. The basic problem was the usual one of finding the right blood sample of Napoleon with the proper amount of DNA in it to allow the computer to be able to locate Napoleon.

The specific date of the Battle of Waterloo was June 16, 1815. The opening shots were randomly fired about eleven o'clock in the morning on a cloudy and pleasantly cool day. Michel wanted to make his time-jump appearance into Napoleon's mind early in the morning. He was sure that, on the morning of the biggest battle of his career, Napoleon would not be sleeping. He expected to find him in the command tent, going over the orders he would shortly be giving to his officers.

The problem was finding the DNA. Dot had told him not to worry, since Bonaparte had died under mysterious circumstances many years after his defeat at Waterloo. Dot was sure that the results of the autopsy performed on Napoleon, to determine if his cause of death was due to poison, would have been carefully preserved. The mysterious circumstances under which he died were still being talked about in academic circles.

She believed that if she gave up some important artifact or rare document from the University, she could talk the handlers of the Bonaparte legacy into making a trade. All she needed was a tiny amount of dried blood to give to Michel's computer.

Michel was sitting there quietly listening to the computer counting down to the final sendoff because Dot had come through once again. He had no idea what she had given up in order to get the vital sample, but whatever it was it had worked, and the computer advised them all that it had the location information all locked in.

After all the usual well-wishes and hugs had been given, Dot handed Michel his copy of the notes she had put together for him on Napoleon. He was going to read it over one last time, so that the information would be familiar to him just as he was ready to go. He sipped his cup of coffee, and adjusted the chair to a more comfortable position as he took up the report.

Report on Napoleon Bonaparte—Prepared by D. Goodman for the eyes only of Michel Nostradamus:

Hello, Michel:

I am hopeful that these are the last briefing notes that I shall be preparing for you. If things go according to thoughts that you and I talked about, then, on your return, you will be a happy man from having completed all of your planned time-jumps. I certainly hope so, and I pray that from that point on, that we will have a "normal" life in both of our special worlds.

What I find so wonderful is that you fit so nicely into my world, which is your future, and I do pretty well in yours, which is my past. It is wonderful to know that we have each other, and that we have so many choices of where to go and what to do. Sometimes I find it hard to believe that you have brought all these things to me.

Much love,

xxx—Doty

Additional notations on Napoleon Bonaparte:

Napoleon rose to prominence under the first French republic as he led several successful military campaigns against the many countries who were attacking France.

In 1779, he overthrew the existing French government and declared himself emperor shortly thereafter.

In the early eighteen hundreds, he fought and won decisive battles against the European allies. These were called the Napoleonic wars, and he won them all.

He rewarded friends and family members with European countries to run for him as part of the French Empire he was putting together.

Napoleon made a major mistake attacking Russia late in 1812. His army had to deal with the terrible Russian winter, and he lost a great deal of his battle-ready troops and materials.

Seeing his weakness after the Russian campaign, the remaining European allies attacked his weakened position and defeated him in 1814. As a result, he was sent into exile to the small island of Elba, where he stayed for just a little over one year. He returned to France from Elba and regained his crown, as the French people were overjoyed at his return.

He took his weakened army to the flat plains of Waterloo, Belgium, where the remaining European armies attacked him immediately before he was able to rebuild his forces. The European armies were under the command of the famous

British general Lord Wellington.

You will soon see and hear all about General Wellington, Michel. It was Wellington's idea to sweep around the side flank of Napoleon's weakened troops. This is where you will be observing during your time with Napoleon. By sunset on the day you will arrive, the forces under Lord Wellington will have caught the French forces in a pincer (two-sided) battle and defeated them completely.

The French forces never recovered from Waterloo, and Napoleon was exiled once again, but this time it was to the fortified and well-secured island of Saint Helena. An autopsy was done on Napoleon's body a few years after his death, and it was determined by the examining doctors that he died of arsenic poisoning. It was never proven, but it was thought that the fear that Napoleon was considering another escape from his captivity led to his being eliminated at such a young age. This was a sad way to end the life of one of the greatest military leaders of all time.

Final additional notes on the importance of Napoleon Bonaparte:

Napoleon married a minor noblewoman named Josephine on March 9, 1796. No living heirs were produced as a result of the union.

Fighting all of the many wars was very expensive. To raise money, he sold France's claim to land in the United States of America. The land was called the Louisiana Purchase. He sold the huge area for three cents an acre. This was the most inexpensive major land sale ever recorded in the world.

Ludwig van Beethoven, the great composer, was a great admirer of Napoleon, and he dedicated his third symphony to him.

To celebrate one of his many victories over Austria and Russia, Napoleon had the world-famous *Arc de Triomphe* built in central Paris. Of course, it is still standing there today in all its glory and fame as a Parisian landmark.

Notes on Napoleon's image and legacy that he left for the world to admire:

"Napoleonic" is a worldwide expression that is used to mean a genius or a political power-house, or just someone excessively ambitious.

Since Napoleon's death, hundreds of towns, streets, ships and even some cartoon characters have used his name. His life story and image have been portrayed in dozens of films and movies. Many books and articles have been written about him.

Napoleon changed the way modern armies were organized. He promoted men to move upward in the ranks based only on their ability and not on who their families were.

Before Napoleon's style of fighting was introduced to the world, two opposing armies would line up against each other on a flat and open area. One side or the other would charge at the other's standing line of soldiers, and hand-to-hand battles were fought. Whichever side had more soldiers to send against the enemy usually would win the fight.

This was completely changed when Napoleon would bring all of his cannons to the front of the battle formations and fire those heavy weapons directly into the enemy lines. After pounding the enemy with cannon fire, his soldiers would then move forward and destroy the shocked and bewildered enemy. This was most successful in the beginning years of his campaigns, before the enemy saw the advantage of using cannon also. After a few years of fighting, Napoleon lost some of his advantages when the enemy began to copy everything he did. This was a great compliment to his genius on the field of valor.

Napoleon also introduced cavalry charges. He would send in mounted horse-soldiers, swinging their heavy swords and charging straight at the enemy, who had just taken a heavy pounding of cannon fire.

Details in brief on the Battle of Waterloo:

Waterloo has become a commonly used term taken to mean a last stand or lost battle. It is a term that had endured from Napoleon's time up to the present.

How it all happened: Napoleon had returned from about a year or so of exile on the island of Elba, and once again he had himself crowned emperor of the French empire. The European world once again began to panic over the possibility of the new rise of France under Napoleon.

Fearing the determined efforts of Napoleon once again, the rest of Europe united themselves and, within one hundred days of his return, attacked Napoleon's standing army on the flat and open field where they were stationed. This was only a small encounter to see if Napoleon was a force once again to be dealt with. And yes, it was determined he was.

The genius of Napoleon was shown once again in this small battle. He completely defeated the enemy, who quickly withdrew from the field of battle. The quick fight against the allies weakened Napoleon's fighting force by about twenty percent.

He then withdrew all his forces and returned to central France to rest and reorganize his men and equipment. He put out an emergency call for men at arms because he knew that the enemy would not give him time to regroup.

Again, the other countries of Europe buried their differences with each other. Their greater fear of Napoleon was the bond that held these longtime enemies together. All the allies united their forces under the leadership of Britain's famous general, Lord Wellington.

Before he could even organize his new troop command, Wellington gave the order to march on France's forces. Wellington did not want to give Napoleon any extra time to put his defenses together.

Note to Michel:

Historians agree that if there was some way that Napoleon could have caused a few months' delay before the united European forces marched against him so quickly, things would have turned completely around. With fresh troops swelling up his army ranks, Napoleon would have won the battle and gone on to bigger and better things.

It was suggested by Napoleon's spymaster, (yes, they had spies and spymasters in those days) that he be allowed to send in several of his specially trained men to assassinate General Wellington. The argument from the spymaster was that without Wellington it would take weeks for the allies to agree upon a new general to lead them, and by that time recruits would fill out the thin lines of the French army.

History does not tell us why this did not happen. The story that was going around at the time was that Napoleon would not dishonor his own reputation by doing something so underhanded as killing the enemy general.

But the real story that came out years and years later was that Napoleon, knowing that he was short-handed and in trouble with the lack of soldiers, did authorize the death of the Duke of Wellington. The only problem was that the duke was so well protected that no enemy was able to get close enough to him to be a real threat.

CHAPTER FIFTY-SIX

Note to Michel from Doty:

Hey Michel:

An interesting thought came to me while I was putting all this information together for you. Wellington has to be the focal point of your "historical adjustment," if you are still thinking about it.

Forget changing Napoleon's plans. Forget about his defeat at Waterloo. If you take Wellington out of the equation, then Napoleon will win at Waterloo and who knows what height the French nation could rise to.

This is just a wild and crazy thought, but one that I thought I should point out to you. You see that I am always thinking about you before all other things.

xxx—Doty

Notes on the Duke of Wellington's battle moves at Waterloo:

As we know, Wellington ordered his attack against the French forces within a few days of his taking over the command of the united forces. The troops under his command were not well organized but there were plenty of them.

Wellington's plan was simple. Since he had almost a two-to-one advantage in the number of his troops over the number of troops Napoleon had, all he had to do was give up a good number of his fighters for an equal number of Napoleon's, and simple mathematics would give him his victory.

With that in mind, Wellington ordered his attack against the French forces within a few days. He refused to give Napoleon time to upgrade his weakened army. He put forty thousand British, Scottish, Belgium and German forces immediately into the field, along with thirty thousand Prussians.

But a frontal attack by his seventy thousand men against a lesser force of France's fifty thousand did not work. At the end of the first day of the battle of waterloo, Napoleon seemed to be doing the impossible once again. Even with a gigantic advantage in men and equipment, Wellington could not budge Napoleon.

Then Wellington came up with a plan that changed the battle from a stand-off into a complete victory for his united forces. He ordered his cavalry to sweep around the end flank of the French forces, who were shorthanded and out of necessity had to concentrate most of their men in the middle of their formations. Once he had accomplished this end run, Wellington was now able to force the French to fight a two-front war: one in front and one in the rear.

Time and the lack of the proper number of troops to fight off the brilliant move by General Wellington made all the difference. Napoleon had to surrender his position or have his beloved Frenchmen slaughtered. He surrendered before sundown, and was taken prisoner by General Wellington himself.

Within a month of his surrender, Napoleon would be exiled once again. This time he was sent to the island of Saint Helena, where, after the passage of a few years, he died under suspicious circumstances.

Doty's short note on "Who was Wellington?":

Arthur Wellington was the first duke of Wellington. He was a native of Ireland. He was a field marshal of the highest rank.

Before the battle of Waterloo, he wrote strategy war books for the British army. After Waterloo, he went on to become the British Prime Minister.

Years later, a very interesting interview with the newly retired British Prime Minister brought out the respect that the world had for Napoleon Bonaparte.

He was asked, "In your opinion, Prime

Minister, who was the greatest military leader that you ever opposed in battle?"

The answer rang out loud and clear from Wellington. "In this age, in any past age, in any future age, the answer has to be Napoleon Bonaparte."

CHAPTER FIFTY-SEVEN

There was no reason to delay my departure any longer. I had read and re-read all of the reports. I was up to date on Napoleon, Wellington and Waterloo. The computer was on standby, and I could not think of any reason not to give the go-ahead.

With a wave of my hand to the onlookers, and a smile on my face, I gave the mental signal to the computer and closed my eyes. I wanted to avoid the uncomfortable few moments that always happened whenever I time-jumped.

I had made up my mind. I knew what I was going to do about changing history from the historic date of June 16, 1815. Anything that happened anywhere in the world up to that date would remain unchanged simply because it was before the 16th of June, 1815. It was from that date forward that changes would be made if I decided to remove the Duke of Wellington from the picture.

I really was going to do it. I was really planning to cause Wellington not to be around to defeat Napoleon. I would not hurt him, of course. I would simply have him kidnapped and kept away from everything until after the battle was fought. In this way, Napoleon would come out the winner and everything would come up positively for the Country of France.

That was my original thought. That was what I was planning on doing. I was going to be a world changer. After all, my real world was back in the fifteen hundreds, and Napoleon's era was in the eighteen hundreds. Not one thing would be any different for my family and friends back home, and that was nice.

But on the other hand, wasn't I being selfish? If I changed things around, what about all the good people and the wonderful things that happened to the world after 1815? What if things went bad and something terrible happened? I would have no control of future events once I started changing things. As the old saying goes, wasn't I better off with the "devil I know rather than the devil I don't?"

It was true that the world, even in Doty's time, had its problems. But people were dealing with it on a daily basis and the human race had come along pretty well. There was always room for improvement, but working on getting better from the inside was a lot healthier for the human race than for someone like me to change things from the outside. And then there was my Doty. Oh, what a man will do for the love of a good woman.

Let us assume that I allowed Napoleon to be successful at Waterloo. Let us presume that the world changed over to everything French. Was that a good thing? What if one of Doty's ancestors, under the new way of the world, had an accident or was never born for whatever reason?

Then I would not have my Doty. I would be there because I was born before 1815, but there was no guarantee she would be there for me, and that would be unacceptable. Life without her was no life at all.

So, there you have it. I would go back just as a visitor with no agenda to make any changes. I will observe my live French hero and see him in action. I will see him at his best, and I will see him defeated. I will see him send out the famous horse soldiers to do their glorious charge. I will see that glorious charge turn into a terrible slaughter in Napoleon's attempt to open up the middle of the enemy lines.

I will quietly slip away from a very sad Bonaparte, who will be sitting alone as he thought about his future, and the exile that awaited him again. I would say nothing about his terrible death, and nothing about how he would become immortalized into mankind's memory forever. I would be there just to observe and then to just move on.

I had just made up my mind.

☙❧

I once again became aware of my surroundings. I was actually inside the mind of Napoleon Bonaparte. I could see and hear perfectly, and noted that Napoleon spoke his French with a distinct country accent. It was probably from his Corsican upbringing.

I could tell that it was early morning because I could see the sun just corning up in the distance. The wind was blowing a bit and that caused the tent entry to flap.

Six officers milled about as they began to exit the tent area. They had obviously just finished their morning briefing and were about to report to their various duty stations.

I felt a deep calmness in Napoleon. I would have thought that on the day of battle he would be a jumble of nerves and energy.

I thought about this for a moment. Napoleon was well known for his detailed planning, and there was probably nothing that needed his attention at this time. The plans were already made, and all that was needed was for his officers to carry them out.

From Doty's briefing papers, I knew that the French were at least twenty thousand men short of their normal fighting strength.

Napoleon had not enough time to put together a bigger force, and if I remembered correctly, his plan was simple enough. It was one that he had used before and that had never failed him. He would lead with his cannons laying down a field of heavy fire, and come at the enemy from different sides of the field. The idea was to catch them in crossfire to soften up their lines.

Then the command would be given for the infantry, with their new and superior muskets, to charge straight ahead at the enemy lines. If he could get enough momentum going and put the enemy back on its heels, he would then follow up with his horse cavalry, which would hopefully pound its way through the enemy defenses.

Napoleon sat quietly at a small desk in the corner of the tent. His aide brought in some tea and sliced-up black bread with a yellow spread of some sort. The sounds of a busy war camp were going on outside, and the shouts and movements were somewhat muffled as Napoleon sat there quietly eating his breakfast.

Having been in the minds of many hosts, both men and women, I could easily tell that, mentally, Napoleon was fatigued. His movements were somewhat slower than they should have been, and I could not detect a sharpness that should have been there. Napoleon was a tired man, and this was not a good thing for the ultimate director of armies on the day of battle.

It was not more than another fifteen or twenty minutes until we were on horseback and riding up and down the formations that stood at attention as we rode by. The lines of infantry were neat and crisp, and it was evident that his men had the greatest confidence in this man who had never lost a war.

After our review of the troops, Napoleon headed his horse up a little rise directly to the rear of the infantry, who were now standing in a ready position. Everything was good to go with all of the French lines, and I assumed that was also true about the

Europeans I could see also standing by on the opposite side of the flat plains of Waterloo.

If I had not known that Napoleon was not hurt or killed in this battle, I would have been very nervous. It was not determined what exactly would happen to me with my mind inside a dead body. I would be entirely dependent upon the computer to step in and bring me home if the unexpected happened.

Fortunately, this was one less thing to consider as I watched seven mounted messengers dressed in different colored sashes pull up and stop in front of Napoleon. These were his direct chain of communication to his officers. He would issue a command to one of the seven messengers, who would dash off to deliver the words to his own company commander. This messenger system seemed to work well, and they were all dispatched as a quiet settled down on the field of battle. Everyone and everything seemed to be in place.

With a nod of his head toward a young soldier who was standing patiently next to him, Napoleon gave the order, and the young soldier fired up a red rocket to signal that it was time for the cannon to begin their firing at the enemy lines.

CHAPTER FIFTY-EIGHT

It was only moments after Napoleon had given the order that the roar of the French cannons took control of the field of action. The enemy cannon fire followed immediately. Explosions were appearing all around us as the French infantry stood at the ready, waiting for their order to go forward.

From what I could see out of Napoleon's eyes, there was much thick smoke. Heavy flying objects darted all around us. And now it was time for the signal that would send the soldiers moving forward. I saw thousands of men, to the beat of a drum, slowly begin their movement toward the enemy lines across the flatlands that separated the two armed forces.

Dozens of reports kept coming in to Napoleon for the next few hours. None of them were good ones, as the lack of infantry was stopping our soldiers from breaking through the center of the enemy's lines.

An unhappy Bonaparte spoke with the captain in charge of a fast-moving, lightly armored horse brigade. He was giving him the usual pep talk about how he needed his brigade of horsemen to break through the enemy's standing center so that the infantry could follow his lead. He told him that the success of the operation was his to achieve, and that great glory lay ahead for himself and for his men.

It was with a heavy heart and a grim smile on his face that Napoleon watched the young soldier mount his horse, pull out his long sword and signal to his brigade of six hundred men to move forward.

At first, they moved slowly down the center of the open field that separated the two opposing armed forces. There was an absolute silence except for the sound of the pounding horses and the wild yells of the cavalrymen as they made their dash across the field.

What followed was a disaster. The enemy cannons were positioned perfectly as they sent cannon shot into the oncoming charge of the light brigade of horsemen.

It was only minutes until the smoke cleared from the first cannons fired by the European forces. It was now clear enough to see that the brigade had turned around and was retreating at full gallop back to the safety of the French lines. The deadly fire from the enemy cannons had taken a terrible toll on the horsemen, and those few who survived the charge barely limped back to our lines.

Napoleon and I could see the enemy soldiers getting ready to follow up their advantage over the horse brigade.

I thought that this would be a perfect moment for me to leave my host. I had no need to see him go through the agony of defeat, as he would soon be forced to do.

As for myself, I knew that I had enjoyed all the time-traveling that I had done. I loved meeting the people from all the different time periods that I had gone to. I think that my favorite guy was Benjamin Franklin, and of course my favorite lady was my own D. Goodman. Unless called upon by fans, editors and others, I planned to only travel with my Doty, back and forth from my time to hers and the reverse.

My final conclusion is that the world, while not the perfect place that I would like it to be, is still the best one we have. I have no thoughts whatsoever about making any changes.

I am going to close now with a poem written by a person, who like myself, was only an observer there to see the happenings on this special day at the Battle of Waterloo.

Alfred, Lord Tennyson, wrote a poem that became world famous and has endured the pull of time.

His poem is a fitting end to my story and to my viewing, of my last hero Napoleon Bonaparte.

The name of this famous poem is "The Charge of the Light Brigade."

(Please take a moment out to read the following pages as I have written it out in full).

Alfred lord Tennyson, was an early example of a modern war correspondent.

He wrote this poem to memorialize the hopeless charge by the cavalry brigade upon orders from higher up their chain of command.

ॐ

THE CHARGE OF THE LIGHT BRIGADE

By Alfred Lord Tennyson
(presented in its original form)

1.

Half a league, half a league,
  Half a league onward,
All in the valley of Death
  Rode the six hundred.
"Forward, the Light Brigade.
Charge for the guns." he said:

Into the valley of Death
  Rode the six hundred.

2.
"Forward, the Light Brigade."
Was there a man dismaye'd?
Not though the soldier knew
  Someone had blundere'd:
Theirs not to make reply,
Theirs not to reason why,
Theirs but to do and die,
Into the valley of Death
  Rode the six hundred.

3.
Cannon to right of them,
Cannon to left of them,
Cannon in front of them
  Volleyed and thundere'd;
Stormed at with shot and shell,
Boldly they rode and well,
Into the jaws of Death,
Into the mouth of Hell
  Rode the six hundred.

4.
Flashe'd all their sabres bare,
Flashe'd as they turned in air,
Sabring the gunners there,
Charging an army, while
  All the world wondere'd:
Plunged in the battery-smoke
Right through the line they broke;

Cossack and Russian
Reeled from the sabre stroke
    Shattered and sundered.
Then they rode back, but not
    Not the six hundred.

                5.
Cannon to right of them,
Cannon to left of them,
Cannon behind them
    Volleyed and thundere'd;
Stormed at with shot and shell,
While horse and hero fell,
They that had fought so well
Came through the jaws of Death
Back from the mouth of Hell,
All that was left of them,
    Left of six hundred.

                6.
When can their glory fade?
O the wild charge they made.
    All the world wondered.
Honour the charge they made.
Honour the Light Brigade,
    Noble six hundred.

ANNOTATIONS

Who was the *real* Michel Nostradamus? A few thoughts and comments from author Bud Seligson

Ever since the sixteenth century, the name of Michel Nostradamus has attracted an ever-growing and very dynamic crowd of myths and mythology. Every major world event in history, from those of his own lifetime to those of 9/11 and beyond, has been followed—but never preceded—by a rash of popular books claiming that Nostradamus had predicted this and that. By "this and that," I mean that the predictions Nostradamus is credited with are so vague and unclear and worded so openly that almost anything at any time could fit into one of his wordings.

Now, I love Michel Nostradamus as a character for this and other books, but I do not for a moment believe that he could really predict future happenings.

Here is my opinion—and only my opinion.

There is a famous ancient character/god that both Roman and Greek mythology often refer to. And I personally have used this wonderful ancient god in a few science-fiction tales that I wrote as a ghostwriter. His name is Janus, and the myths surrounding him are that he has one head on his shoulders with two faces on it. One face looks backward into the past, and the other face looks forward into the future.

The "Janus effect," as I and other historical writers of science fiction call it, gives us an open-ended invitation. If something good, bad or indifferent has happened in the past, then chances are that it will repeat itself and happen again in the future.

Let me take this a little bit further and give us an example of one such event that Nostradamus actually used as one of his special predictions.

Nostradamus lived in the sixteenth century, when there were no provisions as yet for any firefighting equipment. There was a huge fire in downtown Paris, which was near where his village was located. The fire destroyed a large part of the populated area. This is factual. It really did happen and he did witness it.

And so, after seeing a major fire in a big city like Paris, Nostradamus made a prediction. His prediction said that there would be a large fire in a major city. Pretty safe prediction, wasn't it?

Two other large fires did occur within a few hundred years of his prediction and everyone said he had predicted them. Actually, he did. Sort of. The first of the two fires were in London about one hundred years later, and the other was in Chicago (my home town), where Mrs. O'Leary's cow was involved in kicking over a lantern or something.

When he said that major earthquakes were going to shake up the world, once again he was on pretty safe "ground." After several of them happened over the years, his fans were simply amazed.

I could go on and on and list other things that would happen all by themselves, but he wrote about them and so people were shocked and impressed.

I have just a few more thoughts that I want to share with you, so please stay with me a tiny bit longer. Let us talk about world wars and dictators as per Nostradamus.

In Nostradamus's day, the known world was at war even then. France, Spain and England were always fighting among themselves for world dominance. How hard was it for him to say that there would be wars in the future for world dominance?

On dictators, he only had to look in the history books, and find the names of Caesar of Rome, or Alexander the Great of Greece. When Stalin and Hitler rose up, his believers were once again amazed.

And finally, for me, as a writer about interesting characters, Michel Nostradamus is one of the very best. His actions over his lifetime seem to write their own stories. I have found Michel to be a rich and full-bodied individual, full of wants, desires and ideas.

What is also very interesting is that the original parchments he wrote his predictions on have disappeared over the years. All we have left of his multiple and many writings are the bits and pieces that others have put together.

And finally, regarding his world-shaking prediction that the end of the world is near, I say to you, do not worry. The real reason that the Mayan predicting-calendar came to an end, and nothing further was written upon it, was simply that they ran out of room. After centuries of making designs and thoughts on their stone tablets, they simply ran out of space and, immediately following that moment, were scattered all over the known world and were not around to start a new one.

Thanks for the read,

—BUD SELIGSON

WHO IS THE REAL BUD SELIGSON?

Bud Seligson, who was born in Chicago, Illinois, has been a ghostwriter to many of the major well-known writers of today's fiction and science fiction. He is also well known in Hollywood as a "story doctor" for many studios. Bud lives in Los Angeles with his wife, Diane, who is his co-writer and sometime editor.

www.ingramcontent.com/pod-product-compliance
Lightning Source LLC
Chambersburg PA
CBHW020416260626
47156CB00007B/2407